# FLASHPOINT

## Carlotta Carlyle Books by Linda Barnes

# LINDA BARNES

# FLASHPOINT

## *A CARLOTTA CARLYLE MYSTERY*

HYPERION
NEW YORK

Copyright © 1999 Linda Appelblatt Barnes

Library of Congress Cataloging-in-Publication Data

Barnes, Linda.
    Flashpoint / Linda Barnes.—1st ed.
        p.   cm.
    ISBN 0-7868-6317-X
    I. Title.
    PS3552.A682F53   1999
    813'.54—dc21                                                                98-56063
                                                                                     CIP

FIRST EDITION

10   9   8   7   6   5   4   3   2

For Aunt Mary and Uncle Jack, in memory of Chicago summers

# ACKNOWLEDGMENTS

The reading committee came through again. My thanks to Brian DeFiore, Chris Smither and Dr. William J. Smither, Richard Barnes, James Morrow, and Susan Linn. Thanks as well to Ann Keating of IGI, to my dedicated agent, Gina Maccoby, and to the enthusiastic Hyperion team, especially Jennifer Barth.

# FLASHPOINT

# ONE

"*Es iz nit azoy gut mit gelt vi es iz shlekht on dem.*" The thought came to me even as my hand whacked the alarm clock, silencing a wail that cut through the stillness like a tenor sax.

Or as my grandmother, my mother's mother, used to say: "It's not that it's so good with money as it's bad without it."

Morning sunlight streamed through the flimsy bedroom curtains, illuminating a wedge of oak floorboards, an open guitar case stuffed with sheet music, and a once-white sock.

I do not habitually wake to thoughts of cash. I guess it's true: You think about things you haven't got.

I didn't have a steady paycheck. I didn't have a client. I didn't have much in the way of visible means of support. I did have an up-to-date private investigator's license authorizing me to stick my nose into the personal business of folks requesting same in the Commonwealth of Massachusetts. I did own a house, an aged Victorian within spitting distance of Harvard Square. Real estate prices being what they are, I could sell it and retire.

I whispered a silent thank-you for the house, which my aunt

Bea left me, mortgage paid, free and clear, except for monumental property taxes and upkeep costs I can't keep up with. I'll never sell, but knowing I could makes all the difference.

Scooting across the hall, I shivered in the autumn chill. *You are not really cold*, I told myself. Real cold holds off till Halloween, which is why the stingy landlord doesn't turn on the heat till November 1.

I checked the landlord's image in the mirror over the sink. The fluorescents picked up each freckle and magnified it, giving my red hair a greenish glow that spread to my skin, blending with my hazel eyes and achieving a sort of monochromatic, lizardlike effect. In the bedroom mirror, where I do makeup, I look human. Too tall, eyes too far apart, chin too narrow, broken-nosed, but hardly reptilian.

I yanked off my red chenille robe and hung it on the hook. The closed shower curtain brought me to a halt. I sniffed the air suspiciously. The tang of some spray–type ammonia product lingered, indicating that Roz, my third-floor tenant cum housekeeper, might have actually cleaned the bathroom. I studied the sink. It was difficult to tell whether she'd disturbed any dirt.

Had she left the water turned to shower or tub? I always push the knob down after showering so I don't inadvertently soak my head when not planning to shampoo. Roz seems to regard cleaning as an act of sabotage, hiding towels, moving the soap, diddling the knobs.

Why haven't I chucked her into a snowdrift and hired a reputable, bonded cleaning service? Because I'm cheap, but that's not the whole story. I don't know how I've grown accustomed to her, but it's a fact: I have. I need a tenant, to offset expenses, to help me avoid the dread specter of housework. With Roz I know where I am, sort of. Forewarned is often forearmed.

I ripped back the curtain and stood dumbstruck.

Transfixed by the body in my bathtub.

Body. Bathtub. Body in the bathtub. Body in *my* bathtub. My fingers seemed to have lost their power to grip. I couldn't even draw the curtain to make the apparition disappear. A fresh bar of soap nested in the tub's corner, and one large foot was splayed beneath it. The toenails needed clipping.

Somehow I remembered to close the lid before sinking onto the toilet. Resting elbows on knees, forehead in hands, I shut my eyes and vowed to get a normal life even if it meant ringing a cash register at the local Stop & Shop. Tentatively, I shook my head and ran my tongue around the inside of my mouth. No sign of a hangover. I'd never been a binge drinker. Never blacked out. Before. I couldn't recall bringing home a man, and now, here I was with a corpse.

The body grunted.

Instinctively, I snatched a hand towel, which turned out to be way too small to cover what ought to be covered. The phony corpse belched again, its head lolling lazily to one side while beer and dope fumes rose like mist from its hair. I grabbed a bigger towel, draped and tucked, and congratulated myself on not screaming.

He wasn't dead. I wouldn't need to dial 911 and listen to myself confess to a capital crime I couldn't recall committing. With my eyes shut, I counted slowly to five. When I bugged them wide, he remained stubbornly visible, definitely a man; stoned, soaked, stark naked, still lying in my tub.

He had a body honed by workouts, alternately flat and bulging in the right places. Pale, wispy hair clung to his skull. His neck was long and sinewy, his jaw bony, his face turned to the wall. I leaned in to get a better view. Bad skin, pitted by acne. Eyes shut under bristly, dark brows.

It was not a familiar face, not a face I'd seen before. He was breathing deeply now, noisy inhalations, greedy sucking sounds.

Call the cops?

Get dressed, wake him—whoever the hell he was—then call the cops?

His right hand, propped along the edge of the porcelain, caught my attention. At first I thought it might be bruised, but as I inched closer, I saw that the purple blob centered on the knuckle of his index finger was layered and thick. I sniffed at it and knew: paint. Purple paint! Roz might as well have signed her name across his chest.

Quickly, I examined the room's perimeter. My tenant is an artist of sorts, currently specializing in post-punk paint and performance. She's been known to mount rented video cams in her quest to document her bizarre life. If I found a surveillance unit in my bathroom, I'd call the police only after I finished disposing of *her* body.

My outrage soared. Granted, I was glad this wasn't some guy I'd met in a bar, glad I hadn't experienced totally unmemorable sex, but relief didn't go far toward loosening my clamped jaw. Not only did the paint scream "Roz," the man's body type incriminated her as well. She has appalling taste in the opposite sex, choosing boyfriends on the basis of muscles alone.

Very gently, I reached over, made contact with the shower curtain, and tugged it closed.

Shrugging into my robe, I pounded upstairs, letting the towel drop unheeded in mid-flight. Under normal conditions I don't enter Roz's lair. It scares me, with its black matte walls and ceilings, store dummies fixed in strikingly weird poses, black-and-white TVs flickering like lava lamps.

"Roz," I yelled into the darkness. The smell of paint was strong and sharp, and I wondered if she'd switched from her usual acrylics to a more potent medium.

She owns no bed, just mats that she strews haphazardly across the floor. For karate, sleeping, sex. Basics.

"Yo?" I heard her voice, but couldn't distinguish her shape. How did she keep it so dark? Had she bricked the windows?

"Get the hell downstairs."

"Huh?"

"You left some trash in the tub."

"Big deal."

"I mean it. Now. As in *now!*"

I timed her, counting one, one thousand, two, one thousand, as I retraced my steps to the bathroom, clinging to my indignation. If I allowed myself a single laugh, I knew Roz would squeal like a puppy and assume I thought the whole business was way cool.

My cheek twitched. I got it under control.

She took eighteen seconds. Didn't bother to dress. Wrapped in a black sheet—where in hell do you buy black sheets?—she looked like a terrorist from a small Middle Eastern country.

"The tub," I said.

She yanked the curtain, froze for a moment, then roared with laughter.

"Yuck it up."

"Carlotta, I'm sorry! I'm so sorry! I'm really—" She gave up her feeble attempt at apology and whooped until her sheet fell off, flapping to the floor like a strange dark bird.

"I thought he went home," she said. "He was helping me with the murals. I thought he'd spend the night, you know, but he kept sucking a bottle of tequila and got hopelessly drunk, useless, so I told him to go. I honestly thought he'd left."

"In his birthday suit?"

"Cute, huh?"

I studied the body's face.

"Roz," I said quietly, "how old is this boy?"

"What's the diff?"

"Length of your jail sentence, for a start." My mind backtracked abruptly. "Murals? What did you . . . What was that stuff about murals?"

"Hey, it's cool. He's like a bouncer, but he paints, too, and with his bod, I can model the central—"

"The last time I heard the word *murals* it referred to wall paintings."

"You didn't say anything when I painted the attic black," she protested in a small voice.

"What the hell could I say? It was done by the time I knew."

"You're gonna love it. Murals are like total commentary. First, I thought nude guys, but then I thought earth-moving machinery, bulldozers and cranes and heavy trucks, and wham! I had this wipe-out idea, an absolute brainstorm—"

Roz once did a series featuring Smurfs attacking Russian icons. More recently she'd tried her hand at acrylic veggies and sexually enhanced stick figures. Then there was "found art," which she found around my house when she was supposed to be dusting. Like I said, I'm not planning to sell the house, but if I do, the presence of Roz's wall art will not be a major selling point.

I interrupted her flow. "First, I want this guy out of here."

"He'll wake up."

"Not good enough. I want him out now. I never wish to en-counter him again, asleep or awake, even by chance. Is that clear?"

"Hey, just 'cause you're the landlord, you can't, like, dictate my life."

"Get this straight: Ditch him, or move out with him. Up to you. If you choose not to leave, invest in some paint. Heavy-duty latex. Beige. Today."

"No way."

"Two coats, maybe three, ought to cover whatever misguided project you've begun—"

Neither of us had been paying much attention to the body. He chose that moment to stir and groan ominously. As he tried to sit, the skin on his face turned yellowy white. His features twisted. His mouth gaped, displaying the tip—I swear—of a purple-flecked tongue. He was going to be sick.

I was outta there.

# TWO

Scooping an armload of clothes off the hamper lid, I hustled downstairs to the tiny half bath, where I attempted to shower in the sink. After banging my left elbow on the door twice, I gave up. Icy rivulets ran down my torso, dripping on the rugless tile. The towel rod was bare, so I dried myself on the T-shirt I'd rescued from the washing machine.

I wanted a shower, felt a longing for water I can only compare to intense hunger. Thirst I knew I could quench with a cool drink, but my hunger was the kind that required immersion. Water's my element; I swim whenever I can, luxuriate in hot, soapy tubs and pulsing showers.

Groans and grumbles issued nonstop from the bathroom above.

I finished swabbing wet spots, checked the T-shirt's armpits for undesirable fragrance, pulled it over my head, and shook out my hair. The worn jeans had rips at both knees. Strapping on my watch, I eyed the time and decided to head for a place where ripped jeans would provoke no derogatory comments. With my gym bag already in the trunk, there was no need to trot upstairs and risk an encounter with the vomiting hulk. I'd shower at the Cambridge Y, where my early arrival would sit well with Kirsten, our earnest captain, who'd been looking at me askance ever since I'd missed three consecutive weeks of volleyball practice in August. The morning's disastrous opening could be saved and converted into an opportunity to impress her.

I could tell by the record-breaking pace at which I sped the mile and a half to the Y and stomped from car to locker room that I was still pissed at Roz, but I let the anger slip away as I swam twenty laps, then rinsed off the chlorine as lavishly as possible within the confines of a moldy-smelling, plastic-curtained cubicle. By 8 A.M. volleyball time, my fingertips were shriveled and pink.

Next to swimming, I'll take volleyball. Give me two teams on opposite sides of a tall net, the smell of gym socks and sweat, a firm, white ball. Plenty of coed squads exist, but for day-to-day play, I prefer teaming with women, because there are few showboats, and even fewer who'll go out of their way to deck you, although the number seems to be increasing. I imagined Roz across the net and angled a shot at her solar plexus. A middle blocker with a deep southern accent stared at me hard.

"Watch it," she drawled, flashing a disarming smile. "You're gonna lose teeth you keep that up."

"Sorry," I said.

Loretta tipped me an easy crosscourt floater. I smashed it over the net, aiming for floor this time.

"Side out," Kirsten yelled.

My serve sailed too high, way too shallow, turned into an easy dig for a quick woman with dark hair. A small Hispanic woman set it center net for the middle blocker I'd antagonized, but quiet Gwen Taymore, beaded braids bouncing on my side of the net, anticipated her perfectly and saved the point by scooping a dig so gorgeous I wanted to stop and applaud.

*Concentrate,* I ordered myself. *Go for the set.* I hate playing the back row. I grit my teeth and do it for the good of my soul, so I'll remember that cooperation is essential. Most of the time I prefer playing Lone Ranger, but sometimes group effort is the key. And I know I won't get stuck in the back row forever. That's consolation.

I've been playing with the Y-Birds too long to remember. Members come and go but a hard-core element stays loyal, addicted to the movement of ball over net, the give of the wooden floorboards, the smash of fist and ball, the satisfying smack of the victorious point, the kill.

It's fun, it's exercise, and I don't have to interact with machines. I don't have to jog an endless treadmill to nowhere. I do have to put up with non–spa-quality surroundings, but the dues are affordable, and the company's good. For women who've played together a long time, we Y-Birds know almost nothing about each other. It's a restful ignorance, and in our gym shorts and tank tops we all look as if we could hail from the same economic background.

I served five points, which for me is superlative. I don't take full credit: Gwen made three more great digs, reading the opposition's placement like a clairvoyant. After the game, the quick shower, the usual locker-room jive and chat, I thanked her, earning a wide smile and a nod. She turned left out the front door and tagged along with me as far as the corner, hesitating while I stuck five dimes in the slot to buy a *Globe* from a vending machine. She crossed the street beside me, against the light, held the door as I entered Dunkin' Donuts, her eyes fixed on the ground. No single member of the team is as dedicated a doughnut muncher as I am, although each has been known to celebrate a crucial victory with Honey-Dipped or Jelly-Filled.

Gwen was sticking with me like a just-patted pup. I eyeballed the area for a reason, such as a large and angry boyfriend. Some of my teammates know I'm an ex-cop. Relieved that I could see no apparent stalker, I ordered my usual—glazed and coffee with cream and sugar—sat, and cracked the paper.

Drug lords had seized a remote mountain prison in Colombia. Two conflicting conspiracy theories had surfaced concerning the death of Martin Luther King Jr. An outfit called the Jewish Reclamation League had declared a "legal" right to seize artwork looted from Holocaust victims, bang off the walls of museums, if necessary. In the Fenway, rats feasted on garbage while the Department of Sanitation denied any appreciable rodent infestation. This on the front page alone.

Across from me, Gwen lowered her coffee cup with sufficient force to set the contents quivering. A chair protested squeakily as she dragged it over the tile. If she'd wanted to be alone there were plenty of other tables. Four seats were empty along the orange Formica counter. I glanced up and smiled encouragingly. Gwen, a silent young woman of color with a sweet, round face and a grin that lifted the corners of a generous mouth, was a team fixture. I say "woman of color" because my friend Gloria, who used to call herself black, now prefers "woman of color," declaring it hip enough to acknowledge the rainbow of shades between Argentine tan and African noir, yet aware that "African American" might be presumptuous.

Gwen's skin was the color of polished teak, flawless except for the splash of freckles on her nose. She gnawed her lower lip uneasily, opened her mouth several times, then squeezed her left hand into a fist and blurted, "Do you think there's an age at which you—you—you know, l–lose it?"

After battling with the word *you*, she almost made it through the sentence without stuttering, but the *L* of *lose* seemed to catch on her tongue and she couldn't quite spit it out. I waited while she fought to finish, thinking that she never stuttered when she spoke during games, but then she never spoke much at all: What's to say? Good hit, Watch the ball, Whoopee? In her strong and fluid game, I'd seen no hint that her tongue betrayed her.

Ending the sentence, she stared at the tabletop. If not for the speech impediment I'd have thought she was musing aloud, but the question had cost her, in effort and embarrassment.

"Do you mean, lose it in volleyball?" I asked, trying to clarify the subject. "Like lose your skills?" I thought she might be trying to ease into the fact that my serve is weak. I already know my serve is weak. It always has been.

"No," she said, "n–not volleyball. L–like losing your focus, your capabilities . . . l–losing your mind. Is there a certain age?"

I didn't feel that this was an area in which I was a qualified expert, so I asked, "Why?"

Undeterred, she continued, "D–do you think s–senility is there at the end, f–for everybody?"

Senility not being a concept I usually had to deal with over doughnuts, I was tempted by levity, tempted to claim I'd forgotten the question, but Gwen was staring at me earnestly with big wide-apart eyes, almond shaped, almost yellow in color. Curious eyes I'd hardly noticed before, framed with wispy lashes other women might have mascaraed. The beads in her cornrowed hair were blue and green, see-through, like tiny marbles.

I said, "People age differently. I had an aunt who stayed sharp till she died at eighty-nine, but Alzheimer's can hit people in their sixties or younger."

I don't think it was what I said, so maybe it was the way I said it, the fact that I responded seriously and patiently. All I know is that some of the tension in the set of Gwen's shoulders uncoiled and vanished, like a snake disappearing into tall grass.

"I know this old woman," she said softly, and the stammer seemed to subside faintly. *What an effort it must have taken to talk to me,* I thought, and I wondered if she'd been meaning to speak for a while, if she'd waited, procrastinated, stored up anxiety until a childhood stammer returned, or if the stammer was with her always. I wondered how much she minded, if it went away when she relaxed, if it affected her livelihood, her solemn demeanor—made her more physical than verbal.

How old was she? Her unlined face said twenty, give or take two: young enough that "old" could mean forties, fifties, sixties. I prompted her with a cautious nod, sensing a well of untold stories behind the reference to an "old woman," not sure I wanted to tap the source.

She tried several times, finally managed, "W–well, she doesn't live far, just lives over in the F–Fenway."

Boston's Fenway takes its name from the city park that was Frederick Law Olmsted's solution to draining the marshy swamp-lands along the Muddy River. Twisting past the Museum of Fine Arts, it meanders through Longwood, winds out to Jamaica Plain. Tourists think the Fenway refers to Fenway Park, home of the Red Sox, but the true Fenway, much diminished in size since Olmsted's day, encompasses a large residential and commercial community, not to mention the rodent population referred to on the front page of the *Globe*.

"She's acting s–strangely, but there've been problems lately, you know, with the s–sewage backing up, and the blackouts and all. . . ."

Gwen gazed at me as though she wanted me to respond, needed me to respond. The stammer had resurfaced strongly. It didn't like the letter *S*.

"Strangely," I echoed.

"She wants the l–locks on her doors r–replaced. The doors r–reinforced. The windows, she w–wants shutters on the windows, and l–locks on the shutters."

"Not the most effective measures against sewage backups or blackouts," I observed. "It sounds like there've been robberies."

"Y–you know, I b–believe there was one in the building, months ago, but she didn't seem f–frightened then," Gwen said haltingly. I was getting used to the pauses and rushes of her speech. "The building's safe, th–that's what I'm trying to convince her."

There are places in the Fenway I'd gladly move into tomorrow, others where I'd nail the shutters closed and bar the doors.

"Rapes and muggings in the area?" I asked.

"D–drunks outside bars, occasional brawls. N–nothing out of the ordinary, except f–for the electricity going off all the time, and the smell—"

"From the sewage?"

"And when they f–forget to pick up the g–garbage." Gwen wrinkled her nose.

"Some people get more cautious with age," I said. "Is that so bad?"

Gwen made a fist out of her left hand again. The action seemed to help her focus her energy into speech. "She won't g–go out, not even to play bridge. She used to v–visit people. Now she's s–stacking canned goods against the back door."

"It could be some condition that requires medical diagnosis and treatment," I ventured.

"It c–could be, it might be . . . b–but before, you said it s–sounded like she was just being cautious."

"Is this woman related to you?"

"She's my client."

I let a bite of sugar-laced doughnut melt against the roof of my mouth, washed it down with coffee.

"I'm a home health aide," Gwen continued, "and Mrs. Phipps, she's my client. She's a h–handful." She smiled proudly, then surged on. "You m–might have heard of her. She's a regular c–celebrity in the F–Fenway."

I shook my head. "The name isn't familiar."

"She's one of the last t–tenants c–covered under rent control."

"There's no more rent control," I said.

"She's s–some kind of special case. Nobody can r–raise her rent or kick her out, 'cause she's been there so long, and she's a widow and all. So when she talks, they've got to listen, and she's s–starting a tenants rights group, or that's what the article about her s–said. I asked her if it would make her feel better if a professional, s–someone in law enforcement, visited her—"

*Aha*, I thought. *Here it comes.*

"The Boston Police have a community relations department—," I said quickly.

"You," she said. "I–I told her I know s–somebody. She's an odd person. Once she t–trusts you, she trusts you, you know what I mean, but there aren't m–many she trusts. She said she'd pay for your time. She's not rich, though I heard she used to be. She's a c–community treasure. The paper said so."

"A police officer would be better, or someone she already knows and—"

"P–please. It's m–my responsibility. To l–look after her."

This last burst took an eternity to get out, and left her exhausted. The pride in her voice when she declared the old woman her responsibility seemed genuine.

*I'd get paid*, I thought, selecting the essential fact from the halting sentences. Maybe I wouldn't wake up tomorrow with dollar signs hovering over my head like thought balloons.

"Security advice is not exactly up my alley," I confessed. "Maybe somebody from an alarm firm—"

"Oh y–yeah, and what's their a–angle? Mrs. Phipps will have f–five different alarm systems, but will they make her f–feel safer?"

"What would you like me to do?" If it hadn't been for the stutter, I might not have crumbled.

"I promised her I'd try s–someone I know. She doesn't trust s–strangers."

*I'm a stranger,* I thought. *What on earth do you know about me? That I can spike a volleyball?*

"S–see what Mrs. Phipps can do to make her apartment safer. Give her advice about answering her doorbell, using her p–peephole and her door chain. I'm s–scared she'll get a gun, shoot s–somebody. Really I am."

"How old is this woman?"

"M–maybe seventy-five."

Granny gets a gun. Wonderful. Blows away the neighbor boy who stops by to see if she needs groceries. Or the neighbor boy who senses easy pickings. . . . Either way, if I didn't respond I'd wind up feeling guilty and guilt already ranks so high on my list of preoccupations, I sometimes think of printing it on the dotted line under *Employment* on questionnaires.

"Okay," I said, dusting crumbs off my hands, feeling caffeine and sugar surge through my veins. "I'll do it."

"L–let me call her," Gwen said, "while y–you finish your coffee. S–set a time. Great, Carlotta, I can't thank you enough."

"I'll do what I can. No miracles, no promises."

"It eats on me, the way she is. So d–different than how she was. You know, she doesn't have any f–family. Me, neither." Gwen ducked her head and sipped cold coffee, her plastic hair beads catching the light, and I wondered how I could have missed those extraordinary eyes, the way they seemed to gleam when she smiled.

"Okay, make the call," I said.

"If it takes, say, an hour, will thirty-five dollars cover it? She s–said she'd go thirty-five."

It's way below my standard rate, but after a single hour-long evaluation, I could conceivably add Security Consultant to my résumé. So I nodded approval and watched my teammate hurry off in the direction of a pay phone. As I popped the remainder of my doughnut into my mouth, my ears caught an angry burst of Spanish. The hostility in the exchange might have been sufficient to attract my interest; a familiar voice in the mix whipped my head around fast enough to make me dizzy.

It belonged to my Little Sister.

# THREE

"Hey, *pendejo*! Leave us alone!" My Little Sister employs English and Spanish interchangeably, often in the same sentence. Her insult was mild compared to the rest; her voice one of many, all brittle with anger. I caught bits and pieces while my brain attempted to shift linguistic gears.

"Get the hell out!" The loud Anglo male had an accent that turned *get* to *git*. He was immediately swamped by a chorus of derisive comments, delivered in Spanish, concerning the heritage and habits of his mother.

"Goddamn you tacoheads," he continued belligerently. "Don't you fuckin' know you can't smoke in here? It ain't allowed!"

As his volume increased, heads swiveled toward the back corner of the restaurant, where two boys and two girls—correct that, two men and two very young girls—slouched against the orange padded seats of a booth. Coffee was sloshed across the tabletop. Someone had attempted to staunch the flow with an inadequate supply of paper napkins. Plates doubled as ashtrays.

"We no bother nobody." A spokesman emerged from the seated Spanish-speakers, his voice alone an insult, a lazy drawl that couldn't care less.

"You been eatin' one doughnut for two fuckin' hours." The sentence was punctuated by the smack of an emphatic fist on Formica. "Move on—or apply for a job, why don't ya? Why don't ya go to school? Learn good English!"

"School, *malparido?*" The drawl returned dangerously. "School's so out." The man with the drawl stretched his tattooed right arm and rested his hand on my Little Sister Paolina's bare shoulder. I stepped closer to the disputed territory, halting near a wooden partition.

"Go on! Move it!" The man at the open end of the booth stood poised like a waiter about to take an order. He wore the orange smock of an employee over a barrel chest. His hair was blond, buzzed short.

The girl who was not my sister, dark-haired and skinny, laughed and muttered under her breath. All the booth-sitters hooted while a flush crept up the stocky man's neck. I didn't catch his response, but his tone was threatening. I edged behind his right shoulder.

The drawling man's hand no longer touched Paolina's shoulder. It grasped a knife with a black metal handle. His smile revealed a gold incisor.

The sight of the knife immobilized the orange-smocked counterman. His doughy face was white and red, heavily veined. He wasn't a regular employee; I knew the veteran staff.

The scene felt like a freeze-frame camera shot, and time slowed the way it does when there's going to be trouble. I broke the silence.

"Put it away and walk out of here, and nobody will have to do time." I used my command voice, the one I learned when I was a cop. Then I repeated the phrase in careful Spanish: "*Guárdala y sal, y nadie verá la carcel.*"

"Why's he hasslin' me?" The gold-toothed man stared up at me unblinkingly. He didn't want or expect an answer, but I prefer questions to knifeplay any day. His English was heavily accented, but his command of idioms was fine.

The fool counterman was quick with a reply. "Because you're smokin', fuckhead. Whatsamatter, can't ya read?" He must have felt supported by my presence. His voice got louder, as though he wanted to play to a bigger audience.

Goldtooth's knife hand tensed.

"*Quisiera disculpar su proceder insultante,*" I said quietly. "I'd like to apologize for his insulting behavior, but in this city it's the law. If you want a cigarette you go outside. When you're finished you come back in."

"Who're you?"

"Just a cop." My Little Sister's voice sounded amused. I raised my eyes momentarily from the five-inch blade. Paolina's not my blood sister; I'm an only child. But she's been my sister long enough that I thought I knew her.

A lit cigarette dangled from her maroon lips. She'd turned fourteen at the end of August, started high school last month. Her dark hair was swept up and held with a garish purple comb, her eyes gooey with mascara. The man who sat too close to her looked like he was well into his twenties, a stubble-chinned, greasy-haired disaster.

If he stabbed the counterman and wound up in jail, I'd wager it wouldn't be the first time. I'd bet fifty on a previous record based on appearance alone. What? Did he wake up every morning and wonder how best to dress for that ex-con look? His Hawaiian-print shirt was opened to the navel. The waistband of his pants hung around his hips, displaying the dirty elastic of his shorts.

Keeping my voice low, I said, "Paolina, get up and go outside. Wait in the drugstore."

I wanted her out of knife-blade range, out of reach. The man's eyes didn't look crazy, but I couldn't take the chance. While she was near him, she was a potential hostage.

She blew a practiced ring of smoke in my face. The man laughed.

"All this shit over a few butts. *Hijueputas de mierda.* I shoulda brought us some China White," he said.

His buddies snickered. The casual profanity, the drug reference, wouldn't have fazed the regular counterman, but this guy burned red to the tips of his ears.

"Get outta here or I call the cops."

He hadn't believed I was one, and the situation made me glad I wasn't, glad I was no longer required to face off in confrontations like this one, this quintessential cop nightmare. Dumbbells versus dumbbells. Add language barrier, foul mouths, and come out fighting.

I wasn't used to operating as a cop without a partner, a radio, or backup. I wasn't used to having my Little Sister in the picture.

Goldtooth spat another comment concerning the doughnut man's mom. Fortunately only his cohorts and I understood the nature of the observation.

"Chill," I said severely. Then I tried the man in Spanish again. "*Vamos a tratar esto afuera.* Let's take this outside." If I couldn't get Paolina to walk away from the knife, I might get the knife to walk away from Paolina.

"Chill." A deeper voice echoed my own. Startled, I glanced to the right. A Cambridge uniform stood at my side, an unfamiliar bulky shape. I didn't feel relief because I didn't know the cop, and the air was already thick with the musky scent of masculine pride. I trust myself to talk a guy down. Most guys aren't threatened by a woman and they let her sweet-talk them a little, especially the *muy macho* Latinos.

Was I going to have a pissing match on my hands, cops against creeps? All I wanted was to get the blade out of view, the counterman stuffed behind the counter, business as usual.

"*Qué pasa?*" the cop remarked easily, sliding off into a liquid flow of Spanish, addressing the skinny girl across the table from Paolina by name, politely inquiring how her Aunt Graciela was doing with the new baby.

The knife had vanished as if it had never existed. The cop sure hadn't seen it. The counterman, eager to vent, turned to the uniform. With his eyes no longer challenging Goldtooth's, the charged cable that had connected them broke and tension ebbed. Cop and counterman took two paces away from the table.

The girl who was Graciela's niece slid out of the booth, hiked up a bra strap, and disappeared into the bathroom. The quiet man next to her made stealthily for the exit, probably costing the Cambridge cop a collar on a bench warrant. Goldtooth swigged coffee. The uniform seemed an easygoing sort, unflappable. Maybe he'd dealt with the overwrought counterman before. Maybe he'd assume the counterman exaggerated, disbelieve the knife.

I could get the man who'd caressed Paolina's shoulder arrested easily. But how would my Little Sister react if I took an active part in the bust?

The counterman was murmuring earnestly to the cop. On the periphery I was aware of Gwen, peering at me, trying to attract my attention.

"Paolina," I said urgently. "Let's go."

No telling when the magic word *knife* would surface, when the cop would order us to empty our pockets on the table.

Goldtooth said, "Yeah, we're out," as he grabbed Paolina's hand.

"Leave her." I angled my chin in the direction of the cop. "Blade's still on you, right?"

She started toward the exit with him. I jerked her to a full stop. Her cheeks flamed.

He said, "Come by later, *querida*. For you, *chiquita*, I'm always home, *siempre listo a darte lo qué quieras*."

"She's way underage," I said. "Get lost."

"Well, then, how about you, babe?" Anger flickered behind his eyes. "See how good my Anglo is: Fuck you, bitch."

He kissed his fingertips in my direction, then ducked his shoulders, and sped off. I kept a tight grip on Paolina till I saw him jaywalk Mass. Ave. and dodge down an alley. As I made my way to the door with Paolina's hand in mine, the Cambridge cop turned his head and nodded a solemn farewell. I was sure he'd recognize me if we met again.

Gwen, who had appeared behind us, said plaintively, "I'm trying t–to tell you, c–can we make it now? Mrs. Phipps is in s–some kind of trouble."

"Now?" I echoed.

"P–please." The cheerful blue and green beads bobbed in her hair.

I could have confronted Paolina, demanded to know what she was doing dressed like a five-dollar whore, smoking lipstick-stained cigarettes with a bad-news man.

Instead I said yes.

# FOUR

My Toyota was parked on Bishop Richard Allen Drive, a congested street that borders on parking lots and tenements, and ought to run one way, since it only has room for a single lane of traffic. Two right turns took me onto Mass. Ave., where I assured Gwen, tucked silently into the backseat, that I knew the quickest route to the Fenway.

"Good," she said flatly, no stutter on that word. "I don't know what's g–going on."

"Gwen, I'd like you to meet my sister, Paolina." I cast a baleful glance at her overdone eye makeup as I spoke, marveling at her clown-red rouge.

Paolina said, "She's not my sister."

"It's not a blood relationship," I said for Gwen's benefit.

"It's not any kind of relationship," Paolina returned snippily.

I honked a warning at a junk-pile Buick, intimidating him from changing lanes and pulling in front of me.

"I've known her since she was seven," I said. "She used to behave more like an adult."

I drove through icy silence, hoping Paolina wouldn't skip when I had to stop for a light. I wanted to ask Gwen to reach a hand forward and lock Paolina's door, but that would have sent exactly the message I didn't want to deliver.

"C–Carlotta, Mrs. Phipps sounded scared. . . ." Gwen had to backpedal twice for my name.

Pressing the accelerator, I said, "I can drive it in eight minutes. Or we can find a phone and call the cops."

"D–drive," Gwen said.

"What about me?" Paolina inserted angrily. "What am I supposed to do?"

I said, "Wait in the car."

She yanked down the vanity mirror and concentrated on applying more maroon lip gunk. I drove.

I pilot a cab when the investigation business is slow. I've been doing it for years, started when I was working my way through college at U. Mass/Boston. Some say it's dangerous, especially for a woman, but I found the one shift I tried waitressing far more hazardous, what with all that order-taking and forced cheery-smile politeness. Cutting through Cambridgeport on Pearl Street, speeding around the rotary approaching the BU Bridge, shooting down Park Drive, I hit only one red light, and Paolina stayed put, admiring her heavy-handed artistry in the mirror, pouting and pursing her lips.

With legit parking prospects dismal, I pulled to the curb on Peterborough, a narrow street lined with neat, four-story brownstones and minimal patches of lawn. A row of spindly trees struggled to take root in the middle of too much concrete.

As I turned off the engine, Paolina announced, "I'm not waiting in the stupid car."

"Bring her upstairs. M–Mrs. Phipps doesn't m–mind kids," Gwen urged.

"I'm not a kid!"

I said, "If there's any problem, Paolina, you'll get back in the car. When I tell you to do it, you'll do it. Understand?"

Hurriedly, I slapped a chunk of cardboard underneath the windshield wiper. It read: "Car broke down, gone for help." Sometimes it prevents a ticket.

As we sped around the corner onto Kilmarnock, the wind whistled through a playground across the street, carrying the sound of children at recess. Why the hell wasn't my Little Sister in school?

Gwen indicated a yellow brick building and veered toward its concrete stoop. I grabbed Paolina's elbow to steer her to the right. She shook me off. Her chunky purse banged against her hip, emphasizing the tight curve of a too-short skirt. She'd draped her red parka over her shoulders. Her heels were ridiculous pinch-toed spikes.

The building had a security system of sorts. A heavy oak outer door opened into a foyer lined with mailboxes. Underneath each mailbox was a button labeled with a last name followed by a comma and a first initial, neatly typed on posterboard. I approved of the minimal information. If initials were used only for a few, it simply spotlighted the single women.

Gwen pressed the button over PHIPPS, V.

Victoria, I guessed.

We waited. Gwen's lips moved twice, as though she wanted to say something, but each time she subsided without opening her mouth more than half an inch. Paolina darted angry glances at me from under inky lashes.

Static crackled through the speaker.

The system was the latest in 1950s technology, good and solid and full of flaws. If I wanted to break into the building, I'd ring till somebody let me in. Somebody always lets me in. All I have to do is yell a cheerful "FedEx" into the speaker. Takes less time than cracking the lock.

Static again, followed by a sharp "Who's there? Speak up!"

"It's Gwen."

"Thank goodness, thank God. Help me!"

Gwen caught her breath on a sharp intake. The buzzer blared, and we both charged the door, Gwen edging in front, racing up the curving staircase. I trailed a step behind, because there wasn't sufficient room to pass.

Below me, I could hear the clunk-clunk of Paolina's heels. Above: silence, broken by the sound of pounding or hammering. Gwen flew upstairs, peeled off at the fourth-floor landing, wheeling left.

"What the h–hell?"

I heard Gwen's demand before I saw the man standing in front of apartment 4A. His back was turned, so my first impression was of broad shoulders stretching the supple leather of a bomber jacket. His right arm was upraised; what had sounded like hammering was actually knocking.

"Leave me alone!" The voice from behind the apartment door was cracked with age and anger.

The man turned to face Gwen, breathing hard, cheeks flushed. He stood five-ten, five-eleven. His gleaming black hair was caught tightly in a ponytail, oiled so that the toothmarks of the comb stood out like tracks. The pulled-back hair accentuated a jutting nose. His tight jeans were tucked into construction boots so new they'd never walked a working site, but his toolbelt bristled with well-used gear: screwdrivers, claw hammer, steel measuring tape.

The man lowered his hands abruptly, rested them on the belt. "First, she tells me to wait." He bit off each word precisely, exasperation in his tone. "Then she disappears—"

"He's lying," came the dry voice from behind the door. "Lying!"

"She tells me to wait," he repeated, forcing a smile. "I've been waiting kind of a long time and I thought maybe she forgot I was out here."

"Gwen? Are you there?"

"M–Mrs. Phipps, d–don't worry about a thing."

"Gwen, tell that brute he can't force his way in here. He's lucky I didn't call the police, have him arrested!"

"It doesn't sound like she forgot about you," I said mildly.

"The police?" the man muttered. "Hey, I'm not forcing anything. I didn't try anything." He glanced at Gwen, at me, tried the smile until it wavered, managed a weak laugh. "Honest, she went to put on the teakettle, forgot all about me. I was just making a little noise is all, to remind her. I thought maybe she'd gone deaf." He looked as annoyed as a man who'd been fruitlessly door-banging for a while, but there was a shiftiness in his eyes that reminded me of too many misunderstood "innocents" I'd met in holding tanks.

The door yawned open suddenly. In a scarlet dress and tightly wrapped turban, the elderly woman framed within it seemed so autocratic and commanding that her diminutive height hardly registered. "You have no right to demand entry here, Mr. Peritti," she said. "And now that I have a witness to your trickery—witness*es*," she amended, giving me a dismissive once-over, "I trust you'll be gone before this tiff escalates into a major incident."

"Mrs. Phipps," the man said, "you can't keep playing these little games with me. My time's worth money and it's costing me, being out of my office—"

"Go away, then! Can't you see you're upsetting me?" As abruptly as she'd opened it, she banged the door shut. A chain rattled furiously.

He turned to me, shrugging his shoulders eloquently, then tapped the side of his head with his index finger and nodded at the now-closed door. "Old bat invited me to come," he said confidingly. "I called her on the phone, she's sweet as pie, honest. That was probably before she took a big swig from the bourbon bottle."

The "old bat" was far from deaf. Her voice sounded immediately through the door, brimming with indignation. "Gwen, he's lying as surely as he's standing there. Haven't I told you I'd never let him in my home with his measuring tapes again?" The door snicked open and the red-turbaned head reappeared to announce, "You're not half the man your father was, young man!"

"Leave my father out of this."

"I have an agreement with your father, signed and notarized. You can't make me move."

"I just need to take some measurements—"

"Never!"

"Then why'd you tell me to come over?"

"I never did."

"You're the liar." He turned his head and elaborately mouthed, "She's a nutcase," to Gwen and me.

"What's that you said?" the old woman snapped.

"Nothing."

"He tried to break down my door!"

"The hell I did."

"Look at him. He came prepared. Look at that hammer."

"Mrs. Phipps, for chrissakes—"

"I could have you arrested."

"Yeah, sure, why not call your pet journalist and have him tell the whole city what a lousy crook I am? Again? Or are you getting tired of that, lady? Think your adoring public's getting fed up with the same old beef?"

Gwen swallowed, said, "If you want to see Mrs. Phipps, maybe you c–can c–come by when I'm here."

"Look," he said placatingly, turning from the birdlike eyes of the elderly woman to face us, "she gave me permission. Honest, I talked to her on the phone not half an hour ago. She said fine, come, no fucking problem."

"Don't use such language in front of me, young man!"

"You are starting to get to me, lady," he said, pivoting and waving a warning finger in her face. "I don't care what my old man agreed to. Agreements can be broken."

"The city's behind me," she said grandly. "There's nothing you can do."

"Yeah? Yeah?" He glanced tight-lipped at Gwen, then at me. Paolina, on the staircase, remained out of his sight. "Sure, you say it, lady, it's got to be true. Whatever you say." The sarcasm was heavy, the arm gestures wide.

"C–Carlotta," Gwen said softly. "This is Mrs. Phipps's landlord, Tony Peritti."

He said, "If you're a friend of hers, talk some sense into her, why don't you? Believe me, she isn't doing herself any favors, pulling this kind of shit."

"Watch your tongue!"

"There's gonna be a new agreement soon, you better believe it. Maybe I'll bring some people around to look at your space, Grannie. I'm sure my dad put in some kind of clause allows prospective tenants to look at apartments, you know what I mean?"

Gwen said, "Can you l–leave her alone, please?"

"She's lying to you. I swear it. Give her a cup of black coffee and when she sobers up, you ask her if she isn't lying."

"Liar," the old woman echoed, slamming the door again for emphasis.

Peritti threw up his hands, turned, and stomped to the landing, the heels of his construction boots smacking the wooden floor. Ignoring or forgetting the width of the toolbelt, he charged past Paolina. The hammer handle caught the strap of her shoulder bag and almost pitched her downstairs.

She freed herself, stared silently at Peritti, not with outrage, not with the fearful glance of a child viewing an out-of-control adult, but with the level eyes of a woman evaluating an attractive man's wide shoulders and slim hips. That brief, knowing look, the calculating flicker behind her eyes, shook me more than the makeup or the cigarettes or the memory of Goldtooth's hand caressing her shoulder.

Gwen rapped gently on the door as Peritti's footsteps faded.

"M–Mrs. Phipps, let us in," she called.

# FIVE

"Gwen? Has he gone? Who's with you?"

"The f–friend I told you about. And her sister."

The turbaned woman opened the door slowly this time. She couldn't have topped five feet. While Gwen made labored introductions and Paolina tapped an impatient toe, my prospective employer peppered me with hostile looks.

"There's been a mistake," she declared imperiously, hauling Gwen inside while pointedly leaving us in the hallway. The door banged shut, but I could hear plenty.

Mrs. Phipps, it seemed, would have preferred someone else. Someone who not only wore pants but had the right genitalia to stuff down the front of them. Gwen had identified me simply as a "friend" who was an ex-cop, and Mrs. Phipps, being of the blessed generation that grew up obeying the voice of authority when it spoke in a comfortingly masculine baritone, had made unwarranted assumptions.

I was considering whether to leave without a formal farewell, retrieve my Toyota before some relentless meter maid plastered the window with a ticket, when the door clicked open.

"Thank you for your time." The turban accented high cheekbones and a ruler-straight nose, a severe and forbidding combination.

*Not my client, not my problem,* I thought.

Then, boom, Gwen took charge. Paolina and I found ourselves shunted through the door and into an alcove, issued a glass of tepid water apiece, while Gwen and Mrs. Phipps carried on a hissed, whispered, and occasionally shouted conversation. I drained my glass and placed the open end against the wall in an attempt to eavesdrop. That spook stuff's supposed to work, but it never does. I could have heard as much without the show, but I was trying to impress Paolina with my snooping expertise, coax a reaction, maybe even a familiar laugh.

I picked up broken phrases through the wall. While I barely recalled Gwen's last name, she knew mine, knew I was a private investigator as well as a former cop. That I did "important work." Handled cases for "powerful attorneys," which I do, every so often.

If Gwen lost the home-health-aide job, she could take a shot at writing advertising copy. Her skin was beaded with perspiration when she returned.

I said, "I can recommend somebody else. No big deal."

She managed a faint smile. "Mrs. Phipps has r–reconsidered."

"There's no point in my looking around if she won't take my advice," I said reasonably. "I won't charge for the trip."

"She'll l–listen to you, and she'll like it. Don't get mad. It's j–just her way. Took me a while to get her to w–warm up, but once she defrosts, she's nice as they come. Hey, what's your name again?" she said to Paolina. "Why don't the two of us go into the kitchen?"

"All right if I smoke?" my Little Sister inquired sweetly.

"No way," I said, and the only reason I didn't flat out confiscate her cigarettes was because I didn't want to make a scene.

"Mrs. Phipps awaits you in the l–living room," Gwen announced grandly.

Seldom has a job gotten off to a more wretched start. The client didn't want me, and based on first impressions, I'd have preferred to face a smoldering dragon.

Mrs. Phipps was how she introduced herself. She had militantly upright posture to compensate for her slight stature, and beady eyes that tried to bore holes in my flesh. Her nose was so patricianly perfect that it made me want to apologize for my own thrice-broken model. I could only speculate about the hair tucked beneath the turban, but her eyebrows were pure white, startlingly straight, and bushy as caterpillars. Her dress, a long, loose affair, floated from her shoulders. She had the look of a woman who wore a corset for the good of her soul. Maybe a hair shirt. Stockings, by God, in case anyone might come by and criticize her for wearing a housedress.

"Gwen seems to believe you can be of some assistance," she observed icily.

I said, "So, did you give your landlord the come-hither, then change your mind?"

"I'd imagine a security expert would wish to examine the doors."

"Why not lock me out? See how long it takes me to break in?"

I was tutored by an inmate of Cedar Junction, formerly known as Walpole State Penitentiary, Massachusetts's rent-free accommodation for hard-timers, and I'm proud of my skills. I can do most ordinary locks, and I enjoy the thrill of illegal entry, but I hadn't brought appropriate equipment, so my boast was an idle one. I don't make it a practice to carry picklocks, 'loids, or other tools of the trade.

"Can you?" She lifted one woolly eyebrow. "Break in?"

"Try me," I bluffed.

She seemed to seriously consider my proposition. Her eyes were such a startling blue, almost violet, that if she'd been younger I'd have assumed colored contact lenses.

"Your front-door lock seems adequate—," I began.

"Adequate isn't good enough," she interrupted.

"No?"

"You heard him threaten me."

I wasn't certain I'd heard an outright threat, any more than I was sure she knew what security equipment she already owned, so I ignored the landlord business. "The lock's a single-cylinder dead bolt, and you've got both a peephole and a chain. Use the chain whenever you're home, make chaining up as automatic as brushing your teeth, and don't let anybody rush you into opening the door before you check who's outside."

"You have eyes." Her smile was unexpectedly warm. "It seems you use them."

"If the chain's installed in wallboard or plaster, it'll rip out if somebody shoves the door. If you usually carry on the way you did today, I'd recommend a molly bolt, or a new chain unit altogether."

"Go on," she said.

Once she realized I knew my stuff, you could practically see the hairs lie down on the back of her neck. I examined her front door—the chain was screwed tightly into the door frame the way it ought to be—then recommended a back-entry police bar and sash-window stoppers. Fifteen minutes into the grand tour she forgot I was of the wrong gender, and began to treat me like a person.

The apartment she steered me through was compact and contained more plants than artwork. No photographs. The furnishings were sparse, but what there was had been well chosen; each piece looked as if it belonged precisely where it sat and nowhere else.

She lived on the fourth floor at the back. A narrow alley, designed for trash collection purposes, ran behind the property. The rear door led onto a fire escape that was no more rickety or exposed than its neighbors.

I'd be scared of fire if I were seventy-five, living on the fourth floor. Hard to clamber down a metal escape ladder, especially at night. Gwen ought to have the fire marshal visit; fire was a likelier disaster than a break-in, what with stacks of old newspapers and cardboard boxes lining the hallway. But Mrs. Phipps didn't seem worried about fire.

Which seemed to leave burglars, or the man with the ponytail. Since the woman in red was now chattering animatedly, recalling how dreadfully she missed her parakeet who'd died some eight years ago last fall and explaining how much dear Gwen's visits cheered her up, I decided I might as well exceed the call of duty and satisfy my demon curiosity. I was beginning to enjoy the old lady's patter. Just standing near her made me watch my posture, and it occurred to me that I'd been looking for a good home in which to dump my late aunt's parakeet, a mean, skinny bird who answers to Red Emma.

"Would you care to tell me about this dispute with your landlord?" I asked.

"Dispute?"

"How long had he been pounding your door?"

If he'd phoned ahead, as he'd maintained, Gwen's call could have come at an opportune moment, prompting the woman to stage a scene for our benefit.

"How long were you a police officer?" Mrs. Phipps inquired, smartly changing the subject.

"Six years," I replied. "Does your landlord have a key to your front door?"

She cleared her throat. "Mr. Peritti believes he can trick me into leaving."

"Trick you?"

Her bushy eyebrows drew together till they almost met. She lowered her voice to a confidential murmur. "Why does the elevator have an out-of-order sign on the door whenever I want to use it? There's actually nothing wrong with it, you see. And he stops up the drains so the plumbing backs up and somehow or other he gets the city to turn off the electricity. Oh, yes, he has plans for my apartment. Why, I came home once to find him standing in my bedroom—my bedroom!—yammering about loft space and Jacuzzis, and how to attract the right kind of owners for upscale condominiums. He's gone so far as to loose a mouse in my kitchen. Imagine!"

Close as I was, I couldn't smell alcohol on her breath, or detect the telltale scent of mouthwash. My dad used to gargle with Listerine; I associate it with secret lushes. Maybe she wasn't a drunk, but I decided right then that I didn't want to give my bird a new home with someone who registered more than a tad paranoid.

"You saw him in action," she went on. "It's so difficult to trust anyone." She peered at me, pressing her lips into a thin line. "Didn't you enjoy being a police officer?"

"I like working alone."

"Privacy is vital," she agreed. "I need my privacy. I certainly pay for it. How much do you think I pay?"

"I don't know rents in this area."

She brushed back the lace curtain from a window that looked out on an adjacent brick wall. "I won't mention the days when fifty dollars a month was sufficient to live on. If I tell a person what I used to pay, they think I'm a liar or well past a century old." She smiled her quirky smile and raised one eyebrow. "There was a time I didn't pay much attention to the price of things. Didn't have to. Then for years I paid three hundred for this place. Three hundred seemed reasonable. Then four, five, six, and before you could bat an eyelash, seven. Would you believe he wants to raise the rent to nine hundred a month?"

"Move," I suggested bluntly.

"But I don't want to. This is my home."

When someone calls a space "home" in that tone of voice, you get no credit for pointing out that it legally belongs to another party, because "homes" are created, not bought. I considered the living room of Mrs. Phipps's "home." It didn't seem much cozier than she did.

"After all," she continued, "who owns a thing? The one who's cared for it? Suffered for it? Loved it? Who should own it?"

The ceilings were high, the molding ornate, the fireplace mantel swirled with leaves and vines.

"My third husband, Mr. Phipps, was a builder." She stared at me appraisingly, as if to see how I'd react to this unsought tidbit. "I'm only glad he didn't live to see the trash they're slapping up right and left. Might as well make buildings out of cardboard and paste. My Jim did some work for the man who used to own this place, so we got a good deal when we moved in, but that was seventeen years ago, with rent control. Now, without it, where would I go?"

Her voice quivered slightly and I wondered how much of her bravado she donned each morning with her colorful attire.

"Do you have relatives?" I inquired gently.

"None. This is a lovely building, isn't it? Dignified. Solid."

"Mrs. Phipps—"

"Valentine." Her coquettish laugh caught me off guard. "I was born on February the fourteenth. Valentine is my given name. Does that surprise you?"

"I'm Carlotta," I said, thinking that she wasn't my idea of anybody's Valentine. Then, reconsidering, I thought, *Sure she is.* In the short time I'd spent with her, she'd waxed hot and cold, sounded alternately honest and paranoid. If Valentines are romantic and romance is fickle, her parents had chosen more wisely than they could have known.

Extending a hand, she shook mine gravely as though we'd reached some mutual agreement with the exchange of first names.

"Look, Mrs.—Valentine." The first name did not come easily. "Once you get the locks I've recommended, you'll be fine. There's a strong police presence in this area and home invasion is rare; it's sensationalized by TV and newspapers. If you want to feel secure in your home, friends and neighbors are better than the best locks. Do you know the other tenants in your building? To speak to? Do you ever get together with them, have dinner, talk to them—"

"I had red hair once," she remarked. One glance at her faraway eyes and I realized I might as well have been discussing her neighbors with the fridge. "But not such a vibrant shade."

I wondered how long she'd been looking at my hair instead of my lips. My hair has elicited comments from strangers all my life.

"Is it . . . ?" she began.

"It's real."

"You don't—"

"I do not dye it. But I am thinking of tinting it brown, so that people will pay attention when I speak."

"And I had a mouth on me," the woman continued. "And I was flippant with my elders and my betters."

"I see we have a lot in common," I said.

She stared at me until I grew uncomfortable in the glare of her remarkable eyes. "Yes," she said slowly. "I believe we may."

"It's been a pleasure meeting you. Shall I write up a list of my recommendations?"

She crossed the room to a pale sofa, lowered herself, keeping her back carefully erect, and patted the cushion beside her.

When I joined her, she motioned me closer. "I think it's time we got down to business."

I prompted her with a nod.

"What can you tell me about infrared detectors, perimeter systems, microwave alarms, and . . . what were they . . . ultrasonic devices?"

It was an ordinary apartment on an ordinary afternoon. A jay squawked outside the window and I could feel the beginning of a disbelieving giggle rise in my throat. One glance at the woman beside me, at her intense violet eyes, and I suppressed it. She seemed utterly sincere.

# S I X

"Mrs. Phipps," I said as the jay continued its squabble, "I don't know who you've been talking to or what you've been reading, but A, you don't need stuff like that, and B, if you're concerned about paying your rent, you can't afford it."

Nothing I'd seen during the tour would trigger covetous thoughts in a door-to-door salesman, much less a professional burglar. Her TV wouldn't bring twenty bucks from a fence. Was there a rash of nearby break-ins, a drugged-out neighborhood gang desperate enough to attempt fourth-floor digs?

When I inquired about gang activity, she merely gazed at me speculatively. Her nostrils flared and folded as she replied, "Oh, no. Nothing like that."

"Do you keep wads of grocery money in the sugar bowl?"

"No."

"Your life savings tucked away in the mattress?"

"All forty-two dollars and twenty-seven cents," she replied wryly.

"Mrs. Phipps." I was still uncertain whether she was toying with me or not. "You really ought to get together with other tenants. If a neighbor phoned you every night, or somebody came by at six o'clock every evening and knocked on your door, that might make the need for alarms less, um, pressing. Are other people who live here having trouble with Mr. Peritti?"

She stared out the high, narrow window, focal point of the living room even though the abutting brick wall eliminated the possibility of direct sunlight. She sighed. "It's more than locks I'm concerned with. Any fool can get past locks."

"The alarm systems you've mentioned are very expensive," I warned, "and complicated."

"Alarms," she said dismissively. "I'd forget to set them."

"What about a dog?"

"I don't want a pet." Her voice rose querulously. "I asked Gwen for a safety expert, not some do-gooder from the pound."

"I'm not sure I understand what you want," I said.

"I'm not sure you do," she replied astringently, as if I should have understood but was fundamentally lacking in comprehension skills.

"Maybe if you had a cell phone you could carry with you . . ." I suggested.

Her mouth twitched and she peered left and right, as if trying to recall in which room Gwen and Paolina had taken refuge. She beckoned me to sit closer with a talonlike hand.

"Let's not argue," she said.

"Fine with me."

"You're big," she observed. "Tall as a man. That must have been useful when you were a police officer."

"It was."

"I was beautiful," she said matter-of-factly, as though it were somehow all of a piece with my height and her need for new locks. "Not striking or pleasing or any kind of euphemism. So beautiful that men stopped dead in the street to stare when I passed. Men wanted to paint me. My mother said I resembled a fine porcelain figurine. That's how I met my first husband."

I couldn't keep track of where this wayward conversation was

heading. "You met your husband while you were posing for a porcelain figurine?" I guessed.

"For a painting," she said grandly, then spoiled the romantic
effect by adding, "quite a bad one."

"And your husband was the artist?"

"Oh, no," she said, "but no sooner did my first husband see the
painting than he had to find me, meet the model in the flesh. Ah,
well, beauty doesn't last, that's what I know, and neither does love.
No one loves me now, girl, so I have to take care of myself."

"Gwen's fond of you," I said, because her faraway gaze had
turned sad again.

Reaching out, she placed a cool hand on my arm. "And I'm
fond of her, but it isn't love. Don't feel badly about it. Don't dare
feel sorry for me. I've been loved. I've had three husbands, racing
cars, a stable full of horses, and once I lived in a palace. . . ."

She must have noticed the look in my eyes.

"Well, not a palace," she admitted, "but my house had more
rooms than I could count. Don't you believe me?" Gracefully, she
reached up and patted her turban, and I decided it was pure vanity;
now that her hair was no longer red or thick or lustrous, she hid it.

"Should I believe you?" I asked.

"How I wish a great artist had painted me when I was your age,
someone with talent and verve, so I could show you. Even a bad
painting attracted my first husband's attention, though he turned
out to be a rogue, at his age. A catch, people said, because he was
handsome and had family money, but he was a playboy, a *bon vivant*,
people said back then. He had a way with money, lost it with flair.
He collected beautiful things, works of art. He always said I was the
most exquisitely beautiful of them all."

"Well then, you should have talked him into commissioning a
good painting of you," I said briskly, getting ready to flip the conversation back to security.

"I could have talked him into it, if I'd had the time." She
beamed at me. "He let me have whatever I wanted, let me design
an entire gallery to house his art collection—with some assistance, I
admit, but many ideas were mine and it turned out positively stun-

ning. Ten times the size of this, twelve times the size." Her voice seemed to grow to suit the imagined extended space. "Natural light from sixteen arched windows. We went through three architects, arguing, arguing, enjoying ourselves immensely, spending money like water. The best marble, the inlaid parquet floor. It wasn't finished a year when he died. Bankrupt." Her sparkling eyes went dark at the memory, as though a bulb had abruptly burned out.

"I'm sorry."

"Long ago," she said.

"You've made this room very attractive." The compliment fell flat. She'd been describing a chamber in her memory palace and I'd summoned her back to peeling-paint reality.

"My dear," she said earnestly, "tell me, where would you hide something? I find it hard to believe that thieves are fooled by fake rocks and hollowed-out books."

"What is it you want to hide?" I asked with far more patience than I felt.

"That's for me to know."

"Is this some kind of game, or do you really want my help?"

"Don't snap at me. Where would you place something of . . . er, value?"

"In a safety-deposit box," I said firmly. "Let the bank worry."

"No," she said. "Anyone could find the key."

"Put it in an envelope and mail it to yourself," I suggested. "Once it's delivered, just leave it lying around and consider it disguised as unopened mail."

"Recently I saw a bank in a mail-order catalog that looked exactly like a can of tomato soup," she remarked. "It was absolutely realistic."

I found myself beginning to sympathize with the woman's landlord. If she'd started chatting about tomato soup cans while he was on the phone trying to wangle permission to measure the windows, maybe he'd lost his patience and shown up on the doorstep.

"If it's jewelry," I said bluntly, "get a safety-deposit box. Once jewelry's stolen, the pros break it up, melt it down."

"I prefer to keep it near me."

I thought she was teasing, leading me on, and I felt confident she'd eventually reveal her secret. I figured I was her designated audience, here to fulfill her craving for attention, that this locks-and-bolts business was mainly camouflage.

"Do you wear it often?" I asked, resigned to a few rounds of Twenty Questions. She had no rings on her fingers. Her watch was utilitarian.

"You're probably right," she said abruptly, changing the rules just when I thought I knew the game. "I'll take the safety-deposit box."

"I don't sell them. You go to the bank—"

"Don't be ridiculous," she snapped. Her face had shut like a book. No teasing now. No sense of play or fun. We were back to square one. "Do you think I'm daft?" she demanded angrily. "I know how to rent a deposit box."

"Daft" summed it up nicely. Mrs. Phipps's eyes had narrowed as though she'd determined that I dyed my hair after all. You'd never have thought she'd called me "my dear" a minute earlier.

"It's so good of you to drop by," she said airily. "You're a friend of Gwen's, aren't you?"

I glanced at my watch and stood. Fifteen minutes to drop off Paolina, more if we quarreled—

"How well do you know Gwen?" Mrs. Phipps demanded.

"Not well."

"She works hard," the woman said as though we'd been discussing Gwen all along. "She has that trouble with her speech, but I find her intelligent and she doesn't gossip."

I could hear faint voices in the kitchen. I thought Paolina said, "If you don't have a lighter, how about some matches?"

"I'll give Gwen a list of hardware you can buy," I said, "to make you feel more secure."

"You buy it for me."

She stood, smoothing her red dress, and it was clear that the autocrat had returned, scepter in hand. "I dislike having people enter my home, but since you've already been here, I wouldn't mind if you returned. Would you have any difficulty purchasing the items you recommend? Could you install them?"

"Well—"

"I'd pay you, of course. I wouldn't expect you to work for free. We must all pay for what we get."

It's not as if I had a hundred other fascinating and lucrative cases competing for my attention.

Still I hesitated.

"Will you do it?"

"You'll need to give me money for the locks."

"I don't pay in advance."

"I don't want to get stuck holding the goods," I replied levelly. If she'd lied to the landlord, which I suspected, she could very well be lying to me. If she'd just wanted advice about where to hide her favorite earrings, I was giving her an easy out. I did not wish to wind up on her doorstep, banging her door, hollering to passersby that she'd promised to let me in.

She said, "I'll fetch my handbag while you figure out the cost, and keep in mind, I don't need the most expensive thing on the market, and if you happen to know someone who'll give you a discount, that would be fine."

"Thirty dollars," I said.

"Thirty!"

"That's including the discount."

"You'll have to bring me receipts."

"Why? You think Peritti might reimburse you?"

"Hah!" she said. "He'd rather shoot me on sight."

She shook her head at my apparent naivete, found her handbag, which was stuffed underneath a sofa cushion, and laid three ten-dollar bills in my hand. Then three more. She riffled each bill between her thumb and index finger as though she expected it to multiply.

"Will this cover today as well?"

It was five bucks less than she'd told Gwen, but I decided to spot her the five for entertainment value.

"Sure," I said. "You get a discount."

"Thank you. And now, what about collateral?"

"Huh?"

"Collateral," she repeated. "You're taking my thirty dollars, so you must give me, in return, something of equal or greater value. A bank does that."

"Not for thirty bucks."

"It's non-negotiable," she announced. "This is how I do business. My first husband's losses were a tremendous lesson to me."

I fingered my pockets. "I don't think I happen to have anything—"

"Your watch will do."

I held up my wrist, which was adorned with a Burger King giveaway featuring Jurassic Park dinosaurs.

"Oh," she said.

"Let me check my bag," I said. "You never can tell what I'm carrying around."

My gym bag didn't smell great. I rummaged through the contents, figured she'd probably balk at the offer of a sweaty tank top. I grabbed my wallet out of a zip pouch, flipped it open to check my cash-flow situation, thinking that if I had the bills, I'd return her advance, and avoid the whole collateral sideshow.

Mrs. Phipps fixed her gaze on the small plastic window fronting my wallet. "Who's that?" she queried sharply, pointing a finger.

"Paolina. The girl in the next room. When she was younger."

"She's your daughter?"

"My sister."

"It's a lovely shot."

"Isn't it?"

"You should have her painted," Mrs. Phipps advised. "Here, hold it to the light."

Paolina was eight when the photo was taken. It's a simple school job, but none in all the years since has come out half so well. I don't know what the photographer did, but it's obvious what he caught: wonderment, enthusiasm, unlimited potential. I imagined her now, sitting in the cramped kitchen, her fingers drumming the scarred table, itching for a cigarette.

I was unprepared for Mrs. Phipps's sudden lunge.

"You'll come back to get this," she said triumphantly, as she snatched the photo from my grasp.

"I will?"

"You will. Definitely. Gwen!" she called, as harsh and imperious as when I'd first entered.

If I grabbed the photo back, it could rip. Even as I had the thought, Mrs. Phipps thrust it deep in a side pocket of her voluminous dress, and the prospect of tackling her gave me pause.

"It might take me a day or two to buy the locks," I said.

"A day or two. That's absurd! You'll do it this afternoon."

"Are you in danger, Mrs. Phipps? Should I call the police?"

"Don't patronize me."

"I wasn't."

"Two redheads should never argue," she said placatingly.

"Why is that?"

"Because neither one will give up."

I hate redhead myths.

"This one will. I hereby give up," I said. "Please, take your money and give me Paolina's picture."

She got the distant look in her eye. "Oh, excuse me," she said, "what was I thinking? Gwen will stay with me this afternoon, so that will be fine. Keep the money, dear, and could you possibly install those locks tomorrow morning? I'm not going anywhere, you know. Ring the buzzer and pronouce your name loudly, so that I can hear it."

"Yes, ma'am," I said automatically. I might as well have been in grade school, the way she sucked that "yes, ma'am" right out of me.

"That will be all, then." She nodded curtly and disappeared into the bedroom. Gwen emerged from the kitchen, wiping her hands on a dishrag, and motioned me toward the foyer. I got the feeling she didn't want to discuss her client within the confines of the lady's apartment. In a moment I was huddled in the hallway with my teammate, talking softly. When I mentioned fire danger, Gwen assured me she regularly monitored the building's fire detectors.

"Paolina?" I called, raising my voice.

"You th–think Mrs. Phipps is okay?" Gwen asked.

"Is she taking medication that might cause mood swings?"

"No."

"You probably ought to take her to see her doctor," I said.

"B–but she's b–basically okay?"

"Gwen, I'm fine with door locks, but I'm not up on the latest medical diagnoses."

Gwen stared at the floor, disappointed, as though she'd counted on me for reassurance.

"She likes you," I offered, because it was true and because I wanted to redeem myself.

Gwen ducked her head, but not before I saw her pleased smile.

"Paolina!" I yelled. "Come on."

For someone who'd been reluctant to enter and dying to leave, she was slow on the exit.

"Paolina?"

She came flying out the apartment door, her cheeks flushed. Maybe she'd been in the bathroom, applying more rouge. More likely puffing a cigarette.

# SEVEN

"So. Does your mom know you're skipping school?" We were Cambridge-bound on Park Drive. Paolina hadn't uttered a word on the way downstairs; she'd extended her silence during the march to the car and notably failed to join me in rejoicing over the Toyota's ticketless windshield.

"I dunno."

"Have you skipped before? Do you skip a lot?"

She flashed me a sideways look to indicate that she wasn't about to dignify such dumb queries with responses. I drummed my fingers on the steering wheel and outwaited her. When she finally replied, she addressed the passenger window. I couldn't see her expression but I didn't have to; her sneer was audible. "It's not like I might *miss* anything. We don't *learn* anything."

"Nothing? Nothing in math?"

"I hate math."

My Little Sister and I used to play number games, each trying to stump the other with tricky strings of plusses, minuses, multiplications, and divisions. When had her fascination with numbers turned into hatred of math?

Traffic was backed up at the Commonwealth Avenue light. A battered Oldsmobile straddled both lanes and spewed exhaust from a rusty tailpipe.

"What about history?" I tried to keep any hint of desperation out of my voice. "You're taking World History, right?"

"Talk about totally useless. It's nothing but old shit nobody gives a damn about anymore. I mean, World War Two."

If she'd disparaged the Tang Dynasty or the Roman Empire, I might have left it alone.

"Paolina, come on. Hollywood's still making movies about the Second World War. It's in the news. This morning, just this morning, it made the front page—a big story about reclaiming stolen Jewish property. You should read it."

"Why?"

"The article described the Jewish Reclamation League as an offshoot of the JDL."

"So? I don't get it."

Of course she wouldn't get it. I struggled to find words to explain the impact of the Jewish Defense League, an organization newsworthy before she was born, on a country that had bought the image of Jews as passive, scholarly, non-violent victims.

Before I could pick a place to start, she spoke. "Yeah, well, I'm not Jewish. And if you weren't half Jewish, you wouldn't care either, I bet."

*Never again.* The words blinked in my mind like a neon warning on a highway late at night. My mother told me that American Jews considered the JDL an organization of zealots when they adopted their "Never again!" slogan. Assimilated Jews were so certain, she scoffed, that the memory of the Holocaust would long outlive its last survivors. She wasn't. *Never again.* My grandmother wore Nazi numbers on her forearm. My mother had the same tattoo so indelibly inked on her consciousness that it might as well have appeared on her own arm. She described its blue tracks to me so often I grew up knowing the numbers the way other kids knew their street address.

The driver behind me leaned on his horn. The light had changed.

I considered a hundred responses. The only one I could manage without losing my temper sounded about as hollow as I felt. "I guess I need to have a chat with your mother."

No reply. I drove.

Paolina's run-down apartment near Technology Square is surrounded by a vista of dirty lawn, squat brick buildings, and broken playground equipment. It's not as dismal as some—no high-rise Cabrini-Green nightmare—but it's bad enough. I wish I could move her out, but there's only so much a Big Sister from the Boston Big Sisters Association can do for a Little Sister: We can't adopt them, we can't live their lives for them. I know the old self-reliance spiel by heart, but I have my fantasies, and they don't involve my Little Sister dressing like a whore and hanging out with crazy older men.

"You can't talk to my mom. She isn't home."

Paolina waited to deliver this bulletin until I'd already squeezed the car between a sports utility vehicle and a UPS van, a nearly impossible task, accomplished in busy traffic on a narrow street to the accompaniment of rude gestures and honking horns. Give her some credit: I hadn't turned off the engine yet.

"When do you suppose she'll get home?"

"She moved out." Paolina's shrug was way too casual. A curtain of dark hair masked her face as she leaned over to switch on the radio. She fiddled with the dial till she found a hip-hop dance beat.

I punched it off. "What do you mean, moved out?"

"What I said."

"When? Why? Where'd she go?"

"It's no big deal." Paolina sounded defensive, as though she already regretted telling me.

"We need to talk."

"Why?"

Before the conversation degenerated into an adult/adolescent standoff, I decided to change tacks. "You hungry?"

"Maybe."

"Chinese food?"

"Ice cream."

I backed scant inches till my Toyota bumped the UPS van. A red Thunderbird screeched a U-turn, hovered vulture-like, waiting for me to vacate the spot. He'd never fit.

Herrell's, in the middle of non-scenic Brighton with its closely packed liquor stores, bars, and five-and-dimes, serves mocha ice cream to die for. It's tiny—just a counter and five round tables with rickety wrought-iron chairs. I'm a regular customer. It's one of the places Paolina and I used to go, a favorite hangout when she was small. Right now I felt I needed familiar furnishings to cling to, a site where I could remember seven-year-old Paolina, who smelled of cherry Life Savers instead of stale cigarettes.

"You should've called me," I said, once we were seated. *The minute Marta moved out,* I thought.

Paolina had briefly debated between a grown-up, sedate dish of strawberry and a little-kid hot-fudge sundae with mounded whipped cream. The gooey stuff won. I'd ordered my mocha with M&M's Moosh-ins, added a cup of coffee to make me feel like an adult.

She spooned whipped cream. "It's cool. I can take care of myself. We dropped the boys at Aunt Lilia's."

"Lilia knows you're by yourself?" I'd credited Marta's older sister with more brains. Didn't she have a clue what kids were doing these days, unsupervised kids?

"So what?"

"Paolina, you're barely fourteen."

"My grandmother had my mother when she was fourteen."

"So what?" I returned.

"What would you know? You're an old maid."

After a moment's stunned silence, I broke into unrestrained laughter. I tried to contain myself, really I did, but I couldn't help it. I threw back my head and guffawed. I suppose she meant it as a heinous insult, but an old maid . . .

"Stop it. People are looking at us!"

"I'm sorry," I managed, gulping from my paper cup of water, spilling it down my chin. Then I got the hiccups.

"Jeez," Paolina said in an exasperated tone.

"Can't take me anywhere," I agreed.

She licked hot fudge off her spoon, then, diligently, off her fingers. Her nails were frosted midnight blue and each digit bore a ring, ranging from silver bands to plastic gizmos that looked like Cracker-Jack–box giveaways. In the weeks since I'd seen her, the months since I'd paid her the close attention she deserved, her baby fat seemed to have migrated and rearranged itself into breasts and hips. The low-cut red tank and black mini, entirely at odds with her old uniform of loose jeans and shapeless tees, accented the transformation, and the change extended to her face, to newly hollowed cheeks under newly prominent bones.

"Let's start at the beginning. Where's your mom?"

"Marta met a guy. He's okay, I guess, but he doesn't live around here."

"How'd she meet him?"

"In some bar. On the street. What did you think, the public library?"

I kept at it. "And he's from . . . ?"

"I dunno. Some dink town, New Hampshire. He's one of those back-in-the-woods cabin guys. Like the Unabomber, but sexy."

"Sexy," I repeated under my breath.

"Yeah, he stayed at our place once, but Marta said the little kids drove him nuts, and he didn't feel comfortable with so many Latinos and black people around."

"Your mom's a Latina. Didn't he notice?"

"All they were doing is screwing, you know?"

"How long has she been gone?" As soon as I heard my own words I realized I'd failed a major test, realized I should have reacted to her pseudo-adult sexual leer. I mean, somebody had to talk to her about her changing body and her changing mind. It's just that I didn't feel remotely qualified. I am not an old maid: I was married once, for nineteen months, give or take a few days; I've had enough of what you might call relationships to converse in great detail about sex, but I never do seem to come close to figuring out this man/woman thing. I hate to admit it, but maybe it's love I feel so incompetent to address.

"Ten days." Paolina's answer startled me, both in itself, because

Marta had played truant so long, and because I'd been musing about sex and love and what the hell kind of wisdom I could impart on either subject to a girl so young and so old.

Ten days. "Well, I imagine she's planning to come back."

"I guess."

"Fine. As soon as you finish, we'll go to your place and pack a bag."

"Why?"

"You're moving to my house."

"No."

"You can't stay by yourself."

She seemed mesmerized by the tabletop. The part in her long shiny hair was so straight it could have been drawn with a ruler.

"Paolina?"

Mascara glistened on her lashes; her brown eyes were narrow slits. "I wasn't planning to. Stay alone, I mean."

"You can't mean that creep from Dunkin' Donuts?"

"He's not a creep."

"What? Do you want a baby? Do you want to outdo your grandma, have a kid when you're younger than she was?"

"I'm not gonna have a baby! Be quiet."

"You're telling me that—that sleazy jailbird just wants to hold hands with you?" I struggled to keep my voice low, but it came out harsh and furious.

"Diego loves me."

"Finish your ice cream."

"Don't you order me."

"Leave your ice cream! Put on your jacket! We're going to your apartment! You *will* pack a bag! You want orders, I'll give you orders!"

She shoved her sundae away so fast it tilted out of control. Fudge sauce cascaded over the rim, the dish clattered to the floor, and the few people who hadn't already been staring at us turned and pursed their mouths in disapproval and embarrassment.

For a brief moment I expected her newly tough mask to shatter like a cracked shell. Her lower lip quivered and I thought she might lay her head on the table and sob uncontrollably. I wished she would;

if she would simply act like a child again, I could behave like an adult, rock her and shelter her in my arms, comfort her with low crooning murmurs. And then everything would return to the way it was.

She regained her composure. The moment passed, and I wasn't sure it would ever come again.

# EIGHT

Paolina stuffed a brown grocery sack with essentials while I penned a note to Marta telling her where to collect her daughter in the event of her return. My Little Sister must have wept as she packed; her mascara-smeared eyes told the tale, just as the defiant angle of her chin warned me not to mention it.

*At least I can keep her safe at my place,* I thought as I pulled into my drive. From Diego and the rest of the predators who cruise her turf. I have extra space in my old Victorian. In truly lean times I've rented rooms to eager, raucous Harvard students, but I prefer living alone, with only occasional interference from Roz, who usually keeps to her attic when not engineering the removal of bodies from my bathtub.

Jerking open the front door the minute our feet touched the stoop, Roz, now encased in tight black leather and tighter black spandex, announced, "Hey, you were right." Then she launched into an elaborate hugs-and-handslaps greeting of Paolina. My sister seemed to know the ritual.

"Which of the many pearls of wisdom I scatter at your feet struck you as 'right?' " I inquired.

"I deep-sixed the creep. Lousy artist, lousy model, never mind he can't hold his booze. I'm totally raising my sights—guy-wise, I mean. I dialed a friend and we're hitting the bars tonight, trolling for dudes."

The way she was dressed, she could have zoomed straight to a photo shoot, posed for a spread in a weird biker magazine. I shuddered to imagine the guys her getup would attract. She wore her hair shaved to the skull below a left-hand part, flowing, multicolored, and intermittently braided on the right. No beads in the braids, but her boots, I swear, had 5-inch platform soles. Her nails were a color you'd have to call Urban Jaundice.

"Why not wait a day or two, why rush into something?" I asked. So dumb. Paolina and Roz both gaped at me, wide-eyed. If I could have captioned the moment I'd have dubbed it HARK! THE OLD MAID GIVES ADVICE.

I said, "You're on your way to buy paint, right?"

"Nah, you didn't mean it." Roz tugged her neckline to reveal a more generous expanse of breasts. "About the murals. Painting them over, and beige, and that shit."

"I did," I said carefully, reminding myself that Roz could sabotage the groceries, ignore the cleaning, flatten me with a karate kick if she were in the mood.

"Well, I think you ought to see them first," she said. "How can you condemn art? What are you, some kind of Philistine?"

I was impressed that she knew the word. Paolina seemed interested.

"So be it," I said.

Ascending the attic steps, I did sums in my head. How much did Roz contribute in cash and services? If I booted her, how much dough would I need to loot from savings to pay the monthly bills? Would tossing her out rate as a solid investment in my mental health?

Paolina plodded behind and Roz brought up the rear. I waited at the landing till Roz elbowed her way through and flicked on a lamp.

She hadn't bricked the windows, merely stretched black fabric over them, fastened with pushpins and nails. The darkness was nothing compared to the chaos. I couldn't believe I'd been up there that morning, albeit in the small anteroom, shouting and furious, and not noticed the scaffolding that fenced two walls. A crisscross network of ladders and planks turned the larger room into a construction zone.

Rendered with the same care Michelangelo must have lavished on the Sistine Chapel, the murals loomed above. In the heavens, a huge hand cradled a spectacularly realistic Big Mac. French fries sailed across the ceiling like clouds. A huge high-top sneaker, outlined in black, was in the process of being filled in with the same precise strokes.

"Muralism is the most socially relevant school of painting," Roz said earnestly. "Like, Diego Rivera did factory scenes, but the factory has given way to the service economy, personified by the commercial entities we slave for and enshrine."

"Oh," I said.

"You can't see it yet, but imagine the swoosh and the arch as they meet in a symbol of religious ecstasy," she continued. "Is it a clash or is it a comingling of diverse essences—"

"Roz?"

"Yeah?"

"I need to appreciate it in silence."

"Cool."

She waited while I climbed a ladder, got closer to the fries.

"So?" she said as I descended.

"Finish it," I managed, swallowing a manic giggle. Truthfully, the technical expertise was inspiring, awesome. And I could always paint over it. Or sandblast it. And I had an idea.

"Paolina," I said, "the phone's ringing. Are you fast enough to catch it?"

It's almost impossible to hear my office phone from the third floor. Paolina looked as if she were going to object. Then, for the first time that day, she obeyed without a word. *A sign of real trouble,* I reflected.

As soon as she was out of earshot, I said, "If you want to keep this, Roz, we can cut a deal."

"What?"

"You get Paolina to school on time every day this week, next week, too. You pick her up at school. You make sure she's going to class."

"Landlords," Roz muttered darkly.

"And you also make sure she's not seeing a twentyish, mustached Latino who carries a flick knife."

"Then it's a real job." Roz shrugged her shoulders. "Cool. No sweat."

# NINE

Insomnia and I are more than passing acquaintances; we're old pals. I no longer dread squirm-and-shift sessions; I simply toss back the covers and forget about sleep, knowing I can easily pack an otherwise restless night with ho-hum household chores. At 3:00 A.M. I might feed the cat or change the newsprint at the bottom of the birdcage, review the past week's *Globes* and *Heralds* which accumulate in a pile near my desk, shuffle overdue bills.

That night, I had no trouble filling the hours till 4:30. Then my old National steel guitar, nestled in its hard-shell case under my bed, called me. I was in the mood to play low-down Delta blues, with lyrics where *greasy* rhymes with *easy*, and the melody cries for har- monica backup, wailing like the whistle of a northbound train. I couldn't satisfy the urge, scared I'd wake my Little Sister, asleep in her room across the hall. Not playing made my fingers twitch. I couldn't stop wondering how I'd manage as Paolina's surrogate mother for the indefinite stretch ahead.

Damn Marta, screwing a nameless guy she'd met in a nameless bar, who hailed from some nameless New Hampshire town. The number of unfilled-in blanks intrigued me, sparking a plan: Starting tomorrow, I'd hire myself to do a little *pro bono* missing persons work. The idea of action made me sleepy with relief. I know how to find people. It requires dogged stubbornness, which I have aplenty. I have more dogged stubbornness than parental patience, that's for sure.

Before falling asleep, the name "Harry's Hardware" chimed in my brain. I scrawled it on the pad next to the telephone.

I walked the Fenway beat for two months almost ten years ago. In this city—this collection of small towns and ethnic enclaves—a cop remains a cop and is well remembered, because a cop can do a businessman a lot of good or a lot of harm. Harry, of Harry's Hardware and Plumbing Supplies, would certainly remember the rookie lady cop. I could still recall the shocked look on his face when he'd realized that the woman not only knew a Crescent wrench from a socket wrench, she was also a cop. Yes, Harry's would do.

The next morning, I dumped T.C., aka Tom Cat, my intrepid black-and-white mouser, on top of the slumbering Paolina, figuring that since she adores him, she'd neither abuse nor ignore him when he attempted to wake her. Dressed in denim—tighter than her kid clothes but less revealing than her previous day's ensemble—she drank black coffee, consuming half an English muffin only as a favor to me. Roz, bleary-eyed, raced downstairs wearing a T-shirt that read DUCT TAPE SPECIALIST. She owns a world-class collection of offensive tees and has the kind of body that displays them advantageously. This one, possibly harmless on a less well-endowed torso, conjured up, in my mind at least, the image of strange rituals involving bondage and discipline, making me speculate about the success of her nighttime bar crawl. Irritably, Paolina finally agreed to depart for school in Miss Duct Tape's custody.

I headed for the Fenway, where Harry's was located on Ipswich near the Town Taxi garage, with a broken-concrete parking lot for a next-door neighbor. The same yellowed going-out-of-business sign still had pride of place in the grimy front window.

"Hey, hey," the store's namesake called when I entered, setting off the bell above the door. He wore a faded red smock with a logo on the pocket over a white shirt and frayed brown polyester slacks. He'd faded, too, with time, into a squatter, balder, grayer shadow of himself. "How 'bout that Duquette? What's he think, Garciaparra can play the whole damned infield?"

Near Fenway Park, remarks about the Red Sox pass for traditional greetings, in season and out, taking the place of "How are you?" and inquiries about the weather. "Haven't seen you around," he continued, as though it had been weeks, not years since I'd passed through the door.

"Business good?" I asked.

"I'm gone as of the end of the month."

He'd said as much ten years ago. Every day when I'd eyeball his alley door, he'd tell me not to bother: Nobody'd be fool enough to tackle his place, he didn't turn enough profit.

"No, seriously. The whole block's going. This here's the 'Cultural District,' this ain't the crummy old Fenway."

"That mean the rent goes up?" I asked.

"Building comes down first. Then this area's gonna be a gold mine."

"Why? Why now?"

He shrugged. "Who knows? I mean, why do things happen? Maybe the Back Bay's full up."

"People priced out of the Back Bay invade the humble Fenway," I suggested. "Jack up the rents."

"You got it," he agreed. "And downtown's paralyzed with construction."

The "Big Dig," Boston's never-ending, multimillion-dollar, sink-the-Central-Artery project, is hell on commutes. Some taxi jocks had once believed it might improve business, but even they'd had to admit you couldn't earn a buck in stalled traffic.

"So the waterfront revival isn't gonna happen," Harry went on.

"Not till environmental groups are satisfied concerning the fate of the left-handed fiddler crab," I added.

"Hey, the developers are getting itchy. Can't blame 'em. They want to build, and what's left? Us. Here."

"Opportunity bulldozes," I offered.

"And how. I couldn't move either one of my places, this or the sub shop, for years. But now that some of us small guys are getting together and selling as a chunk, the city's scared."

Boston has the distinction of being one of the few state capitals that's also its state's largest city, which means that what the tax-exempt government doesn't own, the tax-exempt churches do, and the tax-exempt universities and colleges enjoy the rest. If Harry's group didn't sell to a commercial developer, the city would see massive revenue losses.

Harry said, "There's gonna be a twenty-screen movie house— What do they call it? Cineplex, multiplex—on Park Drive in the old Sears Building. A new hotel for the BU mommas and poppas, for when they take Junior to school and visit for the holidays. This is gonna be a big money section of town."

"Okay," I said, "but me, I just need to shop and run."

"You're gonna have a hard time come next year," he said gleefully, "unless you want designer coffee or video rentals."

"I've got a list."

"Sorry." He looked abashed. "You know me, I'll talk your ear off."

"Neighbors will miss you when you're gone."

"Hardly any neighbors left," he scoffed. "Just young professionals, got to call a plumber if the toilet gurgles."

"I'm buying stuff for a lady who's lived in the neighborhood seventeen years. Named Phipps. Know her?"

"Just to nod to," he said, after a moment's hesitation. "She's a strange one, isn't she? Over on—what street is it?"

"Kilmarnock."

"Yeah, yeah. One of 'Pretty Boy's' buildings."

It took me a beat. "Peritti," I mouthed. It sounded like *pretty* when you said it fast.

"He's Tony Peritti's kid. They called the old man 'Pretty Tony,' but the kid gets less respect. I hear he dodges behind some real estate trust, but it's old Tony Peritti's kid, remember?"

Old Tony, a school committeeman who'd moved up, or down, depending on your view, to city councillor in the seventies, had been well connected politically. I'd heard he had mob ties as well, but not from an unimpeachable source.

Harry went on, "The kid's not like the old man. Doesn't live in the neighborhood—upscale, fancy dresser. Otherwise okay, I guess."

"You keep an eye out, don't you?" I said admiringly. "The cop on the beat come here for advice like I did?"

"Sometimes." Finally he moved his rump off the stool behind the counter. "The cop's a broad—er, a lady, but it don't faze me. I got used to you, so she's fine."

There's progress.

He shuffled me down a dusty aisle while keeping up the patter. The smell, an earthy blend of metal and manure, transported me to long-ago Saturday mornings, Detroit with my dad, picking tenpenny nails out of high-stacked bins. Along one wall, the display of dead bolts included FM, Master, Yale, and Schlage. A pack of Trilene wood window locks went for $6.49. Police bars were stacked haphazardly in a corner. Harry offered a cup of coffee and twenty percent off, for old times' sake. I made my selections and, remembering his coffee, took the twenty percent.

The morning sky was flecked with high, wispy clouds. The air, caught between Indian summer and the crispness of fall, felt soft on my face. I tucked my purchases into my backpack, on top of the lock-picking tools I'd transferred from my desk to a leather pouch, and set off on foot for the old lady's apartment, thinking of her as "Valentine," not "Mrs. Phipps," determined to make good on my break-in boasts, if she was still interested, then quickly install her new devices.

On the way, I passed two For Sale signs planted on the lawns of brick apartment buildings, three street-floor storefronts with posters in their windows. SPACE AVAILABLE, NATIONAL RETAIL RENTALS had replaced the smaller old-fashioned For Lease cards. *Everything's coming up chain stores*, I thought. A corner lot buzzed with construction workers who whistled like they'd never heard of sexual harassment suits. Ever ladylike, I shot them the finger.

Maybe it was just that Harry had pontificated about neighborhood changes, but they struck my eye everywhere I looked, unex-

pected and more dramatic than autumn's slow progress from green
to brown.

I buzzed Valentine's bell. Would she be stiff and disapproving?
Welcoming, calling me "dear," and brewing coffee?

No static, no answering buzz. Old people don't move that fast,
I reminded myself, although she'd moved briskly enough the day
before. *She's probably in the bathroom; if I ring again it will fluster
her.* I waited.

I pressed the 4A button again, carefully, listening intently although I knew it was unlikely that I'd hear a sound four floors overhead. The buzzer could be broken. I set my backpack down on the
foyer carpeting, scanned the list of first-initial-only tenants, searching
for an asterisk indicating manager or superintendent.

There didn't seem to be one.

*"I'm not going anywhere, you know. Ring the buzzer and pro-
nounce your name loudly, so that I can hear it."*

I pressed every buzzer, one after another, straight down the
line. Waited, trying not to stamp my feet or scream in my impa-
tience.

The speaker box crackled, and I spoke my cheery "FedEx," not
waiting for a person to inquire as to who wanted entrée. The buzzer
sounded. The doorknob felt cool.

I took the stairs quickly, my heavy backpack bouncing against
my spine. I rapped sharply on Valentine's door. Somewhere in the
building a door banged, then another. Someone yelled "Anybody
there?" My throat had closed. I didn't answer. A second deeper voice
said, "Damn kids. I'm calling the—"

I've entered enough secured premises in my time to know that
it's not a great idea. A voice inside me said, *Back off, phone the cops.*

"I am the cops," I muttered.

*Gwen took her to the doctor,* I assured myself.

I rapped on the door of the neighboring apartment. Nothing.
No access to a phone. How to reach—what's-his-name—Peritti,
Pretty Boy, the landlord, the ponytailed man with the bad temper.

My body realized I was going in before my mind absorbed the
news. I'd unslung my backpack, unzipped it, started searching for
my break-in kit before I knew I was going to do it. I lifted out the

plastic sack of hardware, set it on the doormat. My fingers found the leather pouch. I shouted, "Mrs. Phipps, please answer the door," for the benefit of any witnesses, establishing the fact that I was breaking in as a last resort.

I flashed on all the times I'd entered locked apartments as a cop and my stomach lurched as I inhaled through my nose. No smell of putrefaction, none of the death stink I'd dreaded then. Still, the sense of déjà vu clung and filled me with apprehension.

My fingers slipped on the L-wrench, and I cursed automatically. Giving all my attention to the shifting of small metal parts, I flexed and released, manipulating the thin raker pick, until I heard the tiny, rewarding click.

The foyer stood empty and silent. The living room was just as it had been the previous day, every cushion tucked in place.

"Mrs. Phipps," I shouted. "Valentine!"

Her bed was unmade, rumpled as though she'd slept in it last night, but hadn't made it this morning. Valentine Phipps had impressed me as a woman who'd make her own bed with the last breath in her body. I entered the room and crossed to the far side of the bed. People fall and injure themselves, find they can't crawl to the phone.

In the kitchen, the shades were drawn. On the linoleum, a desk phone lay on its side, the receiver off the hook.

I found her slumped on the bathroom floor, small in her belted white robe. Quickly I knelt, barely conscious of the gaping medicine chest, pressing my hand to her neck, searching for the carotid pulse. Something bit into my knee, and as I shifted, I noticed the tile was sprinkled with pastel pills.

Not the faintest movement. I scanned her body for wounds. Her hair, white as her eyebrows, fine and sparse, showed patches of pink scalp. Her eyes were sunken in wrinkled sockets. Her skin smelled of dusting powder. No blood. I knew I should start CPR even though her neck felt icy against my palm. I shut my eyes, saw Peritti banging the door, heard Gwen's worried stutter and the triumph in Valentine's voice. My Red Cross training warred with my cop training, the one urging me to clear an airway, the other ordering me not to disturb the body.

"Don't move!"

My back was to the door. I realized what I must look like, huddled over Valentine's body.

,I said, "Take it easy. Be cool." The voice had ordered me not to move, but I had to see the speaker to read the situation. Raising my hands like a model prisoner, I kept them well away from my pockets.

"Thirty-eight-oh-two," the voice barked. "Get the EMTs." I couldn't make out the staticky radio response. "You, stay where you are."

I never forget eyes met over the barrel of a gun.

When I was a cop I killed a man in the Combat Zone. His eyes were red holes burned into a weather-beaten face, dead eyes, brows hidden beneath a black watch cap. Two months later I left the force.

The woman in uniform had gray eyes. Blond, wispy hair escaped her hat. Her mouth was set in a straight-across, no-nonsense line. She wasn't tall, not even from my vantage point on the floor, but she held all the muscle and authority she needed grasped in her right hand.

Time focused on a finger tucked into a trigger, on the necessary pressure, the impending tug. With one arm outstretched, she offered the narrowest target to returning fire. Her arm was rock steady, the gun an extension of her arm.

*Textbook*, I thought. I wanted to dive and hug the tile, cower in a twisted knot. Instead, I forced myself to smile. Cops don't kill people who smile. If a defeated wolf rolls over and bares its gut after a fight, the victor spares it. A human smiles. And lives.

For a crazy second I wanted to say, "I need my Little Sister's photo back," as if that would mend the situation, but then the idea of explaining how it came to be in Valentine Phipps's possession, the thought that I'd need to explain or else forfeit the image of the young Paolina as surely as I'd lost the original, froze the words in my mouth.

Every trace of saliva had dried on my tongue. I swallowed audibly, managed, "There's ID in my pocket."

"Keep your hands right where they are."

# T E N

I didn't wake up in jail the next morning. That was the good part. Kicking the refrigerator shut with my heel, I balanced an overfilled mug in one hand and a leaky orange-juice carton in the other. No sweat, if I hadn't been trying to elbow the morning paper to my side and the cat hadn't been underfoot.

My neck still had a crick in it from playing statue with Officer Theresa Kiley. Oh, she'd kept at me: Had I done this? Had I done that? What exactly had I touched? Why exactly was I there? Who was I, and could I prove it?

Juice trickled to the floor. I stifled a curse under my breath, in keeping with my new surrogate parent status.

Officer Kiley barely gave me time to respond to one question before hurling another. I knew she was doing her job, but I didn't warm to her, probably because of the gun.

Tossing paper towels in the spilled juice puddle, I stirred the mess with my foot. I sipped at the too-full coffee mug, scalding my tongue.

While she'd played drill instructor, trying to rattle me, the protocol of unattended death unfolded around us. The fire department ladder crew arrived within minutes. As soon as they declared Mrs. Phipps dead, Officer Kiley holstered her gun reflexively. She kept an eye on me. The plainclothes detective who arrived thirty minutes later called her Teri.

Officer Kiley ordered me into the hallway so as not to contaminate the scene—good practice, but aggravating. I couldn't see what was going on, but I assumed the new arrival was checking for signs of foul play. When he asked if Kiley had seen the victim's purse, I volunteered that it might be under a sofa cushion, which is where he found it.

"Looks like a natural," he said, lazily sifting the purse for ID, "unless the M.E. spots a knife in her back when he flips her."

"What's the phone doing on the floor then?" I snapped.

"Who's she?" He jerked his bald head in my direction.

Kiley replied, "Some kind of security consultant. Hired by the deceased. She says."

"Security? You need credentials for that?" the plainclothes cop asked.

"I'm licensed," I said, wishing I knew the guy.

"Dammit to hell." He glowered at me, eyeing his watch like a man seeing his day off evaporate.

Possession of burglar's tools earned me a trip to the station, where I was abandoned in an overheated conference room until the M.E.'s office sent word that no blade had been recovered. Nobody shined lights in my eyes so I didn't break down and confess to murder. Burglar's tools are no big deal, not like an unlicensed handgun, possession of which earns you an automatic no-nonsense year in the pen. I agreed to cooperate; with no client to shield I had no reason to balk. I told all, including the fact that Valentine's death seemed an opportune event when viewed from her landlord's perspective. I also informed the bald cop that Valentine was known to the press, a "neighborhood celebrity," as Gwen had called her. He appreciated the warning enough that, after checking my bona fides and typing up my statement, he convinced an ornery sergeant that charging a Good Samaritan like me would earn the department no praise.

Valentine Phipps hadn't been stabbed: That was the sum total of what I knew about her death as I sat at my desk, fumbling with the newspaper and nursing my burned tongue.

I found an unenlightening paragraph on the second page of Metro, headlined: WIDOW FOUND DEAD. *Widow.* Whatever the hell Valentine had been and done in her life had been reduced to that.

I phoned the Central Square Y again, although I'd gotten no satisfaction the last four tries. I had convinced the receptionist to check out the early volleyball practice I'd missed, but she'd insisted that no Gwen Taymore had responded to her page. And she absolutely *couldn't* give out Gwen's address, it was against every sacred policy of the Y, a statement she reiterated no matter what scam I tried to run. Maybe a new, more pliant woman came on duty at nine.

Same voice. I saved my breath and hung up.

It bothered me that Gwen might have to learn about Valentine's death from the paper, bothered me more that I'd been unable to locate her. The phone company had no listing, not even an unpublished one. I'd tried Taymore, Teymor, even Taimour. I'd phoned several of the Y-Birds; none thought it odd that Gwen had never divulged a phone number.

I flipped back to the front page.

"Start your engines, earthmovers and bulldozers," the column began, "for one of the last non-removable tenants is dead."

It was Peter Breeze's column, left side, beneath a caricature of his bearded face. Boston's hottest commentator, he'd homed to his native city after a stint at Detroit's *Free Press* with maximum publicity a year ago: A FRESH BREEZE IN TOWN, a billboard near Logan Airport had screamed. It took him a while to live that down, but his sense of humor had won out. In an early column he'd thanked his stars that he hadn't been named "Sweep" or "Broom," and ruminated on all the billboards that might have been defaced with worse slogans. On the days I read the paper before consigning it to the floor of the parakeet cage, I read Breeze.

"Not many knew," he continued, "that Valentine Phipps held the line in the Fenway. But the rest of the tenants in her building will learn, as quickly as their leases expire, that progress marches to an implacable drummer."

If Breeze had written about her previously, no wonder she'd been a neighborhood celeb. Breeze was nothing if not a celebrity-maker, choosing "regular" Boston people, singing their praises, probing their faults, using them to populate his urban fables.

"When a neighborhood goes downhill, everybody runs before they're last rat on the ship. But what happens when a neighborhood soars? 'Gentrification' was a key issue when folks got driven out of trendy spots like the South End. That was in the days when people read movie reviews instead of box-office grosses, and didn't know or care about the 'salary packages' awarded to CEOs. Quality of life was debated back then. We thought there might be intangible advantages (not measurable in cash! Were we naive or what?) to neighborhood diversity. We knew that somewhere in Beverly Hills the rich cowered behind electrified fences and Armed Response signs, but, hey, that wasn't the Northeast.

"In today's 'show me the money' climate, the Fenway's been sold down the river with hardly a peep. Except for a few stalwarts like Valentine Phipps, you'd figure no one lived there anymore.

"Money talks, and the poor walk. Hey, it's not discrimination. If you'd been smart enough to buy, not rent, sucker, you could have made a bundle. But you were dumb—worse, you didn't have the bucks—and now you're stuck.

"Most of the time, shamed and unable to exercise what few rights they have for want of a lawyer, people move on. Valentine Phipps wasn't keen on moving. And she didn't have to. To ease our collective conscience, to avoid Dickensian tales of evicted elderly, some formerly rent-controlled, pre-1995 tenants can't be ousted. Of course, many don't know that, not having read the fine print. Valentine threatened to let everybody know, to rally the old guard.

"Outraged at a landlord who tried more than once to invade her home, she decided to change her locks and prepare for a siege. Never again would he enter her premises with his plans to add a loft here, a Jacuzzi there, the kind of upscale modifications that entice the 'right' kind of tenants."

Valentine must have chatted with Breeze as soon as I left, spun him the same tale, complete with Peritti "yammering about loft space and Jacuzzis." I read on.

"Local PI Carlotta Carlyle purchased new locks for Mrs. Phipps yesterday morning at Harry's, a locally owned business that will soon be a memory. When she arrived to install them, she found the last stalwart tenant beyond the need for security."

*Oh, no,* I thought. *Oh, shit.* My name stared at me. Who tossed me to the wolves?

Teri, the lady cop? The bald plainclothes detective? Or Harry? Harry, who'd gotten in a plug for his final final-going-out-of-business sale. Harry was just the kind of guy Breeze would use as a source.

I inhaled and read the final paragraph.

"With the medical examiner's office silent, police neither suspect nor rule out foul play. But if you ask me how to fill in the blanks, I'll tell you: For 'Cause of Death,' write 'Greed.' The pursuit of the almighty buck wouldn't let certain city real estate interests leave Mrs. Phipps in peace. The almighty buck cost a gallant old lady her life."

The end. I cursed Harry for giving my name, and Breeze for using it. I made a second cup of coffee. The milk in the fridge smelled sour, so I sipped it black with extra sugar.

When the phone rang, I picked up on the first ring, hoping for Gwen.

I knew the voice. Mooney.

He didn't need to identify himself, which was good because he didn't bother. Mooney is Lieutenant Detective Mooney, head of Boston Homicide. I used to call him boss. If I hadn't dropped his name yesterday, I'd probably still be at the cop house.

"What exactly did you think you were doing at Valentine Phipps's?" His voice was soft; I held the receiver closer to my ear.

"How are you today? Warm weather for fall."

"You read Breeze's column?"

"Yeah."

"When Breeze talks, the mayor listens, and if you know anything funny about her death I want to hear it. Now, not later."

Mooney's quiet baritone grows on you. So does the rest of the package. I pictured him seated behind his desk, phone tucked to stubborn chin. His brown hair always looks like he meant to get it cut yesterday, his Irish face rates "boyish" even though he's pushing forty. I like the lines around his mouth.

Not without satisfaction, I said, "She was killed, right?" I wasn't glad that Mrs. Phipps had been murdered; I was simply pleased that my gut instinct seemed to be panning out.

"I've got nothing here says she was killed."

"M.E. says heart attack?"

"M.E. hasn't weighed in yet."

"Moon," I said, "nobody dies that conveniently."

"She was seventy-five," he protested.

"So what?"

"People die. Old people die more often."

"Not to order," I said.

"You're giving me intuition."

"What'd you expect?"

"A specific threat. You hear one?"

"To evict, not to kill."

Silence.

I said, "Assuming the medical examiner knows his business, you'll get the news soon."

"You made unauthorized entry."

"Intuition. Nothing to worry about."

"You're lucky Teri Kiley caught the squeal, and not some hot-head." I heard admiration in his tone when he mentioned Teri Kiley. I thought it unwarranted.

"She seemed hotheaded enough," I said. "I made 'unauthorized entry' because I thought I might save a life."

"Okay," he admitted after a pause. I felt my jaw loosen. "Sorry," he went on. "You know what it's like around here when the pols start blowing off steam."

I knew.

"Carlotta, help me out here."

"I told Kiley everything."

"I don't want to read about it in the paper," he warned.

"Me, neither. Especially not with my name attached."

"Okay."

I said, "When the M.E. turns in the goods, will you give me a buzz?"

"Why?"

"Come on, Moon. It's a two-way street."

"I'll think about it."

I wanted to ask if Gwen had been notified, but I'm naturally closemouthed when speaking to police officers. Gwen would be in touch, sooner or later. I might not be doing her a favor, bringing her name to the cops' attention.

The minute I hung up, the phone rang again. An acquaintance at the Cambridge PD claimed he'd seen my name in the paper, and just wanted to say hi. When he mentioned his recent separation, I informed him that the doorbell was buzzing. White lie, but I was not tempted to invest in some other woman's problem spouse.

Get your name in the paper and people ooze out of the woodwork. My phone sounded every ten minutes, with congratulations and commiserations. Breeze had an audience.

I decided to answer one more call before switching on the answering machine.

"Hello." I'm afraid I didn't sound welcoming.

"Ms. Carlyle?"

"Yes." This was an unfamiliar voice. An aluminum-siding salesman? A cold call?

"Are you busy this afternoon?"

"Who is this, please?"

"Um. My name is Bronson Hohen."

I sat up straighter.

"Yes, Mr. Hohen," I said. "What can I do for you?"

"If it's at all convenient, I have some unexpectedly free time this afternoon, and I'd like to speak to you, considering future employment—your employment, I mean. I know it's short notice, but . . ."

Even Bronson Hohen got tongue-tied when it came to hiring a P.I.

"Would two o'clock be all right?" he asked.

I paused long enough to glance at my empty calendar. "I could manage that. Where?"

"My office. One Beacon Street. Sixteenth floor. It's Hohen Music."

I knew that. Bronson Hohen. Hohen Music.

"I'll see you at two, Mr. Hohen."

"Excellent. Thank you."

He hung up, and I did the same, dropping the receiver into the cradle before gleefully rubbing my palms together. Bronson Hohen, the music king! Working for him could be the closest I got to winning Megabucks.

And face it, there was nothing I could do for Mrs. Phipps. She was dead, and she might have died a natural, albeit convenient, death. I'd owe her estate a thirty-buck refund, but with Hohen for a client, I'd be able to afford it.

Damn. I should have asked Mooney to get my snapshot of Paolina back for me. I punched the number from memory. His line was busy.

# ELEVEN

Later in the day, the medical examiner might find that Valentine Phipps had been murdered. Later in the day, I might find myself gainfully employed, courtesy of Bronson Hohen. For now, I donned a windbreaker against the chill and slammed out of the house. Battling erratic traffic as it curved along Concord Avenue onto Broadway, I imagined myself finding Marta at home, maybe baking brownies, wearing a ruffled apron like the moms in fifties sitcoms.

A few years back, Marta was always home, laid up with symptoms doctors had misread as rheumatoid arthritis. Properly diagnosed and medicated, she feels fine.

Aprons are not part of Marta's salsa repertoire, which runs to stiletto heels, heavy eyeliner, and the unshakable belief that a man will rescue her from a life of poverty. She considers youth, beauty, and sex her bargaining chips, and she's scared to death she's running short on youth. She's in her early thirties, around my age, but she's seen more miles; you can tell by her eyes.

The glimpse of a police car to my left made me lift my foot

off the accelerator. I shouldn't carry picklocks, I know, but I'd some-how neglected to remove them from my pack after Teri Kiley— perhaps not such a hard-ass trooper after all—failed to confiscate them. I found myself analyzing the odd note I'd detected in Mooney's voice when he'd mentioned the woman. Did it indicate more than professional approval? Personal interest?

Would I care? Was part of me invested in Mooney as a single male? Did I see him as a comforting body to fall back on when the rush of sexual chemistry that propels me from one disastrous affair to another becomes less of a driving force?

I hoped not. It would be selfish to try to keep Moon—a terrific guy, a friend I love like a brother—off the market. And I hope my chemistry will keep on pumping.

Mooney tells me you can strike sparks and enjoy companionship as well, but I don't believe him. I keep my distance from guys my mother might have approved of.

I parked and locked automatically. In Cambridge, you affix your patent-pending "club" to the steering wheel, lock your doors, chain the car to a sturdy oak, and know it could still get stolen. I trudged through gray grass and broken bottles to the dismal netless basketball court next to Paolina's home. Graffiti defaced the adjacent play-gound. Kids playing hopscotch would have to toss their pebbles on scrawled obscenities.

I kicked a can. It skittered into the roadway. I'd have picked it up, but a bent, old man did the job for me. He looked frightened, as though I might dispute his claim to the five-cent deposit. I smiled, and he scurried down an alleyway.

Great neighborhood for kids.

The security was worse than at Valentine Phipps's place. The basic setup was similar, but one of the tenants had left a stick in the inner door to facilitate break-ins. I know who does it. The woman on the third floor gets drunk a lot and forgets her keys. She hates to climb back upstairs, so she piles sticks by the door, props it open whenever she goes out. With the kind of foresight that stockpiles sticks you'd think she'd remember the damned key. I removed the offending branch and tossed the remaining wood out of sight under a scraggly hedge.

Two flights up. The staircase reeked. Cooking oil and Middle Eastern spices were two of the components, but stale urine won out. No wonder Paolina smoked.

After knocking twice, waiting, I worked my magic on the door. The *snick* of the yielding lock felt like an approving pat on the back. I could get to like this breaking-and-entering thing.

The place was stuffy, unexpectedly hot. I glanced at the wall and saw the thermostat hanging loose, supported by a black band of electrician's tape and two drooping wires.

The door opened into a square box with two dingy windows and a TV. An electric heater, which I unplugged. A sofa and a saggy chair, both draped with faded chenille spreads in lieu of slipcovers.

The bedroom off the kitchen was Marta's. The other belonged to the boys. Paolina used to share it, but after she started menstruating her mother urged her onto the living-room sofa. The door to Marta's room was shut. I knocked again. No reason to downgrade an already awkward situation by barging in on a woman having sex with her lover.

I turned the knob and went in. A thin, yellow bedspread did nothing to make the place more cheerful, just accented the dismal grayness of the once-brown linoleum. The flounced dressing table, the tiny bench, the bulb-ringed makeup mirror on a rickety stand tugged at my heart. It was a grown-up little girl's room. If Barbie lived cheap and didn't mind a mess, she'd have loved it.

The left-hand side of the underwear drawer was tightly jammed, but someone had removed a stack from the right-hand side, a sign of packing. I kneeled, looked under the bed, reached, and groped. Touched dust bunnies the size of gophers. No suitcase, not even a cheap cardboard job.

Quickly brushing my hands off on my jeans, I checked the bathroom, tugging hard to open the sticky medicine cabinet. No toothbrushes. If she'd taken her toothbrush and underwear, she'd probably left voluntarily. But how long was she planning to stay away? What was left to come back for?

Besides her kids?

I couldn't find any notes, not a single scribbled message. No pad by the telephone. No address book.

Into the trash, I thought sourly. Come on, Carlyle, get to it.

I began in Marta's room, with her tiny circular wastebasket. The bathroom next: Kleenex, Tampax, an empty nail-polish bottle, mottled cotton balls. Damn. I headed for the serious garbage, under the kitchen sink.

I'd brought along a section of the newspaper in case it came to this. I spread the sports section on the kitchen floor, although an application of garbage directly to the linoleum wouldn't have done much extra damage.

People still have the feeling, except at FBI offices and Microsoft boardrooms, that stuff tossed in the circular file disappears into the ozone without a trace. Wrong. Investigators like me can come along and loot it freely. If it's on your curb instead of in your house, it's admissible evidence in a court of law.

I wasn't planning to go to court. I was merely trying to find the beginning of a trail. An area code 603 New Hampshire phone number that I could run through a cross-directory, nail a city and street, would be terrific. Even the penciled name of a non–Hispanic man would be a step in the right direction. Hell, I'd take a matchbook from a New Hampshire bar.

I combed through orange peels, coffee grounds, mushy bananas, candy wrappers. The smell was vile, the texture worse. I wished my nose would shut down. I sorted paper waste into one pile, chicken bones into another.

I heard the door behind me swing open. First, I thought it was Paolina. Then, I thought, Marta: *Hey, hell of a way to leave your kids. Welcome home.*

I turned, and the guy from Dunkin' Donuts was staring at me across a hill of garbage, a twisted grin on his face.

I stood. I must not have looked scared enough. His smile wavered. He was long through the torso, but his legs couldn't lift him past five-eight, which gave me the height advantage. His build was slight.

"You want something here?" I asked.

"Hey, just crashin' like the chickie said I could—"

"She changed her mind." I kept my face impassive. "Give me the key."

"*Jódase*, Mama. No way."

"Watch your tongue," I said. "I'll take the key."

"Uh-uh."

"The key."

"*Vieja hijueputa, malparida de la mierda.* Spread your legs, bitch, and you can watch my tongue in action."

The flare of anger seized me so fast, I didn't even realize I had his arm twisted high behind his back until I heard him through the buzzing in my ears, yelling, "Stop! Stop!" The sound sang in tune with the sirens that had raced to Mrs. Phipps's aid too late yesterday, to the frustration of seeing her helpless, alone, dead, when I'd arrived too damned late to do her any good.

I let go abruptly and he dropped to the floor, rubbing his elbow and cursing in Spanish.

I said "The key," one more time in a firm voice, and held my hand out like I expected him to produce it. "*La llave.*" I translated, not because I thought he didn't understand, just to give him more time. Give me more time.

"*Ella no vale la pena,*" he muttered, slapping the metal ungraciously into my palm. *She's not worth it.*

"Right. She's not worth going to jail for." Every action I'd taken belied my words. She *was* worth going to jail for, to me. "And I guarantee you'll do time, you try it on with her. There are plenty of women over the age."

Scrambling to his feet, he regained some of his cockiness. "How's I supposed to know she's so young?"

"Ask."

"*Niñas bonitas son mentirosas,*" he said. *Pretty little girls are liars.*

"Get out."

"Hey." He kept a careful distance. "If it's just her, I'd go. I seen foxier."

"Then go," I said, still breathing hard. I studied his hands. His nails were long and black under the rims. The tattoo on his right forearm was a skull.

"It's dough," he said. "I can't walk out on money. Bad for business, you know?"

*Diego loves me.* I could see the words framed against Paolina's lips.

"I *don't* know," I said carefully.

"Her mama's into me. The way it works, I keep an eye on baby till I get mine. Maybe I take it out in trade, I don't get paid. Hey, hey, cool it. I was just running my mouth. Nothing personal."

*Diego loves me.*

"Get it straight," I said. "I take personally anything that happens to that girl."

"You gonna give me the money her mama owes?"

"I don't believe her mother owes you shit."

"It's business," he said.

"Dope or sex?" I thought the guy might be boastful enough to tell me. Floored by a woman not five minutes ago, his pride would be starting to sting.

"I do parties," he said. "I'm the party man. I make the arrangements, provide the space, and if the guys give the girls money for what they do, I take my cut."

"Did Marta meet a man from New Hampshire at one of your 'parties'?"

"New Hampshire," he repeated thoughtfully. "I believe that could be a freelance gig, but no sweat. *No importa.* I'm reasonable."

For a pimp, he was damned reasonable.

"How much do you figure the lady owes?"

"Three hundred fifty," he said. "I can't let the big bills ride."

"Let me inform you about bad business practices," I said. "Don't waste time on uncollectibles. If I see you near that girl, you're gonna have a visit from INS. *La Migra* isn't like jail, with a friendly lawyer, plea bargaining, and all. It's a stockade and a one-way ticket home. Understand?"

"I gotta get something," he whined. "*Necesito algo.*"

"Get it somewhere else."

He smirked. "I think the little girl, she'll come across with something. A better deal, you know what I mean?"

He must have seen the heat behind my eyes. He moved as quickly as an eel. The door slammed, leaving the apartment unnaturally still.

I slipped the chain home, as much to keep myself in as to keep him out. Part of me wanted to go after him, finish what I'd started, break his damned arm. I sucked in a breath, turned my back to the door, slid down till I was sitting, the stench of garbage forgotten.

If he'd pulled his knife could I have reached a kitchen drawer, grabbed a weapon fast enough? The pulse hammering in my temple said yes, I could have, and wished he'd made the try. The rage that had taken over the day I shot that man, my last real day as a cop, had scared me enough to leave the force. I'd told the shrink then that it was okay, that I was okay, but I was lying, lying, lying.

I stood and shook my head to clear it. I felt limp as a rag doll. I wrapped the garbage in newspaper, moving in starts, like a broken machine. I hadn't found any clues in Marta's trash. I'd let my only lead run away.

I bagged the garbage, took the sack down to the areaway between two buildings, thrust it deep into a dinged metal can. As I approached the car, two teens passed and sniffed the air. I'd need a shower before heading to a meeting with Bronson Hohen.

For Roz's sake as much as mine, I hoped the tub would be clean and empty.

# TWELVE

Number One Beacon Street is a boxy skyscraper that rises from the foot of Beacon Hill. The concrete plaza surrounding it hums with the tread of the well-shod lawyers and executives who work within. The wrought-iron fence of the nearby Granary Burial Ground encloses the graves of Mother Goose, John Hancock, and Samuel Adams. Teens hang out there, wearing oversize jeans that threaten to fall off their skinny hips. Bag ladies push shopping carts filled with empty bottles past the memorial plaques.

I smoothed the jacket of my navy suit, adjusted my turquoise silk tank top, and wondered why Hohen had chosen me to handle whatever urgent matter had arisen. Dee Willis, the singer, is a friend of mine—well, as much a friend as she can be, considering my ex-husband ran off with her. My ex, bass player Cal Therieux, works with tons of recording groups, sessions stuff, and used to be on good terms with Hohen, back when he was more of a hands-on producer, less a mogul, or as close as you get to a mogul in this town. Dee or Cal might have mentioned me. All this flashed through my mind as

I waited for the elevator, got on board, and punched the button for the top floor.

The receptionist, a dark-haired woman dressed in unrelieved black, informed me that Mr. Hohen was running late, would I please take a seat. Her heavily accented voice was low.

Framed gold and platinum phonograph records covered the paneled walls. There was history here as well as in the burial ground below, just a different kind of history. I peered at the small print: Ray Charles, Chuck Berry, Wilson Pickett, Mick Jagger, Bob Dylan. With artists like that in his fold, Hohen probably occupied an industry plateau where he could do as he pleased, or so I imagined. Including work from his hometown. And if he requested anything short of murdering Mick, I'd take the job. A recommendation from Bronson Hohen could keep me employed for years.

"Follow me, please." The receptionist's minimal hips swayed down the corridor.

When I grow up I want an office exactly like Bronson Hohen's. Of course, if I ever truly grew up, I wouldn't enjoy it. Hohen collected—and, it seemed, played with—toys. Three electric trains, beauties, circumnavigated the room, chugging overhead on built-in shelves fitted with O-gauge track and recessed lighting. In a back corner, steps led to a loft from which the designated engineer could operate the controls. Faint music issued from an Alco diesel locomotive: "Atchison, Topeka and the Santa Fe." The steam locomotive belched smoke from an inky stack. The third engine, sleek and silver, was modeled on the Japanese bullet train. I wondered if Hohen had activated them for my arrival.

The putting green laid out on one side of the vast room was no store-bought carpet runner, but custom-built, with flags jutting from three different holes. Bronson Hohen, head down, wiggled his arms and his butt, squinted at a small white ball with utter concentration. I wished he'd been playing with the trains so I could have begged for a turn.

Hohen measured the distance to the cup with steady eyes while I measured him. He stood an inch taller than the Latino man I'd faced off against earlier. He was three times Diego's age, still handsome, elegantly attired except for his bare feet.

The center of the office held a raised platform, almost a dais, lit by low-hanging fixtures over a narrow desk, a slab of wood so exotic I didn't know its name.

Hohen nailed the putt, then lifted his head. His pale eyes seemed to sparkle in a web of fine lines.

"Ah," he said. "Thank you for arranging your schedule to my convenience."

"I admire your trains." I shook the offered hand. For his age he had a formidable grip. "Carlotta Carlyle."

"Sounds like a show tune."

"I didn't name myself."

"You didn't change it."

"It never bothered me."

"Nor does mine, although I sometimes wonder what life would have been like as a Joe or a Jack, instead of a Bronson."

I sank into the leather-and-steel chair he indicated, part of a group encircling a round glass table. The office was huge, incredibly tidy except for a tall stack of newspapers piled on the floor near the desk.

"Is it a family name?" I inquired.

"Yes," he said, apparently pleased by the question. "Precisely. It was in the family. So is collecting." He waved his arms to encompass the room. "Toys, games, trains. I'm glad you like them."

He had a warm smile, easy moves, drop-dead natural charm. His silver hair was beautifully layered, his nails buffed and shined. He pinned his eyes on me and gave me the same full concentration he'd awarded the golf ball.

"Something to drink?" he suggested. "Coffee, tea? It's early for vodka, but I'm not opposed to declaring a premature sundown."

"Coffee," I said.

He tapped a button, murmured. "Yale, coffee for two, please."

"We've met before." He turned to me, studying my face intently.

"Yes." Backstage at a concert, a quick introduction between sets. I'd been with Cal.

"Dee Willis believes I can count on you for discretion."

I said nothing, to confirm how discreet I was. The receptionist served coffee in paper-thin porcelain cups on a silver tray. Hohen took his black. I poured cream and stirred in sugar, grateful for the activity. Small talk is not my strong suit. I waited for him to speak.

He said, "You were involved with a woman who died yesterday, in the Fenway?"

I'd been expecting—I don't know—due diligence on a newly hired company vice president, bodyguard work for an upcoming concert. An assignment to search for Elvis would not have surprised me more than Bronson Hohen's sudden reference to Mrs. Phipps.

"Yes," I said.

"It's a small thing. I don't expect it will take much time, but I would appreciate it if you could handle it personally. If it turns out well, I might have need for, um, someone discreet, at other times. This could serve as a trial run."

He was dangling a very plump carrot before my eyes.

"What is it you'd like me to do?" I asked warily.

He lowered his head, stared up at me with an impish grin. "I would like you to determine whether or not this Phipps woman is, was—well—my grandmother. Don't laugh."

People age differently. At the outside, Hohen looked to be in his late sixties. Plastic surgery may do wonders, but . . .

"Let me explain. I believe I may be her stepgrandson. No blood relationship involved. I'd like to hire you to find out for sure. And, um, to see if she left anything that might connect the two of us— any letters, books, things like that."

"Is that 'left' as in willed? Bequeathed?"

He shifted in his chair, elbows on armrests, hands tented over his chest. "Please. It—my interest in Mrs. Phipps—started with a newspaper column."

He paused, and I said, "Peter Breeze?" to start him up again.

"Yes, his column, but not the one in today's paper. About a month ago. It concerned escalating rents in the Fens, nothing that concerned me, but scanning it, I came across a name that carried me back in time: Valentine."

The phone on his desk shrilled. He strolled over, picked it up, listened for a moment, said, "I'll think about it," in a neutral tone. Then he pushed a button on the console and said, "Yale, dear, could you remember to hold my calls when I'm in a meeting?"

His suit jacket and tie hung on a wooden clothes press. Everything custom-made. The black loafers resting beneath the press shone with a subtle, burnished glow.

He carefully explained to Yale that while he would take calls from Hal, Mel, and Ellis, he would never accept calls from Andy. Period.

I studied his narrow face. His eyes seemed to reflect the eggshell blue of his long-sleeved shirt. The best indicator of his age was the flesh at his throat.

He hung up. "Sorry, she's fairly new. Come join me. I find these chairs more comfortable. I don't know, this modern furniture, who do they design it for?"

I moved to a soft, blue club chair, sidestepping to avoid the pile of newspapers.

"I'm extremely interested in genealogy," he stated. "Are you? Do you long to know the identity of your great-great-grandmother, or whether or not you have any long-lost relations?"

"I'm my entire family," I said.

"That may have its advantages. Although I'm sorry if—"

"It's okay."

"My relationship with Valentine Phipps, if proved, would be a tenuous connection, at best. My grandfather led a conventional existence most of his life, stocks and bonds, blue chip investments, until one day—this is how the family bible goes—he informed his wife he'd hired a young woman of surpassing beauty as a personal secretary, to live and work in his home. He'd never required such a secretary before. She was some forty years his junior, and they spent a great deal of time together behind closed doors. It took my grandmother less than two weeks to sum up the situation and move out. Divorce followed, before divorce was fashionable. Within two years my grandfather was dead. The stunning girl—he married her as soon as the divorce was final—was named Valentine."

"What else do you know about her?"

"Very little. Valentine is an unusual name, and she became Valentine Hohen. The initial given in the newspaper was H.—Valentine H. Phipps, living in the Fenway, refusing to budge. I circled her name, planning to find out if she might be the Valentine who'd married my grandfather, the one in the documents."

"What documents?"

"My family saves everything. Letters, receipts, odd scraps of paper." While talking, Hohen was sorting and signing items on his desk. Normally that would have driven me crazy. I like to have a potential client's complete attention. But with Hohen it didn't bother me. He had so much energy, such juice, snap, and sizzle, that it seemed only natural he'd be able to do two or three things at once. The elaborate phone console on his desk didn't seem like an affectation, just a simple necessity. Maybe the trains and toys and games were necessary, too. He reminded me of a coiled spring, or a controlled whirlwind.

"What is it you want me to do?" I asked.

"My grandfather's papers are in boxes; they're not even arranged by year. I didn't get around to examining them. I intended to, when I saw the name, but I put the matter off. I feel badly about it. If she was a sort of relative, and she needed financial assistance, I could have helped."

"She must have been aware of your existence."

"I was away at school during the upheaval. I didn't attend my grandfather's wedding. None of the family did. I think the couple slipped off to a Justice of the Peace. I never met the woman."

He plucked a Slinky from a nest of Koosh balls on his desk, balanced the metal toy between his palms.

"If this is the same woman who married my grandfather, she was badly treated. No one in my family offered to help her after he died. I simply didn't care. I was only interested in music. Pure art, of course, who would have thought there'd be money in it? I was into the music, and money followed like it was chasing me. But my mother, my late mother, blamed this Valentine woman for spending her inheritance as well as absconding with the few family heirlooms that weren't auctioned off."

"I was in Mrs. Phipps's apartment," I offered. "It didn't look as though there were many items that would qualify as family heirlooms. Even if you could prove you were next of kin."

"How closely did you look?" He'd stopped sorting the papers. The Slinky lay motionless on the desk.

"What, specifically, are you after?" I said.

He moved again, pushing his chair back, elevating his bare feet on a hassock. "First, I'd like to know if this is—was—the same woman who married my grandfather, also named Bronson Hohen, in 1940."

Valentine Phipps had once married a rich man who'd gone bankrupt. The gears meshed.

"I wouldn't imagine there's any chance of finding new relatives, unless she'd been pregnant when my grandfather died," he mused.

"I can determine that."

"Good. Since you worked for her, could you also get access to her apartment? Just to glance around, I mean?"

"Possibly. Tell me, are you looking for—something of value?" I deliberately repeated her words, and as I did, I could almost see the old woman's violet eyes. It seemed to me that they approved of my question.

"Well, I'd certainly like to find out if she left a will. Without becoming overtly involved, you understand. I wouldn't want to upset things if it turns out she had children of her own, from a later marriage."

Two later marriages.

"Yes," he continued, "a few letters would make me very happy. Books. Keepsakes. A will. Do you charge by the hour or by the job?"

It was pure pleasure to negotiate a fee with a rich man accustomed to paying music industry lawyers. We settled easily. I requested a brief note authorizing me to conduct a search on his behalf, as well as a to-whom-it-may-concern letter requesting cooperation from the landlord.

He hesitated. "I'd like to keep my name out of this."

"I can try it on my own, but it would help to have some sort of authority."

"It's because of the media climate. It looks bad. Destitute woman, successful relation."

"I wasn't exactly planning to alert Peter Breeze," I said. "I'll use the letters only if I need to."

He wrote them reluctantly, using plain stationery rather than letterhead. While he labored, I watched the trains, then shifted my attention to the newspaper pile, maybe because it was the only thing in the room that reminded me of my own humble office. At the top of the stack was the *Globe* I'd read in Dunkin' Donuts only two days earlier. Rats in the Fenway. The Jewish Reclamation League. I pondered requesting the front page so I could clip the article for Paolina.

Hohen signed the letters with the same illegible scrawl he used on the check. The check was drawn on First Boston, with "Hohen Music" printed in italics in the left-hand corner. First Boston had a branch not two streets away.

I beamed at the dusky-eyed receptionist as I left, hummed a dance tune as the elevator descended to the ground floor. Yes. I could retrieve Paolina's photo while I got paid for nosing my way back into the Phipps investigation.

Who says it's a bad thing to get your name in the paper?

# THIRTEEN

I deposited the check in my account. First things first.

The uphill climb from bank to State House made me regret wearing my pumps. In Room 272, which houses the Department of Vital Statistics, I filled out forms requesting copies of birth, death, and marriage certificates for the Bronson Hohen who'd died in 1942. Since the records go back to 1848, I thought I had a pretty good chance of learning his young bride's maiden name, and matching it with Valentine's, which I could get via birth, death, or marriage certificates stored among the papers at her apartment. It would take time to obtain the deceased Bronson Hohen's documents, but vintage records are not available on-line. I glanced behind the counter to see if a new clerk might be on duty. I know the veterans. They're not susceptible to bribes. No fresh young faces met my gaze.

When the documents arrived, they'd be the goods—actual proof, not speculation. Till they arrived, I'd follow less certain avenues.

I silently vowed not to break and enter at Kilmarnock Street. Not again. Teri Kiley would bust my ass while Mooney cheered her on. Of course, Gwen might have a key, or know where Valentine kept an emergency spare, but I didn't know where to find Gwen.

I knew where to find Peritti.

I debated whether or not to phone. His office listing was near Kenmore Square, in the Fenway. I decided to show up and punt. Speed seemed important. Once the M.E. cried murder, a call I expected soon, I'd have a hell of a time invading 4A.

Bronson Hohen's office made Peritti's digs seem grimmer and more industrial than they were. The smell of paint and cleaning fluid lingered in the bare hallway and the lighting left much to be desired. Peritti didn't put up much of a front, but if the Fenway, the center of his empire, was going commercial in a big way, he might become as rich as Hohen.

In some ways TV makes my job harder; in some ways easier. I carry business cards engraved with my name and the words *private investigator* in small print. People see *private* and *investigator* marching along together like that, they're intrigued, because of the glut of network PI shows. More often than not it gets me in the door, but then they're disappointed because I'm not cute, don't do gourmet meals, or offer hundred-dollar bills for information I can look up in the phone directory.

I presented my card to a woman who sat behind a desk marked with the generic designation "Receptionist." I watched her long face do the usual double take.

"Wait here," she ordered in a voice so nasal it probably kept her in the temp squad.

While I waited I studied a model of the Fenway, a cardboard mock-up displayed on a low table. Hohen's train set could have sped through it in no time. Major streets were unnamed blue lines, but once I followed the spiderweb tracery to a major juncture and determined that the intersection must be Kenmore Square, I could see that the model stretched from Kenmore south to Melnea Cass Boulevard. I isolated Huntington Avenue, found the Museum of Fine Arts, the Isabella Gardner Museum, the Berklee College of Music, Symphony Hall.

Eight major construction projects were tinted in varying shades of gray. Harry, the hardware man, had underestimated. The Fenway would be unrecognizable if all these structures were built. What did the different colors mean? Were some, the deeper grays, already under construction? Hotels and office complexes. Cinemas. A new Northeastern University dorm was rendered in pale eggshell. The block where Valentine Phipps had lived was covered by a tall gray monolith labeled MILLENNIUM TOWERS.

"This way, please."

It could have been my impeccable card that got me in Peritti's door, but the newspaper lying on the steel desk and folded to display Breeze's column made me doubt it.

Staring speculatively through narrowed eyes from his perch behind the desk, the landlord looked like he was trying to guess my age or my weight. I watched his expression while he connected the dots between the name on the card, the name in the press, and me, the woman who'd watched an elderly lady, now dead, humiliate him. His teeth were blindingly white in his tanned face. With his ponytail and gold neck chain, he looked more like a music industry exec than Hohen did.

He said, "A shock, let me tell you, reading about her death."

I nodded. "Must have been."

Had the cops interviewed him yet? Maybe yes, maybe no. If I were running the investigation I might have been tempted to wait for the medical examiner's report. Then again, I might have wanted to meet him quickly, look in his eyes while I listened to whatever he felt compelled to blurt out in his defense. His first words were intriguing: He wanted me to believe he'd learned about Valentine's death from the newspaper.

He tapped the column with his index finger. "I don't suppose this asshole writer sent you to get my side of the story?"

"No." I didn't volunteer a reason for my visit. He seemed nervous enough to keep speculating. It wasn't warm in the office, but he was sweating.

"Well, I know I want to apologize for that scene at the lady's door. Lost my temper. Honestly, I know I shouldn't speak ill of the dead, but Mrs. Phipps sure lied if she told you she hadn't given me permission to come by. I try to be charitable, you know? I think she was genuinely losing her mind."

The corners of his eyes wrinkled when he smiled. I pegged him for mid-thirties, dressing mid-twenties. "You wanna sit down?" he asked.

"Thanks."

"This newspaper jerk owes me an apology, big time." His nails were short and chewed. "He interview you?"

"No." I yanked a metal folding chair from behind a card table, sat. The office was cluttered. The furnishings were bare-bones minimal, cheap.

"He ought to call me if he wants the true story. It kills me how people hear 'landlord' and see the devil. Sure, that building's got problems, but with her, every time the elevator broke, it was deliberate, you know? She'd phone me night and day with complaints. Am I supposed to control the electricity? Am I in charge of rats?"

He was wound up and on a roll. I didn't say a word, just kept my eyes attentive.

"You think I'm a creep," he said. "Well, let me tell you, I feel for that poor lady, living a rent-control pipe dream, got used to living above her means. It was a bad situation, but it wasn't my fault."

He sounded like a sulky kid: not my fault.

"I own property," I said encouragingly. "I'm a landlord. I hear what you're saying."

"Hey," he said, brightening. "Smart move. Good for you. Then you know how much landlords do for the city, besides paying taxes you wouldn't believe."

"Absolutely." I sat back like I had all the time and interest in the world. Maybe I overdid it. Two lines appeared between his eyebrows and he started working his brain instead of his mouth.

He said, "So, you working for this Breeze guy?"

"I don't work for Breeze or the newspaper."

He laced his hands behind his head, elbows akimbo, and practiced his smile. "You want to rent a place?"

"No."

"So why are you here?"

"You seem like a perceptive guy."

"So?"

"I have a client who'd like to know a few things about the late Mrs. Phipps. I figured you'd know whatever there is to know."

"Yeah, who?" He reacted to the client, not the flattery. Not as dumb as he seemed.

Hohen's name would have clicked. Given Hohen's rep, the landlord would have turned handsprings to do the man a favor. The trick was to generate the same enthusiastic response without mentioning Hohen's name.

The notes Hohen had penned requesting assistance were high deniability items. If I could hand them back, still in their sealed plain envelopes, along with a copy of Valentine's will and an inventory of her apartment, I'd bet on a bonus.

"Somebody who might be grateful," I said.

"I like grateful," he said.

"Your records would list Mrs. Phipps's next of kin, right?"

"Didn't have one. I mean, a long time ago, her husband was next of kin, and I think the husband listed somebody on the form, I'm not sure who. But after he died, old Valentine had nobody."

He hadn't looked it up. Two file cabinets hunkered in the corner behind the desk, but his eyes hadn't flicked in their direction.

"You remember as much about all your tenants?"

"Let's just say she was special. My dad asked me to look after her because she's alone and a lady and all that. You gonna tell me who your client is?"

I said, "Maybe I ought to talk to your father."

"No," he said curtly. "You leave him be. He doesn't remember squat. Hardly knows who I am when I visit."

"I'm sorry."

"As soon as he has a clear moment, the nurses will show him this damn column. Everybody knows it's me Breeze has his hooks into. Man might as well call me a murderer, tossing widows on the street. She could've applied for Section Eight housing, you know? Talked to the BHA or any of the other social service places."

He'd used the word *murderer*. I couldn't help noticing.

I said, "Do you know how Peter Breeze got onto Valentine Phipps's story? Did she call him?"

"She might have. I wouldn't put it past her. But I suspect that cop, the do-gooder lady cop, always yakking at community meetings. That's where I figure Breeze met the old lady. He's that type, man of the fuckin' people, you know?"

I hadn't pictured Teri Kiley as a "do-gooder." Peritti, not waiting for me to comment, raced on.

"That bastard Breeze probably owns a house in some white-bread suburb, cruises into the city to criticize. They kill me, these do-gooder outsiders, especially the ones who get frozen in the past. You know, nothing that's coming will ever be as good as what was. Lousy whiners. That's why we're stuck with Fenway Park. No luxury boxes, no frills, no winners, you know what I mean? Give 'em a shiny new stadium and we'll see some pennants, but no way. Tradition, you know, you gotta love them the way they were. You gotta have the Green Monster and organ music and seats too small for your ass. Stuck in the sixties."

Boston's stuck in the 1860s, not the 1960s.

I waited for him to go on. When he didn't, I said, "How about lending me a key to Mrs. Phipps's apartment? Temporarily."

His ears all but perked up. If he were a bird dog, he'd have pointed. Definitely not as dumb as he seemed. "Why?" he asked after a long pause.

"My client believes he might have been related to the woman."

"And now he steps forward? After she's dead?"

I shrugged my shoulders.

He played indignant. "You'd work for scum like that? Here's somebody coulda taken the lady in while she was alive, and they just sat there, let her live off me—forget it."

"My client wasn't even aware of Mrs. Phipps's existence. If she's the right woman . . ." I let the sentence hang there, gave Peritti a level stare.

"He might be grateful, isn't that what you said?"

"I mentioned gratitude."

"A gratuity, isn't that what fancy waiters call a tip?" He arched one eyebrow.

"Yes," I said.

"Well, much as I would like to help you and your client, I do believe the police have sealed that apartment. I couldn't go against their wishes."

Damn.

Had the M.E. already weighed in? Why had Valentine's phone been on the floor? That phone continued to bother me; even at a quick glance it had looked wrong—not merely out of place, but *wrong*.

"Look, I'd like to do you a favor," the landlord said expansively. "But I don't need cop trouble. It's okay with me, understand, but I don't want cops saying you broke in, stole stuff, and I approved. No offense, but sooner or later this Breeze guy writes about it in the paper, and I can't go home nights without my neighbors looking at me funny."

"I was planning to check with the police. They've probably already located the next of kin." Teri Kiley could have found an address book after I'd left the scene. She hadn't found one before.

"Great. Then there's no trouble."

"You'll lend me a key? To be used if the police allow entry?"

"Well, now, I might want to chaperon you, make sure you don't snitch anything."

"I'm only interested in a will, or information that might point to a next of kin."

"Well, if the cops give you the okay, why don't you stop by again, and then I'll give you the key? Maybe we can have a drink after we check out the apartment. You can tell me more about gratitude."

"Sure." I had the fleeting thought that if I grabbed his right shoe and tilted him back, he'd somersault out of his swivel chair. I'd been hoping for a clear go-ahead, not more fences to hurdle. Should I go straight to Mooney, or try Teri Kiley, who'd be a high jump for sure?

My lockpicks started singing, but I ignored them, and said goodbye without attempting mayhem.

I only intended a brief detour to the ladies' room. While the receptionist was busy chatting on the phone, I strolled back along

Peritti's corridor in search of a likely door. The landlord's face was turned to the window, so he didn't see me walk by. When I left the bathroom, his office was empty.

I could hear his voice boom from the lobby, followed by the slam of a door. It seemed more likely that the boss would step out in the middle of the day than the receptionist.

The call of the fat file cabinets drowned out the singing lockpicks. I resisted momentarily, walked swiftly and silently to the waiting area, eyeballing each office on the way. The employees were out peddling property or leasing out apartments. The model of the Fenway area kept the lone receptionist company. No Peritti.

The cabinets behind his desk were unlocked. His well-organized files were alphabetized in neat folders, separated by apartment address. He owned three properties on Kilmarnock alone.

He'd told the truth: No next of kin was listed on Valentine's lease. After scratching down her Social Security number and date of birth, I scanned the files for a mention of Millennium Towers. Couldn't find the words typed on any of the neat tabs or indexed under a Kilmarnock address. I glanced at Peritti's desktop, saw the fat black wheel of his Rolodex. I spun it to M, found no listing for Millennium.

A slip of paper on the floor caught my eye. I scanned it twice before realizing I knew the phone number, recognized it because I'd called it this morning, repeatedly, each time running into a stone wall: no information given concerning YWCA members.

Underneath the seven penciled digits, Peritti had doodled the letters GT over and over again. Gwen Taymore's initials.

# FOURTEEN

I slid a quarter into the pay phone, dialed the Y. This time, instead of requesting information concerning Gwen, I flat out asked to speak to her, even though, to the best of my knowledge, the Central Square branch rented no rooms. After a pause, a woman declared Gwen "unavailable." When I told her I'd like to leave Miss Taymore a message, the woman said okay. I wondered if the Y acted as an answering service for other members, but I didn't want to raise the receptionist's suspicions by inquiring. I merely recited my number and used the word *urgent*. My next call went to the business phone of the local cop house, since GT on a slip of paper in Peritti's office didn't rate 911. While the phone rang, I tried to reconstruct the scene outside apartment 4A. How had Gwen addressed Peritti? I'd been behind her; I hadn't seen her face.

Would Teri Kiley grant me permission to enter Valentine Phipps's apartment? She'd stepped away from her desk, I was informed after a six-minute, toe-tapping wait that cost me an additional thirty cents, please. Would I like her voice mail? No, thanks. I considered dialing Moon, decided that Teri would interpret it as a leap over her head. In my job, I can always use another friendly cop. And I don't like asking Moon for too many favors.

At Copperfield's, half a block down Brookline Avenue, I got change from the barkeep, settled in with their foyer pay phone and a well-thumbed Yellow Pages. My fingertips traced two pages of Home Health Services listings, jammed between Home Design and Home Improvements. I dialed one of the first—Acme, I swear to God—described my dear mum's plight to a soft-voiced woman, dwelling on financial woes and Fenway location. The voice intimated that I might be happier elsewhere, and, with prodding, mentioned five health-care agencies who might provide aides working the Fenway area. I felt momentarily triumphant.

Up till last year, pay phones in Boston accepted dimes for local calls. Now it's a quarter. Talk about inflation. Five calls later—two bucks and a nickel in the hole counting my first two attempts—I hadn't found a soul who'd heard of Gwen Taymore. I visited the bartender, got more change, made calls to smaller providers ranging from the Fenway to Dorchester to Jamaica Plain. No Gwen Taymore.

I bit my lip and enumerated the facts I knew about Gwen. One: She played a good game of volleyball. Two: She called herself a home health aide. True, she'd never been my client, never acted as more than a go-between, but I felt foolish nonetheless. Was I going to have to stake out the Y?

Teri Kiley remained away from her desk.

I chafed at the inaction. I wanted to get it done today: find the will, retrieve Paolina's photo, clear up the Hohen business before the Phipps case turned into a hands-off murder probe. Instead I phoned my own machine, left a message saying I'd be home for dinner, asking Paolina to wait and eat with me. Then I sipped coffee at Copperfield's bar, steeling myself for what was bound to be an unpleasant encounter.

I arrived at Marta's sister's before five, trudging up the steps to find nobody there. Too early. The woman worked to put food on the table; she wasn't home yet. "Food on the table" sparked an idea. I cruised into Central Square, which isn't far from Lilia's Lopez Street flat. A peace offering was what I had in mind, and McDonald's in a bag was what I got. Overwhelmed by the greasy smell, I bought an extra fries, telling myself it wouldn't interfere with dinner in the least. Oh, no. Thus armed, I drove back to Lilia's and found a slot at the curb where I could watch and munch at the same time.

She had Paolina's little brothers in tow, no doubt picked up from the after-school program where they usually played. The brothers, like Paolina, have dark eyes and hair. Different father, different lives. In Marta's family, boys are treasure, rough jewels worth polishing. Girls are grains of sand.

As soon as Lilia saw me, her face closed and she hustled the boys up the walk. If she could have shooed them fast enough she'd have slammed the door on me. I'd cost her a job once. Marta's older sister is a hard woman who doesn't forgive or forget.

In his hurry, the youngest boy, a first-grader, dropped a sheet of orange construction paper. When he bent to grab it, she yelled. He balked and started to cry. His eight-year-old brother pushed him. That's when I caught up, waving my peace offering.

"Junk food," she said dismissively, but the kids stopped fighting over the crumpled artwork and started screaming for ketchup on their fries.

I made it through the front door.

Lilia lives alone, keeps to herself in an apartment that's a big improvement on Marta's. She doesn't let anyone mess with her. No men in her life, usually no kids, either. She likes things just so, the doilies on the arms of the chairs, the prayer books in neat rows, the plastic flowers in small glass bowls. She'd wedged the boys into her ordered existence, and they appeared to have changed to suit her, becoming sober little adults, intent on eating.

"*Muy bien, chamacos,*" she said when they took the remains of their hastily gobbled meal to the trash. "*Vayan a jugar en el cuarto.*" *Good boys. Go play in your room.*

"Okay," they echoed, solemn little puppies.

"Where's Marta?" I asked as soon as they left the kitchen.

Lilia wiped an imaginary spot off the green plastic tablecloth with her index finger.

"I save you time." She concentrated on the spotless cloth. "I don' know where she is. I don' know when she comin' back."

"Who's the man she went off with?"

"I don' know."

"How long did she ask you to keep the kids?"

"She don' ask. She say a couple hours, but she got somethin' else in mind, you know? She say she got toys for them in bags. Inside I find pajamas. Then I know she stay away."

*I should have gone to the Stop & Shop, not McDonald's, I* thought.

"The boys doing okay?" I asked.

She shrugged.

"What did you tell them?"

"*Nada.*"

She moved into the neat living room. I followed, watched while she plucked at pillows, straightened knickknacks. I didn't expect her to ask me to sit and she didn't disappoint me.

"Look, Paolina can't stay by herself," I said, keeping my voice low and reasonable.

"She don' stay here," Lilia snapped.

"Why?"

Lilia sniffed, patted her pockets for a tissue, ignored my question.

"It's good to keep the family together. Isn't it?" I said.

"I don' think so." She stripped off her shapeless cardigan sweater, draped it over a wooden chair.

"Paolina could help with her brothers."

"No."

"Do you need money?"

"That one, I don' take."

"Why?"

Lilia's mouth pursed. "You know what her mother do?"

"She took off with a guy. Did she mention his name?"

"She call him *gringo*, okay?"

"It's not going to help me find him. Or her."

"She go for the money, my sister. That how she do. You know the big men, the *políticos*, say gonna be no more welfare? What? Marta gonna get work? You think maybe she go to school? You think she gonna keep her place? They gonna toss her out, so she look for some fool, money in his pocket. She gonna marry any guy."

"What's that got to do with Paolina staying here?"

"Oh, you don' know. She like her mother, that one." Lilia's eyes closed like shutters barring a window. "She go with men."

"What are you talking about?"

"You gonna see," Lilia all but shouted. "I don't say *man*, I say *men*."

"I say you're full of it, Lilia."

"You go now."

"A guy named Diego's been hanging around your niece. Thin mustache. Tattooed arm. What do you know about him? His last name? Where to find him?"

"Go."

"He may know where Marta is. If I can find him, I can find her. I'll send her home. You'll be better off."

"Paolina act like *puta*, she don' live here."

A *puta*'s a whore. If I'd stayed I'd have smacked Lilia across her self-righteous mouth. So I left, stomping hard down the staircase, stopping only to squeeze a twenty through her mail slot to pay for groceries for the boys. I drove home too quickly, gunning the engine at traffic lights, the radio turned on high.

I shared take-out pizza with Paolina and steered the conversation first toward Marta's lover, then toward Diego. She refused to talk about either man or anything else that mattered, prattling on about Roz's new flame, who was so totally awesomely cool.

"Yeah," I said dryly, "I'll describe him: six feet something, great shoulders, blond hair, zero means of support, high school drop-out—"

She said, "Small and dark. Good muscles, yeah, but he's smart, gives lectures about art history someplace."

"Wow," I said, "I guess she couldn't find a blond on such short notice."

"He moved in," Paolina said. "And like, she just met him. I don't think she knows his last name."

"Look, Paolina. Roz is over twenty-one, old enough to make decisions for herself, even bad ones. She's old enough to take responsibility. She knows about birth control and—"

"I do, too."

"Honey, there's a time when your body is way ahead of your brain. With your body you can do anything a grown woman can do; give birth to a baby, no problem. But can you afford to raise a child? Do you have the wisdom to teach your child to be a decent adult?"

"Nobody would have kids if they waited till then," she scoffed. "You don't have kids."

*I have you*, I wanted to say.

Sex blinds you, I wanted to tell her. The dark urge gets so strong that your pulse hammers deep in your gut and common sense deserts you and you wind up handing your key to scum like Diego, linking your bright future to his dismal past. You wake up one morning to find that you're trapped behind doors you thought were open, and your mother's sad song becomes your own.

Her unlined face said that I knew nothing, could tell her nothing. Is pain the only teacher?

After midnight, restless, unable to sleep, I yanked at the twisted sheet, sat upright. The smell of paint was heavy. Since I'd rescinded my order to paint the third floor beige, I couldn't help wondering what artistic activity was occurring overhead. Were Roz and the new boytoy painting each other? Could body-painting cure insomnia? Sex doesn't. I had trouble sleeping with Cal, trouble after the split, during my one-night-stand, get-even phase. At least good sex gives you something to concentrate on when you can't sleep. I sat cross-legged and smelled paint fumes and hugged my pillow and imagined what my former lover, Sam Gianelli, might do with a can of paint. I've taken lovers since Sam—hell, I got married after Sam—but he's the one I think of in the night, the one the word *lover* conjures up. Where was he now? Somewhere in Florida, maybe, one leg a little shorter than the other because of a disaster I should have seen coming, a disaster I failed to prevent.

Mooney hadn't called. The eleven o'clock news hadn't led with "Murder in the Fenway." But something had prompted Teri Kiley and her colleague to seal apartment 4A. Why hadn't Mooney phoned? I wanted to hear his voice, tell him about Peritti's scale model of the Fenway and Hohen's connection to Valentine, run it by him the way I used to. Get him to stop waiting for the damn M.E. and open an investigation.

But not till I got what Hohen wanted, earned my keep.

I replayed Lilia's obstinance. Did she know where her sister was? I pictured Diego, saw him repeating my words, saying "New Hampshire" with a flicker of interest in his voice. He'd known something. Or I'd told him something he hadn't known. Either way, it had been a mistake to run him off.

A little after two, Roz started moaning and howling. Roz makes noise when Roz makes love, and most of the time I sleep through it, or find it amusing. This time I closed my eyes, stuck my head under the feather pillow, and hoped that Paolina slept like a drunk.

# FIFTEEN

She started in again first thing the next morning. By 6 A.M., Roz had roused the entire house, squawking like a randy hen greeting the dawn. Then, when I crossed the hall to Paolina's room, I found her smoking in bed, killing off a withered gloxinia by using its terra-cotta pot as an ashtray.

"But my mom lets me," she whined, while I flung open the windows and dispensed statistics about dying of smoke inhalation in a flaming bed long before lung cancer has a chance to strike you down.

"I'm not your mom."

"I know. Believe me, I know."

"Time to get dressed."

"I can't. I forgot to wash my clothes."

"Wear them dirty. All the smoke, nobody'll notice."

"Carlotta, quit it." She turned on her side and stared moodily at the curtained windows of the house next door.

"Look. You don't go to school, the truant officer goes searching for you at your apartment. He asks around, finds out you've been living there by yourself, or not living there at all. First thing you know, your mom's been evicted to make room for somebody on the waiting list, you and your brothers are in court, and you're lost forever in the Department of Youth Services."

"I'll go tomorrow. You can write me a note."

"And lie about how sick you were today?"

"Like you've never told a lie before."

"I'll write that you have terminal lice," I offered. "Nicotine poisoning. Body fungus."

"Oh, good. Multiple choice," she said.

"Multiple choice," I agreed. "Would you like to, A, get dressed and go to school, B, get dressed and go to school, or C, get dressed and go to school?"

She flopped over onto her stomach. "None of the above."

Roz, rosy, glowing, and smug after morning lovemaking, trotted downstairs to take charge of my budding delinquent, shooing me out the door with assurances. Not only would she keep an eye on Paolina, she'd run Valentine Phipps's SSN for me, see what she could forage from the on-line world of credit bureaus and databases.

Roz is a Net master, an info wizard, a cyberspace queen. Yet another reason to keep her around, I reminded myself as I started the car's engine. The wipers quickly cleared the windshield, but dampness lingered in the morning air and I shivered with the chill. Heading east on Memorial Drive, I squinted into the rising sun, steering with one hand while fumbling in my backpack until I located my sunglasses. Even with them on, I had to lower the sun visor; the glare off the Charles was blinding. Traffic crept along.

I still made it to the police station before Teri Kiley's shift began. Schmoozing my way past the desk sergeant, I ignored the elevator in favor of the stairs and lurked impatiently outside the locker room.

And I'd branded Peritti's surroundings grim. Here, individual offices were nonexistent. Overcrowding and lack of funds had knocked the entire third floor into a warren of cubicles. Gray waist-high dividers screamed "cheap," and the noise level was so high nobody would notice if cops routinely lost their tempers and started firing rounds into the walls. One group of uniforms clustered around a sputtering coffee machine, two plainclothes officers yelled into phones while scribbling notes on spiral pads.

A balding cop hollered, "Mrs. DelVecchio, please, could you say that again?" He nodded as he crooned, "Now, did her teeth fall out, or did he knock them out? Wait. You're saying they were already in the glass?"

Officer Kiley, when she finally arrived, looked frazzled and less than enthusiastic about company. Would I excuse her while she finished some paperwork? She'd caught a burglary squeal day before yesterday, forgotten one of fifty zillion forms that had to accompany the suspect to the holding tank. Without waiting for me to respond one way or the other, she hunched into a chair, her fingers clicking at a keyboard, a blank expression on her face. Not a touch typist, she was quick and sloppy.

She didn't glance up when the phone rang or when a brief shouting match erupted across the room. I took advantage of her blinkered state to stare and speculate.

The uniform made her hard to pigeonhole. Clothing choices tell more than favorite colors; they speak to income level, class, aspirations. All I could glean from her uniform was that it looked freshly laundered. Points for personal hygiene.

I'd been taken with her gray eyes at our first meeting; they'd looked fierce behind the gun. Altogether, she'd made quite an impression; I could easily have picked her out of a lineup, what with her high forehead and tip-tilted nose. Her streaky yellow hair had probably started out blond and gotten darker with age. She wore it cut so short the barber had buzzed the back of her neck.

I thought the short haircut was a mistake; it made her look vulnerable, that bare neck.

She wore earrings, small dabs of gold that seemed to be her only concession to vanity. No makeup on good clear skin. Mid-twenties. No rings on her fingers, a sharp edge to her chin. As she typed, her eyes had a half-closed, veiled look, though occasionally she opened them wide, peering at the keyboard like she might need glasses.

Her cubicle decor was minimalist. Other officers had family photos; she had file folders. Others had Garfield posters, art museum calendars; she had two looseleaf notebooks and a spiral pad. Her coffee cup sported a bank logo; a giveaway, not a declaration of loyalty. On a shelf, a copy of *Arts and Antiques* magazine made me wonder if she might have tastes too expensive to indulge. On the other hand, she could have nabbed the mag in a raid.

Her space reminded me of Mooney's spartan office. I found the comparison disturbing.

She leaned back in her chair, flexed her shoulders, and sighed. "Seems like all I do is paperwork. My desk is filthy."

"Doesn't look too bad," I said.

She gazed at me steadily. "When you were a cop did you type all day?"

"Pretty much." *So, she checked me out,* I thought. *Well, if I were a cop, I'd have checked me out, too.*

"I had a chat with your old boss."

"Oh."

"How'd you get on with him?"

I scanned her face, but it seemed innocent enough. When I worked for Moon there was a brotherhood of guys who talked up the lie that I'd slept with him to get my detective's shield.

"Fine," I said.

"Seems like he'd be okay to work for."

"You want detective?" Usually I sing Mooney's praises. I noted my reluctance to outline his virtues for Teri Kiley.

"Who doesn't?" She glanced from left to right, lowering her voice. "I want out of here, that's for sure. I keep thinking I do more typing than anybody else. Are these guys that much faster at the paper shuffle? Or do I look like somebody's secretary?"

"Not mine."

"It's easy to turn paranoid, imagine they're putting one over on you because you're a woman."

"Just 'cause you're paranoid—," I began.

"For instance, I'm so paranoid I don't think I've got a chance at making your buddy's squad. The pressure's off to keep a lone woman on the squad."

"Huh?"

"You were the lone woman, right?"

"Yeah."

"I mean, hey, we don't discriminate: Look, we got one black, one Latino, one woman. . . . You know the deal. That's how it used to be, but lately the bosses don't even care about tokens. I figure I can say that to you, but anybody else hears me, it's paranoia city."

Laughter erupted from a group of three male cops gathered by the coffee machine. One made a lewd gesture; another fake-punched him in the gut.

Teri Kiley noticed me notice them. "Guess what they're discussing."

Briefly I wondered which squad-room tale about Teri I'd been chosen to embellish. Was I the lesbian lover of the bull-dyke cop, or the loyal wife come to rescue my man from her sleazy clutches?

"Football?"

Teri leaned back in her chair and almost cracked a smile. "What can I do for you?"

"Give me the okay to enter Valentine Phipps's apartment."

"Today you want my okay?" She leaned heavily on the *today*.

Briefly, I explained what I'd been hired to do, carefully leaving Bronson Hohen's name out of the tale. She twisted a short lock of blond hair, regarded me with a cool, gray stare.

"So, did anybody find an address book?" I asked. "That could save me time."

"No."

"How about a will?"

"No. The landlord ought to have next of kin."

"But he doesn't."

"No?"

"He gave me his permission to search—if the cops are finished." I lifted the end of the sentence to make it a question.

She gave me a question back. "Seemed routine enough, didn't it?" I read a challenge in her tone that may or may not have been there.

"Depends. Did you find pills underneath the body as well as scattered around it?" I asked.

She shot me an appraising glance.

"Hey, I used to work with Mooney." I admit it, I was showing

off. A scattering of pills, added for effect while Valentine lay unconscious on the floor, would cry "setup," staged death.

"The report's not in." She might as well have said, "None of
your business." That's what she meant.

"Then why did you seal the scene?" I asked.

"Orders," she responded succinctly. "Because of press interest."

"I, for one, don't intend to talk to the press."

She let my statement float for a while. "Something's bothering
you. What?"

Very effective, I thought appreciatively. She'd coupled a caressing tone with Mother Confessor earnestness.

"Nothing," I said.

"Come on, you don't check your instincts when you leave the
job."

"You're imagining things." I kept the annoyance off my face.
She may have routinely tried that shit on perps, but I wasn't falling
for it. Sure, I was troubled about Valentine's phone being on the
floor, about Gwen's disappearance, about finding Gwen's initials in
Peritti's office, but there's a long distance between troubled and spilling my guts to a cop.

She stuffed the document she'd just typed into a manila envelope, licked the flap, securing it with a vehement slap. "Okay. Here
it is: I'll crack the door for you, if I get to tag along for the ride. How
about it? You mind?"

It would cramp my search for Paolina's photo. "Would it matter
if I did?"

"Not at all," she replied.

# SIXTEEN

I considered various ways to lose Teri while exiting the cop house, walking the half block to the parking lot, adjusting the passenger seat in the battered unit. A short cop had previously parked his butt there and smoked three packs of Camels, from the look of it. Ashes spilled from the crowded tray onto the damp, gray carpet mats. Teri pattered on about the weather cheerfully enough, but I didn't hold up my end of the talk. I missed Mooney's restfulness, his way of handling events one step at a time, never lurching too far ahead, never falling behind, either. This woman moved too much for my taste, touching the buttons on her uniform blouse, tapping the steering wheel with the flat of her hand.

She was a decent driver, I'll give her that. She cruised with the ebb and flow of traffic, didn't oversteer or ride the brake.

"Key?" I asked.

"We'll stop by the super's apartment."

"There is no super."

"He's two doors down, holds keys to all Peritti's places on Kilmarnock."

Peritti hadn't told me that. I was annoyed that Teri had the scoop.

"If he's not home, you can always break in again," she remarked dryly.

Demonstrate lockpicking to a cop? Not likely. To my relief, the super was only too glad to award the keys to a woman wearing a uniform. One look at the blue suit and the yeses tripped eagerly out of his mouth. I remember when people behaved like that toward me.

*Even if I can't grab a will or a marriage license,* I thought as I waited in the cramped foyer for Teri to open the door, *I might locate an address book with a listing for Gwen Taymore.* Gwen could tell me if Valentine had ever mentioned her first husband's name or his successful music-biz grandson.

Teri and I agreed to snub the elevator in favor of four floors of exercise.

"So your client hasn't seen the woman in years," she mused at the first landing.

"Never saw her," I corrected.

"But if she happened to own anything, he feels entitled. For all the loving care he gave the old lady."

"*If* she turns out to be the right woman, and *if* she has stuff that belonged to his grandfather, he'd simply like it restored to his family. He's not out to screw anybody."

"Sure."

The hallway outside 4A was quiet. She slit the seal with her pocketknife.

"No scratches," she observed as she worked the key. "Nice pick job."

"Thanks."

"If I knew your guy's name, I could tell you if I saw it on any documents."

*Nice try,* I thought.

Valentine Phipps's apartment, empty less than two days, smelled faintly of mothballs and unwashed clothing.

"No desk," Teri called from the living room. "Not in here, any-way."

Twin advertising brochures sat on top of a cluttered console in the foyer along with a fat paperback *Gone With the Wind* and a hardback *Heroes of the Bible*. A coffee mug bristled with pens and pencils. A tin container held breath mints.

No bills. Nothing of value.

I composed a mental floor plan of Valentine's apartment. Hall-ways and rooms. Furniture. I figured the more detailed description I could give Hohen, the better.

"Where do you want to start?" Teri was watching me suspi-ciously.

"The kitchen." When there's no den or office, the bedroom's the most likely spot to find personal papers.

"Okay."

I yanked on disposable plastic gloves as we walked through the living room. So did Teri. They're standard issue for cops. It's not fingerprint avoidance anymore. In this age of AIDS, cops—public and private—who come into contact with more body fluids than they'd like, feel naked without gloves.

If I found Paolina's photo in a kitchen drawer, I could say, "Hey, I must've dropped that," in an easy voice. Or say nothing and stash it in a pocket. What if Teri picked that moment to watch?

I began with a drawer to the right of the sink, methodically emptying it of folded-up recipes, rubber bands, Scotch tape, and string. A plastic bottle of Elmer's glue had leaked onto a pile of paper clips.

At what age should you clean your cupboards and prepare for death? The idea of someone pawing through my stuff the way I was pawing through Valentine's haunts me. I want a funeral pyre, with all my foolish acquisitions burned beside me, so no one will know about the wrong, wrong, wrong lipsticks I've purchased, the padded bras, the pinch-toed shoes, never worn, still in their boxes, mum-mified in tissue paper.

I doubt my environmentally correct Cambridge neighbors will tolerate a pyre. Maybe Roz can host a deathbed yard sale.

Teri started by the light switch and worked to the right. I began near the pantry, marching to the left like the Yiddish words in my grandmother's books. I could sense the cop observing me. It could have been to see whether I snitched anything. Or she could have been merely curious about how I worked. I'd once had the job she now wanted, on Homicide, and given it up. She had a right to be inquisitive.

Valentine had devoted one small drawer to department store perfume samples. Why? Had she considered them something of value?

The phone still lay where I'd last seen it, on the floor. The plastic casing was cracked. That's why it had looked so odd. . . .

"You believe she was murdered." Teri's voice echoed my thought so precisely it felt as if she were reading my mind.

*I know it.* I didn't say the words aloud because I was afraid she'd order me off the scene, gloves or no gloves. I forced my gaze away from the battered phone.

"There's nothing here," Teri said.

"Maybe, when the landlord first crashed her place, Mrs. Phipps decided to dump her personal items."

"Throw them out?"

"Some. And hide the rest. She asked me where I'd hide something if I needed to."

"She wouldn't hide something as commonplace as an address book. Everybody has an address book." The cop slammed a drawer shut for emphasis.

"We'll find it, then."

"Sorry, I didn't mean to snap or sound so—I don't know— sharp. I hate doing this. A person's family ought to sort things out after they die, or friends. Not strangers . . ."

We continued the search, strangers to each other as well as to Valentine Phipps. I tried playing "Do you know so-and-so?" inserting the names of cops I'd worked with, but we didn't share many acquaintances. I've worked alone a long time, and I never enjoyed an easy camaraderie with my fellow cops, except for Mooney.

The only noise was the shuffle of paper, the click-clack of rattled objects. Then Teri sighed. "I wouldn't leave a will in a kitchen drawer."

I wouldn't, either. I might leave a photograph in a kitchen drawer.

"Okay, let's divide up the rooms. Living room, kitchen, bedroom, and bath. Quite a few closets, those boxes lining the hall . . ." I tried to make the place sound like a full day's work, small as it was, thinking maybe she'd leave, hoping she was booked for an afternoon court appearance.

"Where did you tell her to hide her stuff?"

"I didn't tell her to hide anything."

"But you said—"

"She *asked* me, where would I hide something if I had something to hide."

"What did you tell her?"

"Safety-deposit box."

"So we might be looking for a key," Teri offered slowly.

"Which could be anywhere. Say, did you find a number for the home health aide?" I kept my voice casual. "She might know where the woman kept her stuff."

"Nope. But if we have to locate her, we will." She spoke with assurance, as a representative of the big police machine. Then she added, "I'll try the living room." She wasn't about to abandon her post and head back to the station.

"I'll take the bedroom." I tried to make it sound as if it wasn't my first choice.

I stood as close to the center of the room as possible, given the double bed, and spun a slow three-sixty. The bed was unmade, its shabby quilt trailing on the floor. The three-drawer dresser was cheaply constructed of pine. A darker wooden bedside table held a brass candlestick lamp. Blue was the basic color, dark for the curtains, pale for the quilt. White sheets.

No visible heirlooms or objets d'art. No silver-framed photo of an elderly gentleman bearing a family resemblance to Hohen.

I shifted uneasily, and as I stared and pivoted my anxiety grew. The bedside table's single drawer hung open a quarter inch. The middle drawer of the chest hadn't been closed correctly. The corner of a three-by-five throw rug was furrowed; a slight ripple marked its center, as if it had been hastily shaken and replaced.

Taken separately, each was negligible. Together, the marks stood out like a roadside billboard. Someone had searched the room.

I hunkered down, peered under the bed, felt carefully beneath the mattress. Then I opened the drawers of the bedside table, probing them diligently, even though I knew other fingers had already done the same.

I'd had the impression Valentine was speaking of jewelry when she'd asked what to do with "something of value." Women keep jewelry close to the bed. Burglars know that.

Hohen had stayed cagey about his "family heirlooms." As far as I knew, he could have been hoping to regain the family silver— or the family eggnog recipe. Had he believed his mother when she accused her father's widow of theft?

Who'd searched the bedroom? Why hadn't I noticed it before, when I'd entered yelling Valentine's name? I'd been moving fast, focused on finding her, but—

"Hey!" Teri's exclamation came from the living room.

"What?" I was surprised at how offhand my query sounded.

"Come in here, okay? I don't like this." Her voice was harsh and uneasy.

"What?"

"Here. What does that look like to you?"

She pointed toward the space between the sofa back and the sofa cushions. I knelt to get a better angle, saw a green plastic cylinder plugged by a white cap.

"Pill bottle."

She leaned forward and snagged it in a gloved hand before I could suggest photographing it as it lay.

"Probably nothing."

"Yeah," I agreed. "Still . . ."

She held it to the light, displaying a label from a CVS Pharmacy. "Novodigoxin. Point five milligrams." The small warning tag declared DO NOT TAKE THIS MEDICATION WITH MILK OR DAIRY PRODUCTS.

Heart medicine. Digitalis.

Teri studied the label as if she were committing it to memory. I wondered if she knew what it was. I knew because my Aunt Bea had something like it before she died. If she felt pain in her arm or her chest, she'd stick a tablet under her tongue.

.

Teri turned the small vial in her hand. "Prescription's current. Not expired, not old."

"Wouldn't have done Mrs. Phipps much good, hidden in the couch." I followed Teri into the kitchen, watched as she removed a plastic grocery bag from a collection beneath the sink and dropped the pill bottle inside.

"I've got an idea," she said.

"What?"

"Let's go see your pal Mooney."

# SEVETEEN

Moon works out of the old D Street station in Southie, where the bosses have stashed the homicide squad for years, mainly as a sop to the neighborhood. Lately they've been threatening Moon with a move to the new headquarters on Ruggles Street, so he can push more paper, be "responsive to fellow commanders," in department-speak. Mooney likes D Street. Me, I get nervous in Southie. The defiant Irish-American pride grates. The residents always treat me as one of their own, as if my red hair and semi-Irish appearance give me the key to the city. Their assumptions make me uncomfortable, make me feel as if I'm operating under false pretenses.

Teri, backing the unit easily into a skinny space in the lot, seemed to know her way around. She hadn't talked much during the drive. I'd watched her eyes sweep the crowded streets the way a cop's eyes are supposed to, noting illegally parked delivery vans, a broken street sign, a group of marauding teens in leather jackets. She radioed her whereabouts and destination, scribbled in her log-book.

At D Street, Moon inhabits the only space with a locking door that's not devoted to toilets. We checked in with the desk sergeant, who smiled knowingly and told us how to get there, although I hadn't forgotten.

Teri ran a hand through her hair, stretched her lips nervously in an experimental smile. It shocks me, but the truth is the troops are afraid of Mooney, who doesn't terrorize me in the least. Of course, when I got to know him, he had neither the title nor the rep he now enjoys. Then, I was too young to perceive the pecking order among cops, sufficiently naive that I rated people solely on ability. Dumb.

If competence frightens you then Mooney ought to scare the wits out of you. If you do the job, you've got nothing to worry about from him. Teri tugged the hem of her uniform jacket, took a breath before banging the door.

"C'mon in."

He stared at the two of us for a moment, removed his reading glasses, and slid them into his top drawer. He got the half-glasses when he turned thirty-nine. So he could remember his age, he said, and slow down.

"You under arrest?" He lifted his right eyebrow.

"Not even amusing," I told him.

"Hey, Theresa, what's up?" He awarded her a wide smile as well as her full name. The way his voice caressed "Theresa" made it sound more intimate than a nickname. I glanced at him sharply.

His gray-green shirt was tucked into belted khakis. He didn't look like a cop—more like a professor who worked out at a serious gym. His reading glasses had left a red welt across the bridge of his nose. For a minute, I considered the muscular body under the shirt, the way I might look at a man I'd met over a pint of Guinness in a bar. I wondered if I were seeing him the way Teri did.

"Have you got the lab report on the Phipps death?" She seemed unaware of any undercurrent. "The elderly woman in the Fenway?"

"She trying to turn it into a murder?" He jerked his chin in my direction. "She may need the work, but we don't."

"I'm afraid she may be right." Teri sounded apologetic. "Something's come up. If you want to give it to a homicide dick that's fine, but if you're shortstaffed, I'd appreciate a chance to run with it."

Did Teri's voice turn warm and throaty whenever she spoke to male officers? Did I use the same trick? I hoped not.

"If there was anything to run with, I'd turn you loose," Mooney said. "But it's a clean death."

"Almost," I interjected.

"Carlotta, the M.E. just came in with a nice myocardial infarct. The woman was under a doctor's care—"

"We know she was. Why don't you tell him, Teri?"

She squared her shoulders, indicated me with a nod. "She's working for a possible heir. I accompanied her to the decedent's apartment to carry out a will search."

"You went with her."

"Seemed a reasonable precaution."

"I don't think Theresa trusts you," he said to me. "She's smart."

Was I reading more into a mutual exchange of glances than I should? Teri hadn't let on that their relationship extended beyond a few casual hellos and her interest in joining the homicide squad. I thought back to Moon's comments on the phone. What exactly had he said about her?

Teri still looked him in the eye. "I found a pill bottle—prescription, for heart medication—stuffed behind a sofa cushion."

"Odd place to find it." He returned her glance.

Her cheeks flushed. "I was looking for an address book, thought it could have slipped down—"

"Good work," Moon said.

I broke in. "Mrs. Phipps died in the bathroom. It's no stretch to imagine she could have been looking for medicine. The cabinet was open, pills scattered on the floor."

"You're telling me she misplaced her pills?"

"Number one," I said, more brusquely than I meant to, "the woman's bedroom shows signs of a previous search. Unless the police forgot to tidy up."

Teri's eyes narrowed. "No way."

"And number two . . ."

Moon aimed his eyes at the ceiling. "I don't want to hear this."

"The telephone."

"What about it?"

"When I discovered the body, I noticed the phone had been knocked off the kitchen counter."

Moon took a breath. "Okay, I'll bite. Sick woman can't find pills, tries to call doctor, knocks over the phone."

"Her pills were hidden," I said.

"Misplaced," Moon corrected.

"Take a close look at her phone."

"Why?"

"It's broken."

"No dial tone?"

"The case is shattered."

"So it fell on the floor." He raised an eyebrow at Teri, as though inviting her to join him in deriding what he used to call my "overactive imagination."

I lifted his desk phone, gave a quick tug to make sure the cord was long enough, then tossed the whole thing. It landed with a satisfactory smack and a ringing aftershock on the wooden floor.

Both cops protested, Mooney shouting, "Hey! What do you think you're doing?" while Teri gave an incoherent cry and slapped her hands over her ears.

I bent and picked the phone up off the floor, returning the receiver to the cradle, displaying its undamaged case.

Quietly Mooney murmured, "Yeah, I see, that's a problem."

I placed it back on his desk. "These old phones don't crack. Ma Bell knew how irritating they can be, made them pretty damn well shatterproof. Imagine if you had to replace your phone every time you heaved it across the floor."

"So what are you telling me?" Moon leaned way back in his chair.

Teri, who'd been flipping through her notebook, lifted her head. "I may be onto something. I've made a lot of calls, and the deceased woman's home health aide doesn't seem to work for any registered health care firm."

"That's not exactly a criminal offense."

Which was why I hadn't mentioned it, or the fact that Tony Peritti had scrawled her initials on a slip of paper.

I may have dropped the phone, but Teri dropped the bomb. "So I kept on checking. And this Gwen Taymore, the health care aide, she's got a record."

I opened my mouth to protest, to say it couldn't be true. "What kind of record?" is what came out.

Teri seemed pleased at my reaction. "I ran it last night. I don't have every particular, because part's a sealed juvie, but there are multiple prostitution busts, and petty theft." Her cheeks were an attractive shade of pink, her eyes bright.

"Good for you." Moon pinched his nose where the red marks lingered. "Sounds like we'd better move on this. Could be the aide was present when the lady started having an attack, withheld the medication, even broke the phone."

"Why?" I asked.

"We don't need to worry about why yet," Moon replied. "Let's find the woman and talk to her."

Teri nodded solemnly, but a smile played around her lips.

"Theresa, you're on it," Moon said.

No wonder she was smiling. She was staring at a promotion.

"Carlotta," he went on, "I appreciate your contribution. But as of now, you're out."

"I'll help."

"You're a civilian. And you're out."

Turning to Theresa, he gave her his full attention. They were "we," the cops, coworkers. I was an outsider. Teri took a seat on the corner of Moon's desk. He smiled. Was that all I was sensing, a cordial relationship between colleagues? Their mutual admiration left me in the cold.

"If you find a will," I said, "call me."

I'm not sure they heard me leave.

I spent the afternoon at the Y. I checked the gym, the locker room, the pool, exchanging greetings and gossip, easing conversations around to Gwen Taymore. None of the members I spoke with seemed to know where she lived. She hadn't called in to retrieve her messages, and her answering-service arrangement with the Y was unofficial. The woman in charge of the front office turned scarlet when I told her about it, and declared that the privilege, if it existed, would immediately end. A teary-eyed receptionist named Doris swore she hadn't known she was doing anything wrong, that the agreement with Gwen predated her tenure. The other three staff members knew nothing concerning Gwen's whereabouts. Nothing.

I went home.

# EIGHTEEN

I was out.

I read about Guinivere Taymore's arrest in the paper the next morning, which is not my favorite way to learn the sports scores, much less news concerning a woman I know—a teammate. Hell, I hadn't even gotten her name right; I'd assumed Gwen was short for Gwendolyn. I scanned the story twice, three times. Maybe I have an attitude problem, but the questions journalists pop are rarely the ones I want answered, and the stuff they leave out is exactly what I yearn to know.

I wondered if the cops had located Gwen through her parole officer.

On page 5, a feature writer quoted a medical ethicist who believed that many elder deaths could be linked to medical care given by unqualified aides, but that, "mercifully," most of those deaths were without malice. He discussed cases where rich old folks, neglected by their busy-busy kids, were fed cat food and bilked out of large estates.

Peter Breeze had plenty to add in the Metro section. About our scheming treacherous times, about elderly who were considered prey instead of family, about cities selling their hearts for dollars. Short on facts, long on wind, he laced into landlords, but never linked Peritti and Taymore.

Gwen's photo ran on page 1, a head shot with a stunned doe-in-the-headlights look. *"Caught in the act,"* it seemed to say, as though her eyes had already agreed to a plea bargain. Her attorney, a public defender I'd never heard of, declared his client the victim of a rush to judgment, demanded a change of venue due to prejudicial press coverage, and admitted that while he'd hate to play the race card, well, there it was, staring him in the face.

Boston has a rep as a racist city, the BPD as a racist department. In the recent past, Boston cops have arrested black men for spitting, routinely rousting them when they had no resemblance to a suspect beyond shared skin color. DWB is still a recognized offense: Driving While Black in a white suburb. Any heavily publicized black-on-white crime fans the flames.

Health aides who violated the trust of elderly clients were decried in editorials. "Not even the strongest locks can keep out the 'helpers' we welcome into our homes," one trumpeted. Gwen's arrest had touched some vast, untapped guilt about elder care, some dread anxiety.

I flung the paper down with a snort. I needed hard information, a fact I could use to chisel my way back into the case.

I checked my refrigerator door, which doubles as a giant magnetic bulletin board. Roz owed me facts, computer-search results on Valentine Phipps, but they weren't on my desk, and I couldn't locate an apology or explanation amidst the clutter of expired coupons, one-time-only offers, and concert updates.

As I mounted the stairs, the paint smell thickened. Tolerable at the second floor landing, it grew nearly unbearable as I approached her door. I kicked my shoes into each step as vehemently as possible to warn of my approach. I didn't hear any lovemaking yowls. It was almost ten.

The tenant—the tenants—were awake and about. Up, you might say.

Roz, strapped into some kind of mountaineering harness, appeared to have tethered herself to the ceiling. Her gear looked equally appropriate for high-altitude fresco-painting or sexually deviant behavior involving whips.

The smallish, dark-haired new boytoy was very much a part of whatever it was. Descending from a metal ladder, he waved a paintbrush in a manner that might have been threatening if he hadn't been barechested, wearing Jockey shorts, and covered with yellow-green acrylic that clashed with the ornate tattoo on his right forearm. Roz adores tattoos, has a few killer designs of her own.

Where the hell does she find them? How does she fill her bed night after night, with no appreciable gaps between men? I've never seen her with an unattractive mate, so she has physical standards, at least.

The mural had taken a turn. The arches and swooshes and magnificent Big Mac had been joined by defiantly political symbols, the Stars and Stripes, the Star and Crescent, a retro Hammer and Sickle. Roz, it seemed, wasn't painting after all. She was busily suspending plastic netting from dangling cup hooks.

If she fell, I wondered how the hell I'd explain it to an insurance adjuster.

She glanced down. "Hey, Carlotta, this is the installation part. We may do a big spider, a conceptualized spider, with sort of a Deco feel. Then we're going to add actual bugs—"

"Think again."

"They'll be encased in a Plexiglas cube. I'm hoping for lizards, too. K-Rob has newts and thinks they'd be cool. And some of those stuffed Florida alligators, so there'll be death and life juxtaposed—"

"Much like the living death of the capitalist market system, as indicted by the mural." The boyfriend seemed entirely at home in Jockeys and paint. "Here, the flat representationalism of the cheeseburger is ensnared by the dimensionality of the plastic netting, the presence of the trapped insects and lizards symbolizing the spiritual prison of organic decay—"

"Pleased to meet you." I offered my hand. "You're K-Rob?"

"I'm an artist." He gave me the full effect of huge dark eyes under hooded lids. His lush eyelashes were coal black.

*Oh, yeah,* I thought, *a bullshit artist.*

"I didn't sign up for the lecture," I said. "Roz, if one bug escapes the Plexiglas, you're history."

Unfazed, K-Rob continued, "Damien Hirst employs a Lucite box, containing the head of a cow and maggots. I don't think he's had any trouble, with either escaped maggots, or wandering cow brains, so I wouldn't worry."

He rambled on while I made a mental note to check the health and welfare of T.C., the cat, and Red Emma, the parakeet, lest they become part of this surrealistic menagerie. This guy was not a typical Roz trophy. For one thing, he could whip out complete sentences.

I decided to get my information and depart. "Roz, did you get me the skinny on the Phipps woman?"

"The one the nurse killed?"

"She isn't a nurse, and she may not have done it."

"Oh." The way she said it, *oh* meant "fat chance." So much for the impartial press and the enlightened citizenry.

"Roz, did you do the search?"

"Yeah, yeah, sure. The printout's like, in the kitchen, where did I put it? I was eating peanut butter, so I probably stuck it in the cupboard. Sorry."

"Okay."

"When the installation's finished, Carlotta, we're gonna stage a viewing."

"Wait a minute. This is my home."

The boyfriend started back up the ladder. "Yeah, but it's her art. She makes it, she owns it."

"She owns my walls? That's news to me."

Roz interrupted. "K-Rob does stuff for the Museum School. He'll be photographing my work."

I thought maybe he should do a video. She could own the video. Not the walls. The Museum School is associated with the Museum of Fine Arts. It's a prestigious place.

"Is that how you met? Classes?" I shouldn't have asked, but I was curious. It seems to take me forever to meet a man I might sleep with. Mooney's image passed before my eyes: slim khaki hips, hastily removed spectacles, the mark on his nose. Had I waited too long, was I merely lonely or horny, or was I getting carried away by the idea of Mooney with Teri? Did Moon seem increasingly desirable only because another woman found him attractive?

Roz chuckled. "Classes? Uh-uh."

"Mutual friends?"

"Introductions, you know, they get so old."

"I grabbed her," K-Rob contributed. "The minute I saw her, I knew. She's art."

. "Lust at first sight," Roz chimed in.

No matter how badly this lovefest ended, I resolved not to feel guilty, to ignore the niggling voice that told me she'd never have met Mr. Jockey Shorts if I hadn't ordered her previous lover out.

"Paolina's at school, right?"

"Sure."

"How do you know?"

"We made a deal. I trust her. She's cool."

"Roz, I take this seriously."

"The Rindge and Latin truant officer will call me pronto if Paolina does a bunk."

"And what about the guy? Diego?"

"No sign of him."

"Damn," I muttered.

"Huh? You're disappointed about that?"

"Things have changed. I want you to locate him."

"Why?"

"Doesn't matter. I'll write a description. Take it to the Cambridge cop house and ID him. Somebody there's booked him for something, I'll bet. I want his address, a place he hangs."

"When?"

"Now."

"Are we talking time and a half?"

"For speedy results."

Pondering beige paint, I retreated.

I found the printout in a kitchen drawer under some silverware. I studied it closely, searching for flaws so I could feel better about throwing Roz out of the house, but she'd done her usual superlative job.

Not that the job was tough. With a Social Security number, if a person's alive and in the system, doors open and barricades crumble. But some know how to massage databases better than others, and Roz has an innate nosiness that pays off.

Valentine Hohen Barryman Phipps, nee Hayes. *Hohen.* That nailed it. Born in Southie. Switching names with husbands, no wonder women get lost in the cracks. I didn't take Cal's name when we married. Maybe I'd always known it wouldn't work. Maybe Valentine always thought it would. More likely just the fashion of the times.

Valentine had stayed married most of her life. When her first husband, Bronson, died, she'd married one Edgar F. Barryman within the year. Using CBD Infotech, Roz had found no trace of my client's long-dead grandfather, only a sketchy employment history centered around art supply shops for Barryman, who was still alive and using his MasterCard in Iowa. I wondered if he'd ever painted a mediocre portrait of Valentine. Despised by her in-laws, had Valentine returned to a previous lover?

When they divorced, she'd married Phipps, James A., seven months later. When Jim Phipps died, she'd gone it alone.

Valentine was once joint owner with right of survivorship (along with Phipps) on a low-priced duplex in Jamaica Plain. That was the extent of her property ownership. She'd been infrequently employed, clerking at convenience stores.

A medical history check would take four to six weeks, Roz had noted. Mooney'd get it faster.

I picked up the phone and dialed Bronson Hohen. Got his secretary, classical music, then the man.

After an exchange of hellos, I informed him that Valentine had once been married to his namesake. "I don't have documentary backup yet, but I've ordered it. If you need immediate proof, I can—"

"I'm glad you called. Um, I've been keeping up-to-date, reading the papers, and I've been in contact with the police."

My heart plummeted. "Oh."

"I discussed things with my attorney, probably should have brought him in right away. He advised me to make my interest clear. To the police. He also told me, since it's a murder case, that you'd no longer have access. So I won't be needing your services. Unless you happen to have already located the woman's will . . ."

I had to admit I hadn't. According to his lawyer, it was less than certain that his step-relationship to Mrs. Phipps would prevail in Massachusetts courts if the lady had died intestate. On his attorney's advice he was probing his grandfather's records, sales receipts, and such. The lawyer said he still had a chance, courts being reluctant to forfeit personal property to the state.

He assured me that he was grateful for my discreet assistance, asked me to return the notes he'd written.

I tried, but when it became increasingly obvious that I wasn't going to be allowed to elbow my way into the Phipps case courtesy of Bronson Hohen, I hung up.

Stared at the ceiling, ate a slice of white bread smeared with peanut butter, went back to my *pro bono* Marta search.

Paolina's mother hadn't called, which implied she was still off with her New Hampshire man. I debated another one-on-one with Lilia, who had to know some small detail. I could peruse the newspaper again, reading the paragraphs with small-type titles, like JANE DOE FOUND IN QUARRY.

The jangling phone interrupted my cheerless thoughts.

"Carlyle," I answered tersely. I ought to be more upbeat over the phone. Hell, I ought to be more upbeat in person.

"Henry Fine."

"Do I know you?"

"You know my client, Guinivere Taymore."

"Yes." Bingo. Henry Fine was the public defender who'd been quoted in the morning paper.

"She'd like to see you."

"The desire is mutual."

"Are you busy this afternoon?"

"Not at all."

"Great. Two-fifteen. Nashua Street jail. Use the side-door entrance."

# NINETEEN

Dumpy, damp, inadequate, filthy, antiquated, hopeless. Pile on the derogatory adjectives, but remember, the Nashua Street jail is merely a temporary holding facility. The suspects will be arraigned soon enough, bused to Concord or Walpole or Framingham, home to the female prison pop. Small comfort, you might think.

Camera-toting news flacks hung near the doors, hoping Gwen would show prior to deadline, waiting to click that shot, prowling in case she struck the national fancy, morphed into a *Court TV* sensation. I didn't know which was worse, this pseudo-celebrity, with paparazzi straining at the leash, or the forgetful fog that usually descended on Boston when a person of color was imprisoned.

One look at Gwen was enough to snap me out of general misgiving and into specific dread. Her breathing was quick and shallow. Prison garb shrank her a size. Her hair looked drab and lifeless. With her head lowered and eyes downcast, she appeared so defeated that I surmised she'd already copped to hiding Valentine's medicine, awarded Teri Kiley the details.

The newspapers hadn't mentioned a confession, but wouldn't

the prosecution love one. Valentine Phipps had died of natural causes; conviction would be a tough nut without a confession.

I tried to see it: Gwen and the tiny woman arguing. The pain of an impending heart attack. The race to the bathroom. Gwen snatching the pills. Valentine going for the phone. Gwen smashing it—using what? A cooking pot? A hammer? What had the cops found? Gwen shoving the pills under the couch cushion. Leaving Valentine to die.

Why?

A late salary payment? An accusation of theft? A stake in Peritti's real estate empire? Something of value?

The guard, a big woman who'd had her dental work done in a Soviet gulag, indicated a chair. I sat. The big woman's eyes said I might have passed muster at the other checkpoints, but she didn't have to like it. Gwen's handcuffs were connected to a chain around her waist, her feet hobbled with shackles.

The guard promised to stay within hollering range. Warned us that we'd be observed via video cam: no touching, no passing of articles. Departed. The small, cool chamber smelled of disinfectant; a high, barred window offered no view. I could hear muffled traffic, the clatter of an elevated Green Line train.

Gwen tried to rest her shackled hands on a gouged wooden table. She didn't seem to be marshaling her thoughts or attempting to shape words.

"You okay?" I ventured.

It took almost thirty seconds before she managed a no. Then she stared at the floor some more.

"Aren't you going to say you didn't do it?"

"You th–think I did?"

I ran the scenario again. Leaving Valentine dying on the floor. The image made me wince. "Hey, I hardly know you. For example, I thought you were a home health aide."

"I am."

"Not buying."

"B–but—"

"For which agency?"

"For myself. You s–sound like a cop."

"Yourself?"

"The underground economy, the p–poor folks' economy, okay? Work for cash."

"And what exactly did Mrs. Phipps pay for?"

"Cleaning, shopping, help with the bills. Reminding her to t–take her medicine."

She knew about the medicine. No way around that.

"What do you think I should have called myself? The m–maid? The n–nigra help?" Instead of sinking lower beneath her collar, Gwen's chin tilted defiantly. I was glad she had some fight left.

"Don't yell unless you want Jaws to come running," I advised.

Her hands clenched. The tendons stood out in her forearms and I wondered what games she played besides volleyball. Basketball's big in prisons. So's weight lifting.

"How'd you work it?" I asked. "Getting the job?"

"B–bumped into her at the supermarket. Old folks go Wednesday mornings, soon as they cut the coupons out of the paper."

"Spell it out for me. I'm not following."

She pursed her mouth in exasperation. "I help her with her b–bags. I say h–how hard it is, carrying and toting, and how I helped my aunties when they were getting on, and p–pretty soon she asks how much I charge. That's how you do it."

"Wouldn't she ask for references? From your aunties?"

"I don't have any aunties." Her voice pitied my stupidity.

I waited a beat. "Peritti."

"What?"

"I don't suppose you told Mrs. Phipps you worked for him."

"Where'd you get that? C–cops saying that?"

"I'm saying it."

"You're wrong."

"I know he left messages for you at the Y."

She sucked in a breath. "So what?"

"So I figure he set it up, you working for Mrs. Phipps."

She opened her mouth, closed it without making a sound. Her bottom lip looked raw, as though she'd chewed it.

"L–let's leave him out of this." She glanced up at the video cam in the corner of the room.

"It can't read lips."

She made a disparaging noise, a *humph* sound.

"Why'd he call you at the Y?" I asked.

"You tell the cops he did? H–has he talked to the cops?"

"You're in here. He's not. Draw your own conclusions."

"I'm here b–because I'm a con," she said bitterly.

"There's probably a little more to it."

"I didn't hurt Mrs. Phipps."

"How much did Peritti pay you?"

"For what?"

"The mouse in the kitchen, the out-of-order sign on the elevator."

"He . . . N–no."

I raised an eyebrow. There was a different note in her voice. She knew what I was talking about.

"He mentioned stuff like that once," she mumbled softly, almost like she was talking to herself. "It was a joke."

"So you spoke to him."

"Forget I s–said that."

"Gwen, for chrissakes—"

"Leave him out."

"Why?"

Silence.

"He talk to you?" she asked finally.

I didn't deny it.

"It's j–just . . . just gonna make things worse."

"Gwen."

"Okay, s–so he leaves me a message sometime. S–since when's that incriminate me? You think I'm working for him, because he leaves me messages?"

"I suppose he could be working for you."

"Get this: I'm d–dating him. B–boyfriend. Girlfriend. You know. W–we go out." Her chin tilted even higher. "Sometimes we stay in. Know what I mean?"

*It's j–just gonna make things worse.*

I could see how it would.

Interracial couples used to be a rare sight in Boston, but no more. That doesn't mean they're universally accepted. Would an average jury buy a relationship between Gwen and Peritti that had more to do with sex than with Mrs. Phipps?

Would I?

I pictured them: both good-looking, both eye-catching, with his ponytail and her beaded braids. A phone number and initials on a slip of paper. Why hadn't I considered it from the start? Because they'd behaved like strangers in front of Valentine's door. But mostly because I remembered tales about Peritti Senior. Old man Peritti, city councillor during the busing riots, a presence at the front of marching mobs, advocating all-white schools.

"C–can we talk about something else?" Gwen asked.

"Like, did he know you're an ex-con?"

"Look, can you help me? Or you'd rather nose into my sex life?"

"If he set you up, Gwen, you walked into a helluva frame."

She didn't believe it. Her mouth opened to deny it, then her eyes narrowed, and she clamped her lips shut.

"You met him at Kilmarnock Street?"

"No," she snapped.

I waited but she wasn't volunteering.

"How?" I demanded. The descriptor "like pulling teeth" was made for such moments.

"D–dancing at a club." I imagined her amber eyes and wide smile under flashing lights. Music pulsing, no one would hear or care about her stutter.

"Where?"

"Avalon."

The Kenmore Square club was well within Peritti's stomping ground, not five minutes' walk from his office.

"When?"

She shrugged.

"Gwen, before or after you started working for Mrs. Phipps?"

"About the s–same time."

"Before or after?"

"I'm not s–sure. What the hell's it matter?"

"It may be the only thing that matters. Come on, Gwen. Did you set him up—and use me to witness his fight with Mrs. Phipps— or did he set you up?"

"I didn't—"

Her words stopped so abruptly that she looked like a run-down battery toy.

"Cops ask you about him? About the timing?"

She revived enough to shake her head no.

"Don't answer if they do," I advised.

She nodded grimly.

"What do you know about the property he owns?"

"He's got M–Mrs. Phipps's building, a few others," she ventured cautiously.

"What about Millennium Towers?"

She lowered her already negligible volume. "I'm not getting him in trouble."

"Gwen, wake up. You're in trouble, not him."

"He'll be in trouble. His f–family's full of racists."

"You're the one in trouble. What about Millennium Towers?"

"Never heard of it." She made the announcement directly to the corner video cam. I couldn't tell if she was lying or telling the truth, but I could tell she didn't trust our "privacy."

"C–Carlotta, they gave me a P.D. It's all over his f–face how I've got a record and he's defending me because he's got to. He doesn't care what happens to me."

She paused, waited for me to speak. I didn't bother reassuring or contradicting her.

"He wants me to plead, says it's manslaughter easy. I won't plead. I–I won't do time for nothing."

"Gwen, how sick was Mrs. Phipps?" I'd considered mental illness a possibility, the way Valentine had skittered from topic to topic, alternating between imperious and imploring.

"She was mostly okay. She had a couple spells where she had to take a pill, put it under her tongue. She wasn't supposed to get upset, which is why I was so angry with T–Tony. He shouldn't have yelled at her."

"When?"

"When you saw him. Even if Mrs. Phipps lied to him, he didn't have to yell."

"You told him about her medicine."

"No."

"Never?"

"N–never."

"Gwen, I'd think that one over, because you may want to change your mind."

She slammed her shackled hands on the table in frustration. Then it was my turn to gaze at the corner video cam, as a warning to her to calm down.

"I w–want to go to her funeral." She got the words out in a whisper. "Who the hell else is gonna go?"

The start-and-stop pace of her speech kept me off balance. I think of myself as a gifted lie detector, flatter myself that I can hear the off note, sense the edge of terror behind the eyes of a skilled liar. Gwen's halting sentences would drive an expert with full oscillating lie-detection gear crazy.

"She t–trusted me," Gwen announced emphatically, like it was more important than any nuts-and-bolts fact.

"Why?" Valentine Phipps hadn't seemed a trusting soul to me.

"She knew about me."

I hadn't asked Gwen about her prison history. She was defensive enough. I figured her lawyer'd fill me in.

So I didn't dig. All I said was, "You told her."

"After a while. She liked secrets. The w–way it happened, she wanted me to have a key to her place, but she was worried about it, a little. So we t–traded. I gave her my story and she gave me her key."

I've heard stranger tales in prisons. But not many.

Gwen's teeth flashed behind a smile, and she looked momentarily pretty again, like a carefree sister of the woman in jail. "She had odd ways of doing things. B–before she'd give me money for the groceries, I had to give her something to hang on to, didn't matter what it was, a nickel even, she just wanted something in exchange. A token."

Like my photo of Paolina.

"She trusted me," Gwen repeated firmly.

"Boyfriend borrow your key?"

"N–no."

"You didn't use it the day we went to Mrs. Phipps's apartment. Remember? You waited till she buzzed us in."

"She took it back."

"Why?"

"I d–don't know."

"When?"

"When she s–started getting scared."

"Did Mrs. Phipps ever say she'd heard from someone claiming to be a relative?"

"No."

"Did she mention someone named Hohen? Or Bronson?"

"No."

"Did she keep anything unusual in her apartment?"

"Like what?"

"Old stuff. Papers, a collection of letters. Keepsakes. Something of value," I finished, consciously parroting the old lady.

"Something m–missing?" Gwen asked warily.

*I helped him design a gallery,* Mrs. Phipps had told me proudly.

"How about artwork? A painting?"

Gwen shrugged.

The guard filled the doorway with her bulk. "Two more minutes, that's it." She disappeared.

Gwen's eyes searched the perimeter of the room, found no escape route. Her chest rose and fell as she began breathing rapidly again, the way she had when she'd first been ushered inside.

"Okay, Gwen, I need to know what the cops have."

"My record."

I pinned her eyes with mine till hers faltered and she looked away. It's an old trick, but it works.

"S–somebody says he saw me."

"In the building? Or in Mrs. Phipps's apartment?"

"In the building. That night."

"Somebody you know?"

She shrugged.

Being seen in a building in which she legitimately worked didn't sound insurmountable. A decent attorney could handle that, plant a seed of mistaken identity. Had Peritti come forward as a good citizen, given the cops something juicier?

"And s–somebody else says he heard me, night she died, arguing with Mrs. Phipps."

"Did the two of you have an argument?"

"I never argued with her. I t–told the cops."

"Look, if you argued, admit it. Someone could have heard you another day, mixed up the time—"

"I never argued with her."

"The cops would ask where you were. At the time this witness says you were yelling."

"That's a p–problem."

"How?"

She didn't answer.

"You were out with Peritti?" I guessed. Didn't want him involved, so she didn't use him as an alibi. How dumb can you get? Didn't she realize—

"No."

"Where were you? Who with?"

"Home. Alone. What's it matter? I'm a b–black chick with a record. She's a white lady in the newspapers."

"I know these cops—," I began.

"Cops," she spat, with all the disgust in the world.

"Okay, where's home?"

"Cambridgeport."

"You live under your own name?"

"Taylor. Glenn T–Taylor."

"Why?"

"Ever have old friends look you up?"

"Yes."

"The kind of friends I used to make, I'm better off this way."

"Is your phone listed under Glenn Taylor?" No wonder I hadn't been able to find the woman.

"Don't have one."

"Don't have one?" I echoed. I couldn't imagine life without one.

"I p–pick up my messages twice a day. People want to talk to me, they can do it when they see me."

"What about work? How can you get a job if you don't have a phone?"

"If you've got a phone, p–people can always find you."

She had a point. "How did the cops find you, Gwen?"

"Bus station."

Damn. She'd been running away. Almost as good as a confession.

"How did you find out she was dead?"

"Tony."

"He phoned you?"

"I just told you, I don't have a phone."

"Then—"

"I was over at h–his place when he heard."

"Ladies." The guard loomed in the doorway. "Time."

"Please." Gwen's volume dropped so low I could barely hear it. "A favor?"

"What?"

"Please. Go by my place, feed my cat, water the plants."

The big woman hovered. Gwen lifted her hands, as though an imploring gesture might convince me where words had failed. The chain rattled; it pulled taut and yanked her hands level with her waist.

I wouldn't chain a dog; that doesn't mean there aren't plenty of humans I'd like to see under restraint. The guard tapped her toe impatiently, stuck out her chin, and glared at Gwen like she was daring the smaller woman to make a break for the door.

"How do I get in?" I asked.

# TWENTY

Pickets walked the pavement outside the jail. I wouldn't go so far as to call it a well-organized demonstration. One heavy-set black man wearing a navy suit braced a sandwich board that read FREE SISTER GWEN! across his broad shoulders. Two slight, dark-skinned women in scarlet choir robes waved placards: POOR IS NO CRIME and NAT-URAL CAUSES: ARREST A BLACK. Shoppers and businessmen gave them a wide berth.

Years ago, white Charles Stuart shot and killed his white, preg-nant wife in the Mission Hill section of Boston, ten minutes after they attended a preparing-for-childbirth class at nearby Brigham and Women's Hospital. Though badly wounded, he struggled to give the cops a description of the black man in a jogging suit who'd done the deed. The BPD bought it, ran a civil-rights-stomping manhunt through the black community that resonates to this day. Months later, caught in a vise of accusations, Chuckie jumped to his death off the Tobin Bridge.

The district attorney, the police department brass, all the suits had to know Gwen's arrest might rake up old resentments. A videographer shot film, which naturally led to increased fervor, a snatch of a gospel song. Impressed by the music or the color of the robes, a news photographer snapped stills.

I walked through Haymarket toward Government Center. The wind caught my hair and for a few seconds I thought I could smell the ocean. Then a traffic light changed and the salty tang was replaced by exhaust fumes.

"Well, hey, let's do some brainstorming on this," Henry Fine, the public defender, suggested twenty minutes later.

His gray suit had marched off the rack at a bargain outlet and looked like it still might have a wire hanger stuck up the back. His thin tie was an assertive red. He had a tanned, angular face, topped with gingery curls.

"So, hey, brainstorming," he went on. "I don't have a lot of time for this today. You mind answering a question? How you figure she should dress? For court appearances?"

"I'm wasted as a wardrobe consultant." My confidence in Gwen's acquittal at the bar was rapidly ebbing.

"Okay, yeah. You're an investigator, right?"

"You ran background on me, right?" No way a lawyer would put me next to Gwen without doing a cursory check.

"Look." His narrow shoulders elevated, then lowered abruptly. The knot in his tie was slightly off center. "I know the client's enthusiastic about putting you on the team, but the department doesn't have funds to pay outside help."

"Really?" The public defenders' office always pays. Not well, not in a timely manner, but the check eventually hits the mail. "High-profile case like this? No funds? Wouldn't that make a news flash?"

In the ensuing silence, I settled myself in my creaky chair, indicating that I wasn't about to leave.

His mouth tightened. "So, did your interview suggest an area of investigation?"

My desire to confide in Henry Fine was low. I didn't have much feeling for his skill as a litigator, but he'd already lied to me about money and we'd barely met.

"What I mean is, I'd hate to use you to cover old ground," he continued earnestly, "when it might remove you as a character witness. You could do Gwen a good turn as a witness."

"You think so?"

"If this goes to trial, I'll tell ya, the sentencing phase is gonna be crucial." He leaned forward in his chair and his voice turned suspiciously salt-of-the-earth folksy. "Juries don't want to hear a defendant's virtues sung by a parole officer or anybody involved in corrections. You'd be—"

"*If* this goes to trial . . ." I let the phrase hang in the air, my emphasis firmly on the initial word.

"Hey, you want coffee?"

"Sure."

He retreated to the hallway. I wondered if he was planning to use the phone, wondered which Beacon Hill politico might have an afternoon appointment disrupted by a call.

His desk was stacked with file folders and unopened mail; a framed photo of a dog was half hidden by a crumpled bag of Cheez Doodles. He kept folded newspapers on the floor, piled under fat law books. When I moved a political flyer aside, the corner of a folded yellow sheet protruded, a program insert from a Sunday service at New African Baptist Church.

Behind his desk, the wall was speckled with photographs, some framed and hung, some merely thumbtacked. Most featured Fine shaking hands with another suit. Some were autographed. I recognized the names of several local big shots, up-and-coming guys with reputations as movers and shakers.

The coffee, when he brought it, was pale and sweet in Styrofoam cups.

He resumed his seat behind the desk. "I'll level with ya. Way I see it, we're looking at a chance to frame the debate."

I nodded. The coffee was cold.

"First thing, this is not about that old lady as a victim. We rephrase it: This is about Gwen Taylor as a victim."

"Taymore," I corrected.

"Whatever. Look at her. Yeah, she's poor, she's black, she's got a record, but she's trying to make a living. She's not on welfare. Can't be making much money, but she's out plugging. Not asking for a handout, getting by on her own. She's a hard worker."

He paused as if he expected a show of enthusiasm, maybe a round of applause. I nodded again. It was enough to keep his mouth moving.

"We've got a coroner's report saying heart attack, for chrissakes, and a terrific-looking female client, photogenic as hell. I've got a black community that's been quiet lately, simmering, you might say. I've got an upcoming election. If I spin this right, there's no case. I've already tried to convince Gwen that this doesn't need to be any major to-do, but you can really do her a favor, woman to woman, and all that. Tell her not to fight this. I'm talking a plea all the way down the ladder to involuntary. No risk, probably a walk, a maximum deuce at Framingham."

His optimism didn't jibe with the outrage in the newspapers.

"What's the D.A. going for?" I asked.

"First degree." His hand strayed to his tie, failed to center the knot. "But it's just an opener. He's not getting any first degree."

"I don't know about that."

"I'm saying we can turn it into a different case than what the D.A. thinks he's got. If she's willing to plead."

"What if she had an alibi witness?"

"Cops say she doesn't."

"Cops aren't working for her. I would be."

"You want to waste time, bill the state, milk it for what it's worth like everybody else, okay, just as long as we both understand it's a waste of time." He stared at his desktop like he expected to find a discernible grain in cheap Formica, then glanced up with narrowed eyes. "What do you know about your pal Gwen?"

I shrugged.

"Most women, they've got a record, it's prostitution, bad checks, petty theft. Your pal's got assault on her sheet, and that's gonna hurt. She clobbered two other inmates at Framingham."

If I were confined to Framingham it would only be a matter of time before I clobbered someone. "And why was she there in the first place?"

He glanced at his office door to make sure it was tightly shut, lowered his voice. "Her sheet's loaded. If this were a three-strikes-you're-out state she'd never have been on the street. We're looking at prostitution raps; we're looking at drug offenses. She ran a scam on johns in the Combat Zone."

In the Zone, it's hard to tell the scammers from the scammed.

"Look, two witnesses put her at the old lady's, where she says she wasn't. Not one. Two. So as far as fighting this on the merits of the case, I'd take a pass if I were you."

"Her motive?"

"Come on. The cops have an overheard argument. Ex-con gets angry. Still the press could turn, become our ally."

I liked the way he included me with that "our."

"Realistically," he went on, "if Gwen is a friend, talk her into a deal. A plea down to involuntary is not to be dismissed lightly, and the prosecution might eat it. Nobody looking to be governor of the Commonwealth wants to crucify a black girl, especially if they're already holding prayer meetings for her in Roxbury churches."

Like New African Baptist.

"Were the pickets your bright idea?" I asked.

He lifted one eyebrow, and a self-satisfied smile settled on his lips.

I matched the smile with one of my own. "I want to speak to the two witnesses who put Gwen in the building the night of the crime."

"Well, I guess the budget'll stretch that far. Why not try to get racist responses, make somebody use the N word?"

"And I may want to interview the other tenants."

"Don't get greedy. If you can't get a rise out of the two pri-maries, forget it."

"You misunderstand me. I intend to put in some serious hours investigating this case."

"No bucks."

I finished my coffee and tossed the cup in the trash. "Yeah? Well, how much are the pickets running you? Or are they unpaid stooges? You messing with churchgoers, telling them how transpar-ently innocent dear Gwen is? As a legal maneuver?"

His lips tightened and the smile disappeared.

"You could wind up reading about yourself in the newspapers. Do you usually attend services in Roxbury? At New African Baptist? Or are you perhaps using religious zeal in pursuit of what some might see as a desirable political outcome?"

Desirable for Henry Fine and city incumbents, not necessarily for Gwen Taymore. Pleading her guilty to involuntary would move a potential racial confrontation quickly off the front page, which could lead to political favors for Henry Fine. He'd be the man who'd extinguished the campfire before it became a raging blaze. In an election year, his payoff could be huge; if not in cash, in favors.

There was no downside for Henry Fine. He wasn't going to spend any two years washing prison laundry.

He interlocked his fingers, clasping his hands and centering them on the blotter. "How's this? I sign your ticket. You get hours and expenses, within reason."

He'd definitely bought the pickets.

"I'll be in touch," I promised.

# TWENTY-ONE

Cambridgeport isn't far out of the way, so I decided to feed Gwen's cat and water her plants before heading home to switch my blackmail-the-lawyer outfit for comfortable sweats. I didn't mind the detour. On the contrary, the prospect heartened me; if Gwen could still fret the ho-hum details, she hadn't abandoned the hope of seeing cat or philodendron again. Plus I intended to snoop. I considered fascinating items I might uncover. Letters from Peritti, perhaps.

I blasted my horn as a green Land Rover veered directly into my path, braked abruptly, and turned into a side street. The driver never bothered to signal, left me pondering the benefits of trading my Toyota for an M-40 tank.

The rest of the drive passed more smoothly. Swiftly as well, as my mind strove to accommodate first the reality of Gwen's prison record, then her intimacy with the son of a notoriously racist former city councillor. I found it amazing that I could play shoulder-to-shoulder with the woman, game after game, and sense so little about her past, or her present. Perhaps not so amazing; in grammar school, hadn't I assumed all my classmates were only children like me, who ate their breakfasts in kitchens like mine with moms and dads like mine, who argued and threw lamps and disappeared from time to time, to lead union marches or get quietly, despondently drunk?

I watched pedestrians hurry along Memorial Drive, tried to peer beneath surfaces, peel away veneers. Was the energetic woman in the navy suit the attorney the two-inch pumps and pinstripes proclaimed? Or a busy mom of six dressed in a factory-outlet find? Or both? The streets hummed with anonymous walkers, as full of untold stories as unopened books.

The green Buick with a ding in the passenger side wouldn't have read "cop car" to most folks, but I happen to know that Moon's door won't open, making for an undignified scramble over the gearshift lever if you're riding shotgun. He refuses to get the ding fixed, insists it gives his car character while keeping it shy of perfection. In Boston's hostile traffic climate, he maintains, an undamaged vehicle is a target.

The Buick was parked in front of Gwen's building. I considered turning tail, returning later to a clear field. On the other hand, a postponed visit might mean another police-sealed door.

The clapboard siding had once been painted blue, but most of the color had faded to weathered gray, and the porch sagged dispiritedly. In the vestibule, a cheap hand-lettered sign told me the place was both commercial and residential; a chiropractor and a palmist shared the ground floor while tenants were housed above, two families per floor—except on five, where Gwen lived solo.

Moon could be knocking doors, checking Gwen's alibi. Homicide commanders don't usually do their own door-banging, but Moon isn't run-of-the-mill. He likes to get his hands dirty.

So do I and it's a good thing. In the vestibule, per Gwen's instructions, I inspected a sickly looking rubber tree, whose planter should have contained wood chips, dirt, and a small plastic bag shielding two keys bound together with a yellow twistee. I came up empty. No key in the damn pot. Plenty of dirt under my fingernails.

I pressed the button under the mailbox labeled G. TAYLOR. Pushed it again when I got no response. A third time and I was rewarded with Mooney's brusque "What?"

"Greenpeace," I yelled into the speaker.

"No, thanks."

I rang again. "Salvation Army. Masspirg. Hare Krishna. Bread Not Bombs. Bakesale."

"Come on up." The resignation in Mooney's voice said he'd recognized my voice.

No elevator. I climbed four flights and seemed to come to the end of the staircase. After wandering the hallway past 4A and B, I found an unmarked door that opened onto steep wooden steps so narrow my shoulders almost brushed the walls as I ascended.

When Mooney cracked the door at the top, I caught a glimpse of Teri Kiley in the background.

"You looking for me?" He didn't invite me to join the party.

"Gwen asked me to water her plants."

"Of all the lame ones."

When I tell the truth no one believes me.

A single unshielded bulb lit the hallway.

"If you were coming to water the plants, what were you planning to use for a key?" Mooney inquired.

"Gwen keeps a spare buried in the planter in the vestibule."

"Then why ring?"

"It's gone missing."

"When did she tell you about it?"

"This morning. I'm now working for the public defender." I stared up at my former boss from three steps below. He's tall—six-four—but I was used to our eyes meeting at more of a level.

He moved aside.

"What the hell," I murmured involuntarily as I ducked through the doorway. I took three steps, then halted because there was no place to go.

Gwen's home consisted of a windowless, one-room, slope-ceilinged attic. The "walls" were pink insulating material covered with gray paper backing, or occasionally, a thin plywood panel. The warped linoleum felt chilly through the soles of my shoes.

"What kind of apartment is this?"

"Illegal." Mooney moved further into the cavelike space, stooping so his head wouldn't hit the rafters.

To the right, a hot plate balanced half on, half off a countertop made from a wooden shelf and two concrete construction bricks. A refrigerator smaller than a hotel-room minibar hummed irregularly in the corner. If I moved my left foot forward it would have kicked Gwen's bed, a thin mattress on a metal frame in the center of chaos.

No phone was the least of her problems.

Along the most substantial of the "walls," she'd rigged a closet pole. Shirts and jeans lay crumpled on the floor nearby. I glanced around with growing understanding. Gwen's plants wouldn't need watering till someone rerooted them in unbroken pots. Broken dishes littered the floor near the refrigerator. Cops don't yank clothes off hangers or smash crockery.

The two large cushions had probably rested side by side and served as a couch before someone tossed them helter-skelter. The small TV, dumped off its metal stand, rested in a pile of kitchen utensils topped by a dented coffee pot.

"Cat still alive?" I asked.

"Wandering around somewhere. Yowls a lot."

"Anybody feed it?"

"Not me."

I waited a beat. "Too bad it can't tell you who broke in."

"Who says anybody broke in?"

"Well, if he didn't, he must have used the key I didn't find in the planter."

Wearing gray slacks and a matching sweater, looking slender out of uniform, Teri Kiley abandoned a cardboard box she'd been rooting through and got up off the floor. She was short enough that she didn't need to watch her head. "Somebody after drugs, maybe. An addict."

"Who instinctively searched the planter?" I inquired.

"A flowerpot's not the most original hiding place."

"And I suppose Gwen labeled the key with her apartment number just for this hypothetical addict's convenience?"

"She has a prior drug conviction," Teri reminded me pointedly. "She probably knew him."

Ouch.

"Plumbing?" I asked.

Moon nodded toward the far corner. "Hallway—if you can call it that—behind the shower curtain. Leads to a closet with a sink and a toilet."

"A shower?"

He shook his head. "Just the sink."

I guess she used the Y for more than messages.

He shifted uncomfortably, keeping his head low. "Landlord never intended this space to be let, he says. His nephew manages the building, admits to renting it as a 'favor' for a friend of a friend, which means he pockets whatever Gwen pays him."

"Can't be much." I turned my attention back to the devastation. At Valentine's place the signs had been subtle. Here, the search had been hurried and destructive. Signifying two different perps? It would be so much simpler with one, a phone-cracking pill-hider who'd been looking for a particular item at Val's and, failing to find it, seeking the same prize at Gwen's. I liked that.

"What do you suppose they were looking for?"

Moon cleared his throat and shot Teri a glance that warned her against speculating out loud. He recognized my question for what it was, a fish hook, baited and dangling. I smiled. It felt like old times again. I know how Mooney's mind works. Or maybe I kid myself that I know how Mooney's mind works.

"Don't tell me drugs," I said. "Not here. If Gwen were dealing, she'd live in a decent place."

"Who says they were looking for anything?" Mooney leaned his weight against the now-closed door, the only surface that looked solid enough to support it.

"Well, what are *you* looking for?"

His turn to smile. "None of your business. Teri, did you finish with the bathroom?"

"Almost done."

"Let's wind it up."

She retreated behind the plastic shower curtain. Seemed like it was just the two of them. I wondered how that set with the rest of Mooney's team. Were they jealous of the new kid? I waited a moment to see if Moon had sent Teri off because he had news he wanted to confide in private. He didn't speak though, just stared off after her.

"Motive," I said. "That's what you're searching for."

"How do you figure that?" He took the bait, but he knew it was wriggling. I could tell by his eyes.

"The pills belonged to Phipps, her own medication. So the means were at the scene. As far as opportunity goes, I hear you've got somebody who'll put Gwen in the building."

"Two somebodies."

"But juries crave motive. If you could find loot Gwen lifted from Phipps's place—"

"It's a routine search."

"If it's so routine, why are you here?"

"I want to play it by the book. It's moving fast, this case, what with TV and the press. I feel like we might be railroading this chick. I mean, look how she lives."

Marta's crummy apartment was a palace next to this.

He blew out a deep breath. "But what am I supposed to do? Not arrest her because she's poor, black, and has a record? I'm going to take heat on this, so I might as well be up front in the investigation. And we're short of personnel, anyway. I drafted Teri for the duration. I might even make it a permanent thing. You approve?"

He'd lowered his voice so it was barely above a whisper.

"Of Kiley?"

"Yeah."

"She'll do fine." I wanted to say, Why the hell ask me? What? Am I the expert on "chicks"? You need my blessing? I hoped it was just a subject-changer, a trick to throw me off balance.

"She's something else," he murmured.

I didn't want to chitchat with Mooney about Teri Kiley, now

or ever. Didn't want to find myself imagining their easy camaraderie on the drive back, shared department gossip, watercooler jokes, the quick scoot over the gearshift.

One night, when I was working undercover, drafted out of Homicide into Vice despite my protests, wearing a thigh-high skirt and skin-tight top, freezing my ass and seething at an assignment that was little more than coming on to sorry johns so I could bust them, my hidden radio crackled with Mooney's voice. A source had warned him of Combat Zone trouble, of an undercover who'd been made, and he wanted me out fast. Vice knew; they should have warned me. They didn't. I remembered racing down a treacherously icy sidewalk, leaping into Moon's Buick. If I hadn't kicked off my heels so I could move more quickly, the crowbar that sailed out of the dark and struck his passenger door might have damaged me instead.

I liked the fact that Moon had never gotten the dent fixed. I didn't relish the image of Teri Kiley clambering over the gearshift, even if she wore slacks instead of a mini.

I forced my focus back to Mooney's voiced doubts. If he was uneasy in his gut about Gwen's guilt, I was pleased. He'd keep sifting till every detail fell into place.

Carefully, as though testing me, he said, "I think she did it for her man. I hate it, but that's the way it seems."

"Sounds like a corny country song."

"Yeah? What rhymes with Peritti?"

"He talk to you?"

"Why shouldn't he?"

"What's his version?"

"Version?" Moon folded his arms across his chest. I was tempted to follow suit. The chill in the air made me wonder how Gwen managed in winter.

"How they met, when."

"Dancing."

"Avalon," I agreed.

"He'd noticed her in the neighborhood, going in and out of his building, so it was easy to strike up a conversation."

No help for Gwen there. Peritti admitted to approaching her, yes, but only because she seemed familiar. In other words, she'd already started working for Phipps.

Mooney brushed the hair off his forehead. "I'm not reading him as a total innocent."

"Good." I had a sudden vision of Peritti, not in his office, but standing in front of apartment 4A, wearing a low-slung toolbelt. Would a blow from his hammer have cracked the phone, or smashed it to bits?

Moon hurried on. "He spins her a tale about how much money he'd make if he could sell the property, and she thinks he'd marry her and she could have everything, if that stubborn old lady weren't standing in her way."

"Okay. Then who trashed this place?"

"Peritti," he returned dryly.

"Why?"

"Because he agrees with me. He thinks she did it. And he's worried she may have kept a diary, saying how she'd do anything in the world for him."

"No."

"Why?"

"Peritti's never been here. I'll bet he doesn't even know where she lives."

"Why?"

"Look around, Moon."

"Everything's upside down. Place isn't at its best."

"At its best, is this a love nest? A turn-on? Come on, would you want to get naked in here?"

As soon as I said it, I knew I'd made a mistake, crossed a forbidden line. Mooney and I hadn't worked side by side in years; we weren't brother and sister any longer.

His right eyebrow arched and he glanced at me in a way that confirmed my fear. At least he didn't say, "Is that an offer?" He didn't say it, but that's what he was thinking; he was thinking about getting naked and, dammit, so was I.

"There are probably rats behind the insulation," I added quickly. "If we listen we can hear them scratching."

"Carlotta, you know how they say love is blind? Well, sex is stone blind, deaf and dumb to boot. Guy interested in screwing isn't checking the decor." His voice was husky.

*What did Teri's place look like?* I wondered. I caught myself before I asked him for a description.

"Moon, we're not talking about a blow job in an alley or a one-night stand. Gwen said 'boyfriend-girlfriend.' "

"Who knows what Peritti calls it."

"Good point. What *did* he call it?"

"If you were still on the force, I could tell you."

"She didn't bring him here." I made myself sound more certain than I felt.

"Where's your evidence?"

I started to say, "The bed's too small," but the bed seemed suddenly large, prominent, as if it had ballooned to take up all the space in the attic. I considered saying, "Because I know her," but I didn't know the woman who lived in this one-room disaster. The Gwen I knew played volleyball; she was quiet, reliable, beautiful. How could she live here and look the way she did, with her hair kempt, her clothes clean?

She'd lived in a cell. This couldn't be any worse.

I had the uneasy feeling that Mooney could read my mind. I snatched at a straw. "The old lady's place was searched, too. Do you think Peritti's responsible for that? Or is that supposed to be a co-incidence?"

Moon considered it, glancing around the room, focusing on anything but the bed. "Okay. I'll get a scene unit in to do prints."

"Okay," I echoed, relieved.

"Don't get your expectations up. I doubt we'll find anything out of the ordinary. Just Gwen and the boyfriend."

"Still—," I began.

"You maybe ought to hope Peritti masterminded it, and that Teri and I can pin it on him, because we did find a will."

The way he said it, I knew the will was bad news. The way he said "Teri and I" sounded like bad news as well.

"It leaves everything to the hired help. Of course, it may get tossed out in probate. Undue influence. Somebody like Bronson

Hohen contesting it. You could have mentioned Hohen, by the way, if you were in a confiding mood."


It took me fifteen minutes to coax the shivering tabby out from behind a sheet of plywood. Five to find a rusty can opener. As I emptied a tin of chicken parts into its dish, I thought about taking the cat home.

I decided against it. I had enough strays at present.

# TWENTY-TWO

Maybe I just wanted to play with the electric trains.

I found myself pulling a U-turn in the middle of traffic-choked Mass. Ave., earning righteously upraised fingers and wrathful honks. When I regained control of my vehicle, it was aimed toward Bronson Hohen's downtown office. When that sort of thing happens I run with it.

Maybe I wanted to hear the Santa Fe diesel sing its song while it chugged around the track, easing off to a siding when the steam locomotive blew its whistle.

He was in, and busy. His secretary, Yale, in black again, remembered my name, but was reluctant to buzz him even to inquire if I might beg an interview. I leaned heavily on her desk, planting myself in her field of vision, not moving, not intending to move. I have experience at being a pest, years as a cop. You can't insult me.

She caved eventually, with a grimace that tightened her lips to a pout. If I could wait, he'd see me within the hour. I wished he kept his toy collection in the outer office. I'd have been satisfied with his stack of old newspapers.

Yale wasn't overwhelmed by chores. Her nails clicked occasionally against the computer keyboard. Once, an incoming fax kicked a machine into life; the phone jangled twice. The pace was not the quick tempo I associate with a busy company. I wished she'd abandon ship and leave me with the computer. At five, she stretched and smiled and gave the impression of a non-clockwatcher.

Hohen hadn't been prompted by any genealogical whim when he'd hired me to determine whether Valentine had wedded his grandfather. I'd never believed that. I'd believed the size of his check. In the back of my mind I'd thought, how much could he need an inheritance? A wealthy man like Hohen?

He'd never requested that I do anything illegal.

How wealthy was he? Record companies are not the most stable businesses. They get bought and sold and traded and become parts of conglomerates, and most of them are headquartered in New York, L.A., or Nashville, not Boston.

The second hand on my watch moved slowly. The only reading material was a cluster of glossy magazines on the glass coffee table. I scanned breathless chat about recording artists, "superstars" I'd never heard of, whose claim to fame consisted of one "best-selling," "superhot" "megahit." *What will we do when we're all superstars?* I wondered. *Who'll be awed by our magnificent presence?*

A scruffy group of androgynous teens shepherded by a conspicuously well-coiffed older man bustled out of Hohen's office. The teens wore holes surrounded by scrappy tie-dyed cloth. They were talking the lingo, mechanicals and residuals and title credit and on-the-road perks. They had attitude; every other word was *fuck*. I thought I recognized the older guy as the former tenant of a prison cell, a habitual whistler some wag had christened "Felonius Monk," but I couldn't be sure.

Hohen looked wilted, but he summoned a smile and a show of enthusiasm.

"They're going to be huge," he said, after their noisy, air-kissing departure.

"Who?"

"The trio. Call themselves Monster Grunge, but we're renaming. We have an entire division that mostly names bands, can you believe it?"

I shrugged.

His smile disappeared. "Sometimes, I swear," he said, shaking his head, "bands get together five minutes before I see them. Pluck a star from this group, a star from that—*voilà*—a supergroup! There's no chemistry. No sound. I'm not talking about this group, not these kids. Please don't quote me. I'm not having my greatest day."

"Does that have anything to do with Valentine Phipps?" I asked.

He closed the door of his playroom/office. The trains were motionless. His pale eyes seemed suddenly tired, so drained of vitality that he almost looked his age. "I'm saddened—shocked by what I've seen on TV and read in the papers. First there was outrage, but now everyone seems to have so much sympathy for that black woman, and no one seems to care about Valentine at all. She was lovely, you know, truly lovely."

"I thought you'd never met her."

"I never did." He was unfazed. "There was a portrait of her in the hallway of my grandfather's house. Did you see that preacher on TV, carrying on about the insult to the black community, calling for forgiveness rather than hate? It sounded as though he believed she was guilty as hell."

"You know about the will?"

"The police informed me, as a courtesy. It makes things look worse for the health aide, don't you think? If the TV idiots knew about the will, maybe they'd stop talking about what a perfect victim the Taymore woman is. Damn, if I'd known Valentine needed nursing help, I could've found her someone reliable."

"You're upset."

"Not about the will, dammit, about her dying over nothing. I had so much to ask her. I wanted to know more about my grandfather, flesh out the family tales." He picked up his Slinky, ran it through his nervous hands. "Well, at least I know she was the right woman, thanks to you. And I hope to be permitted to go through her belongings to see if she kept letters from my grandfather. I'd be gratified by letters, any family memorabilia."

"Memorabilia," I repeated.

"Yes."

"What sort of memorabilia?"

"Letters." He shrugged. "Diaries, anything concerning my family."

He was good at lying. *Anyone in the music business would have to be*, I thought. But he was lying.

Oh, I know, who do I think I am, a lie detector? Yes, I tender delusions of grandeur concerning my truth-discerning ability, but I keep myself humble by remembering that all humans lie. It's *why* they lie that's fascinating. And as to that, usually, I don't have a clue.

"Your grandfather was a rich man, wasn't he?"

"What does that matter?"

"I'm working for the attorney defending Gwen Taymore."

He looked like he'd eaten something that didn't agree with him.

"Can you help me out on this? Did your grandfather give his young bride a special engagement present, a fabulous wedding ring, something small and valuable—"

"Sounds to me like you're trying to hammer nails into the black girl's coffin."

"Did your grandfather give his wife valuable presents?"

"All my grandfather's property was sold at auction to pay off the debts of his estate. He'd speculated wildly in his last years, in art and real estate, as well as love. My mother thought he might have been going senile for some time. She was shaken by his death, and the monetary loss, the whole family was. Suddenly I had to foot the bill for my last year of college; my mother moved from Beacon Hill to the suburbs, which she felt deeply, as a humiliating comedown. I'd be fascinated to know if the police have found something."

He was fishing now.

"Your grandfather's name was Bronson, like yours?"

"Yes," he said testily.

"And he was a collector? Like you? Did he collect toys?"

"Did the police find something at Valentine's flat? Or at that woman's place, wherever she lives? If they did, they haven't informed me. They should."

I shrugged.

"Do you know?" he asked.

"If I knew what you were looking for, I might be able to pose the right questions. The officer in charge of the investigation is a good friend of mine."

He grabbed a blue-and-yellow Koosh ball off the wooden desk, moved it nervously from his right hand to his left.

"I brought those letters you gave me," I added, "requesting cooperation when I was trying to get into Mrs. Phipps's apartment. I never used them, never mentioned your name. They're still sealed."

"Thank you."

"I know how to be discreet." I laid the envelopes on the desk.

He tossed the blue-and-yellow sphere into the air, caught it, and squeezed it tightly in his fist.

I think he might have let something slip if Yale hadn't waltzed into the room with an air of aggrievement and a fat sheaf of papers.

"Excuse me, but it's getting late, Mr. Hohen, and these contracts need to go out tonight."

"I'll be right with you, Yale."

I expected her to leave. She stared me coolly in the eye, stood her ground, and announced, "I'm holding calls from the coast on two and four."

Hohen sighed. "Please see Miss Carlyle out."

"But—"

"If I need you for anything, I'll call." His words were devastatingly polite. If I'd been a musician I'd never have sung in this town again.

# TWENTY-THREE

Rush hour snarled Beacon Hill, so I followed the lane-of-least-resistance rule: Insert car in fastest stream, get out of downtown clog, use less-traveled side streets. I don't mind distance or direction as long as I'm moving. I look on newly discovered streets the way I imagine Christopher Columbus regarded New World islands after months at sea. I like nothing better than navigating an alternate route from point A to point B, and successful routes come in handy in my fallback career as a cabbie.

The car across the street from my house wasn't a neighborhood regular. The man inside, crouched low in the driver's seat, was reading a newspaper. Instead of turning into the drive, I kept rolling at a steady twenty-five, made four right turns, and circled, considering options.

I toyed with the idea of blasting my horn as I pulled up behind the gray Ford, but if Mr. Inconspicuous was from the police, which I expected, or the FBI, which I thought a possibility, or the Mob, an organization with whom I've come in contact over the years, he might prove sensitive to loud noises, react badly by pulling a gun.

I made do with slamming the door as I exited. I didn't expect to come face-to-face with the caricature over Peter Breeze's column. He had one shaggy eyebrow, just like the drawing. His nose was hooked, but not as hooked as the exaggerated cartoon. He didn't bother to introduce himself, which I read as flaming arrogance.

"Nice house." His voice was full of suspicion. It wasn't a compliment; he was asking how a lowlife like me could afford to live among the Cambridge intelligentsia.

"I like it," I said.

"I ran a profile on you. It's not what I expected."

"It's mine."

"Trust-fund babies don't usually join the cops."

"No trust fund. Not that it's your business." Damn, I could see why people seemed to blurt out their lives to journalists. He'd set me up, mouthing a false assumption for me to deny.

"I'm a reporter," he offered blithely. "Everything's my business. Can I see the house?"

"You want to report about my house?"

He cracked a thin smile. "I'd like to talk to you, and if you let me in the door, I have a better chance."

"What do you want to talk about?"

"I've got a photo: you entering Nashua Street jail this morning. You went to visit Guinivere Taymore."

"No comment."

"I'll ask one of my Metro news buddies to run it," he said smugly, "along with your name."

I do my share of the kind of work in which an investigator benefits from anonymity. The way Breeze voiced his threat, he had to know that. Celebrity might seem cool to the grunge group in Hohen's office; I could live without it.

"A little blackmail courtesy of the fourth estate?"

"Nobody wants to talk to me anymore," he said modestly. "What am I supposed to do?"

*Look for an honest job,* I thought.

"Come in," I said.

The stink of turpentine spilled onto the stoop as soon as I unlocked the door. It filled the foyer. Breeze's nostrils fluttered and he kept a careful distance from the walls as if expecting to encounter wet paint.

"Redecorating?" he asked.

"Involuntarily."

"Should we talk in your office?"

"How much talk do we need to prevent my picture from running in the paper?"

He peered up the staircase, took in the foyer's high ceiling, complete with the brown water marks that would knock down the price if I were selling. His eyes swiveled from the hallway to the arch leading to the living room.

"Look, I'm not a bad guy. I'm doing a piece on urban renewal, how it's another name for sticking it to the poor. Maybe, living here, you could care less."

I motioned him toward the arch. "Watch the step."

"Ex-cop in this neighborhood. Hard to believe, surrounded by certified Cambridge bleeding-heart liberals."

"Do you get paid to stick labels on people?"

He seemed puzzled by the living room. Its graceful mahogany reflects my late great-aunt Bea's cameo-and-lace sensibility rather than my own more eclectic taste.

He said, "The town's labeling Gwen Taymore guilty. Agreed?"

"They seem to be doing that. Have we talked long enough?"

Uninvited, he sat in the straight-backed client chair opposite my rolltop desk. I took the desk chair, which is more comfortable.

"I think Gwen's getting the big screw," he said. "I don't think she's even the story here. Agreed?"

"No comment."

"Off the record." His eyes were deepset, blue-gray, and he knew how to use them. I put him in his late thirties. He dressed well. "Even without the racism angle, this would be front page. She's black, yeah, but she's a home health-care worker, which is a hot-button job these days, what with foreign nationals bilking the elderly, itinerant 'buddies' killing old coots in their beds after borrowing the car keys. I'm already hearing that Gwen Taymore's been signing Mrs. Phipps's name on her checks for three months."

"Where'd you get that?" I asked, thinking, *Oh, great, Henry Fine tells me he can spin the press, plead down, while the press, in the person of the* Globe's *leading columnist, is saying the story rates front page, plus or minus the racism.* Who was doing the spinning?

"Where'd I get it? An unnamed source."

"I doubt that Gwen stole from Mrs. Phipps. You can quote me."

"Wow," he said, "that's juicy. Look, I want to backtrack the story, refocus it. Mrs. Phipps believed her landlord was out to get her and I don't see why that angle is suddenly so far off. If Taymore's in the picture at all, it's the landlord who put her there. I hear they were seeing each other, the landlord and Gwen Taymore, which would kill old man Peritti, who's a white supremacist from the get-go. Let's say the son takes after the old man, you think he'd be evil enough to promise Gwen Taymore marriage on condition she does the old lady?"

It wasn't far from Mooney's pet theory.

The reporter said, "Aren't you going to deny that a relationship exists between Peritti and Taymore?"

I leaned back and laughed. "And then you print that P.I. Carlotta Carlyle denied it. You use my denial to legitimize your crap."

"We'll have to have dinner sometime."

"Not in this life," I returned with a smile.

"Do you know anything about Phipps's husband?"

"Why?"

"Somebody phoned, left a message suggesting I ought to check him out, said it would make a dynamite story. All I've got is that Mr. Phipps was a carpenter who died, which might make a Christmas column, but nothing more."

He was onto the wrong husband. Didn't know about Hohen. Yet.

I said, "You never know what'll make a good story. For example, have you visited Peritti Real Estate?"

"No."

I stood up. "Since you're on your way out, let me make a suggestion. A photo of the model in Peritti's office, the brand-new revitalized Fenway, might make a better visual than a shot of some P.I."

"Thanks."

"And you might try reading your own newspaper," I suggested.

"What?"

"Pull up all your stories on the Fenway. Two, three years back ought to cover it. Rat infestations—that was just a few days ago—and garbage that doesn't get picked up, and a string of electrical blackouts . . ."

"The Fenway flood," he muttered.

"It's hard to manipulate rainfall, but that could've given someone an idea."

A low purring noise came from his throat. He stuck his tongue between his teeth and started scribbling quick words on a yellow pad he'd snatched from the pocket of his button-down shirt.

"You're talking—what—some kind of sabotage? To move the residents out, make way for the developers."

"Just a possibility." I felt like I'd tossed a juicy bone to a ravenous dog. I wouldn't have to worry about my picture in the paper now.

Our eyes met and Breeze smiled the way a snake might smile if it had lips. He stood up and turned to go. I doublechecked the lock behind him.

How far would he run with it? Standing by the refrigerator, wondering if I'd lunched, and on what, I ate two slightly furled slices of Swiss cheese.

Then I searched the crowded refrigerator message board. I found two coupons for cut-rate cat food and a note in Paolina's writing that said "band practice tonight."

I mounted the stairs, hesitating on the second floor, sniffing fumes.

"Roz?" I called.

"What?"

She was home. She sounded alert. I blinked my eyes, took a breath, and went upstairs for a visit. I couldn't see her. I addressed a question to the air.

"What band?"

"Huh?"

"Paolina. Band practice."

"It's like a school thing. Concert band, not a ska group, no funk. I pick her up at eight."

She was above me, practically ceiling height, lying on a narrow board that straddled two ladders. One bare leg hung over the side. Her toenails were painted black. I could see her hand pressing a sponge onto a deep green section of mural.

"Want some work?" I asked.

"No baby-sitting." The sponge dabbed at the ceiling, paint dripped, and she muttered under her breath.

"Millennium Towers. A building project in the Fenway. I want to know all about it, plans, principals. I'll write it out, put it on the fridge."

"Fine. You want it fast?"

"Yes. Did you talk to the Cambridge cops?" It was fun to imagine the stationhouse reaction to Roz.

"Oh, yeah. Hang on, okay?"

Both legs appeared. The toes on her left foot were magenta. The rest of her descended, shrugging into a long denim shirt. She'd been working in the nude and her spectacular shape was splotched with greens and yellows.

"Maldonado," she said. "That's your Diego's last name. Cops know him well. Skull on his forearm, right?"

"That's my boy."

"Officer named Schultz volunteered to pick him up, pleased to do you a favor. You dating him?"

"Where can I find Diego, Roz?"

"Depends on when."

I sighed. Marginal guys often have no regular base of operations.

"Dude's got a schedule," Roz offered.

"How about tonight?"

"Friday?" She closed her eyes. There was a smudge of yellow over her left nostril. "Riley's on Western Avenue. Usually shows up around eleven, with a couple girls."

"Pimping?"

"Amateur. Keeps his string with him, Schultz says, invites guys to party. What the girls do depends on what the guys pay."

"Diego have a party place?"

"It floats. Motels, different sites—which aggravates your cop."

"Not my cop." Jay Schultz and I went through the academy together. No chemistry.

"Okay."

"Let's do some barhopping tonight."

"Paid? Terrific. What should I wear?"

I glanced at her. "How about something sexy?"

# TWENTY-FOUR

Roz was late, which left me nursing a Harp on tap, brooding at a bar. Intending only to review facts, list reasons Gwen should or shouldn't languish at Framingham Correctional, I found myself drifting down speculative lanes. Did Teri Kiley appreciate Mooney's small talk for what it was—some of the finest course work she'd get in her cop career? Now that Mooney'd climbed the ladder to become a boss, he seldom teamed with anyone. Did Teri appreciate her luck? Did Mooney miss having a partner? Did he miss me?

A barstool is a rotten perch from which to contemplate a might-have-been relationship. I've been that route. Loneliness tends to endow the loser on the next stool with the sheen of romance.

I sipped slowly, reviewing the apologetic note I'd left for Paolina, the few fast-food evening meals we'd shared since she'd moved in. I was doing a sub-par substitute-mom job. Still I pondered offering her a permanent home, abandoning the search for Marta.

Paolina grew up thinking she knew her father. Jimmy, her brothers' dad, didn't hug her as warmly as he hugged the boys, never roughhoused with her, but she'd assumed it was a "boy-girl" thing.

She called him Dad; he never denied it. She'd learned the truth only by eavesdropping, by mistake.

*Newsweek* once ran a color photo of her biological father. An undercover DEA agent snapped the picture, spiky Andean peaks in the background shrouded in mist. The caption: COLOMBIA'S DRUG BARONS SETTLE DISPUTE. Of the five men in the shot, two are still alive, including Paolina's dad.

Her father by blood, Carlos Roldan Gonzales, a man of many aliases and enemies, sends an occasional cash package. I act as go-between, launderer, what have you. The money's earmarked for Paolina's college years. If she drops out of high school, then what?

Where the hell was Roz? She knew the agreed-upon meeting time. The bar hadn't been tough to find. The nearest neighbors were autobody shops. Some patrons had come straight from the job, wearing overalls with names stitched over the breast pocket. At first I wondered why they hadn't bothered to change, then I realized that visible proof of employment in these parts was a true come-on to the opposite sex. The heavy smell of grease blended with cigar smoke. Probably half the clientele worked at dismembering and reassembling wrecks, then waltzed over to the bar, drank, and drove.

The place was big for a neighborhood joint, which meant no roomful of regulars nailed me as an intruder. Crossed pool cues provided decor; the motif was overstated, considering the one lonely pool table. The light was yellowy and low, the walls knotty pine, the carpeting an unfortunate golf-course green that hadn't worn well. Interspersed among the overalled men were enough high-voiced women that one of three TVs over the long wooden bar was tuned to women's basketball. The players looked sharp on defense.

I sat at the bar and let what passed for ambiance wash over me, absorbing the jukebox disco, the smell of spilled beer, the clatter of pool cues from the back corner. The TVs' ghostly presences were by and large unconnected to the sounds of the place.

I didn't hear what I was listening for: the tinkling rush of Spanish. Diego and entourage still hadn't shown up by the time Roz made a late-by-thirty-two-minutes appearance. I let her tardiness slide.

"Plan?" She eased onto the stool to my left. I only needed to raise my eyes as far as the mirror to realize the redundancy of telling

Roz to dress in a sexy fashion. She could wear a cop uniform blouse
and look like a floozie; the overstressed buttons would come undone.

She'd abandoned the leather, but she still projected tough.
Black was the color and tight was the style. Her tube top stopped at
her midriff and her skirt didn't start till after you noticed a lot of
ribs and abs and the gleaming ring in her navel.

"We'll need to improvise."

She ordered a Bud from a bartender who sprinted to serve her.

"Roz," I advised, "turn off the high beams."

"Huh?"

"Dim the signals you're shining at the Coors-hat guy."

"He's cute," she protested.

"Roz."

Too late. The hatted dude at the table sent over more beers. If
the atmosphere didn't chill, Roz and I would have to start holding
hands to discourage offers. The corner of my mouth twitched. I
hoped I wouldn't have to discuss, much less resort to, same-sex-
preference subterfuge with Roz.

"Where's the boyfriend?" I posed the question to encourage her
to keep her focus at the bar.

She shrugged.

"Odd name, K-Rob."

Another shrug.

"What's he do?"

Most of Roz's lovers are bouncers at weird establishments.
One's a karate instructor.

"Research," she said.

"Into?"

"Art, history. Libraries, museums. I think he's doing a talk at
the Fogg tonight."

Harvard's Fogg Art Museum is world renowned. When I tried
to envision K-Rob lecturing in the plush auditorium, my mind
balked. I tried placing him in the well-lit galleries instead, stealing
items off the walls or swabbing floors with a mop.

Diego arrived at eleven, two Latinas in tow. I stared at them
sharply. Each reminded me of Paolina's mom, with shared emphasis
on thick eyeliner and dark red lipstick. One wore her tangled black

curls in the same loose style as Marta. The other had cropped her hair and dyed the top layer a shocking platinum. Her eyes had the snap and sparkle, the vitality that used to characterize Marta's. Neither woman had the hard air of the practiced hooker.

"Here he comes," I murmured to Roz.

"You want me to beat the shit out of him?" she asked.

"I'm aiming for subtlety."

"Does he know you?"

"We've met."

"That could be a problem," she remarked.

I wore midnight blue silk tucked into skinny black jeans. My blow-dried hair—I rarely smooth my thick curly hair—was sleekly parted on the left. I'd used makeup.

"I'm in disguise," I said, "but I'll let you handle him just in case."

"Handle him?" She wrinkled her nose.

"Flirt. Vamp. Take the man's mind off business, Roz."

"This could cost you extra." She regarded Diego judiciously.

"It's for Paolina," I said solemnly.

She sighed and yanked her tube top an inch lower.

"I'll give you the signal," I said.

"Where'll you be?"

"I'm betting one of those charmers knows Marta. I'm betting they can't drink beer and keep out of the john."

Fifteen minutes later the ladies had focused on a quartet of heavy-drinking construction workers, leaving me to admire the speed and precision with which they worked.

Diego seemed cast as a benevolent brother. He did fine, didn't overplay his hand, seemed amused at his "sisters' " bold antics.

The one with hair like Marta's sat on the lap of a red-faced blond. She wasn't shy and she moved around enough to give him a thrill and a preview.

"Let's do it," I said to Roz. "When the ladies leave the bathroom, come visit me there."

"And if they don't hit the loo at all?"

I shrugged. "We'll go to plan B."

The rest-room door was marked with a massive W upon which some clever soul had painted nipples in the appropriate locale. Inside: one sink, two stalls, fluorescent lighting, and a printed warning to employees to wash their hands.

The grim lighting provided inspiration. Okay, tell the truth, the way I looked under the grim lighting gave me the idea. Accentuating the negative, I dampened my hair in the sink, rubbed the blusher off my cheeks. I entered a stall, waited, reading the obscene graffiti on the wall, flushing the toilet as I heard the outer door creak open. A buxom lady in Capri pants entered, so I canceled my first performance.

I got luckier the second time. When my quarry entered, both women chatting amiably in Spanish, I moaned and clung to the side of the stall.

"*Cuidado!*" the dyed blonde advised her friend warily, afraid I'd vomit on their shoes, I guess.

I slid to the floor, groaning and burying my head in my hands.

"*Pobrecita,*" the tangle-haired one murmured. Six-foot-tall women are not easy objects of pity unless they're on the floor, which was why I chose to take an early dive.

"Please, you are sick bad?" Her English was more hesitant than Marta's.

"*Tengo unos cólicos menstruales los hijueputas,*" I mumbled. Cramps. What awful cramps. From then on, the conversation was entirely in Spanish, and they professed themselves delighted with my accent and vocabulary, a tribute to Paolina's coaching. I told them I'd grown up in Bogotá, where my dad had worked for a mining company. They were both Dominican, I learned to my relief. No danger of shared childhood remembrances.

Damn, they were nice. Almost innocent. They never assumed I was some lying chickie on drugs, for instance. They clicked their tongues and dampened harsh paper towels to lay on my brow. Between stints in the stalls, they inquired whether I wanted a message taken outside to my boyfriend. One offered me a Tampax from a tiny purse, telling the other she hoped she wouldn't get her period tonight because it looked like the *cabrónes* were anxious to have a good time.

"You better hope you get it soon," the other laughed.

We were pals by the time I informed the tangle-haired lady, my new *amiga* Zita, that she looked familiar. When I asked if we could have met through Marta, I saw no suspicion in her eyes.

It wasn't like I'd rushed in and flashed a badge. I was one of the girls, a needy one at that.

Sure she knew Marta.

I had to work more quickly than I'd have liked, because I was afraid the construction crew quartet would grow impatient. And then Diego would pound the door. If Roz slipped up.

I knew Marta's children's names, how tough she'd had it since Jimmy'd returned to Puerto Rico. Friends of friends, speakers of the same language, Zita and I were practically family.

The dyed blond was dispatched to soothe the guys and fetch me a glass of water.

Eagerly I asked Zita if she expected Marta to drop by later tonight.

"I miss her," I said. "I'd love to see her."

"She's maybe getting married!"

Such good news almost made my cramps subside, I told Zita. She seemed to know little about the bridegroom, not even his name. He was a gringo, yes, but I already knew that.

Zita wanted to chat about her hopes for a winter cruise to the islands.

Blondie reappeared.

"Hey," she said, "the *pendejo* wants us out there now."

"You gonna be okay?" Zita was solicitous.

"You're an angel. Could you get a message to Marta for me? Or tell me how to find her? I owe her money."

"You do?"

"If she's getting married, she can probably use it. A new night-gown, you know?"

Blondie laughed. "Better a bottle of perfume."

At this both women laughed and chattered, and so I discovered that Marta's intended ran a fishing camp, small run-down cabins on a lake that might or might not be called Silver Pond. The ladies had visited late one night, gotten too blasted on tequila to make the trip home, slept on the ground. It had rained and the smell of fish had not been pleasant. Hence, perfume.

I wondered whether the campsite was one of Diego's movable party sites. New Hampshire seemed too far away.

"If I want to go up, how'd I find it?"

They had only the vaguest recollection. Neither drove. It had been dark and late.

"When you're real close there's a sign."

Zita thought it had something to do with *tumbas* and *cementerios*.

"Graves," I suggested. Blondie nodded.

Graves's Cabins, Silver Pond, New Hampshire.

Zita dug in her purse for an aspirin, gave me a pat on the shoulder. Both women, advising strategic repairs, offered to lend me cosmetics. I thanked them, said I'd rest till the cramps subsided.

They waved as they returned to duty.

When Roz entered ten minutes later, I instructed her to dump Diego, offering to wait and give her a ride home. She smiled wickedly, said dumping him would be a pleasure indeed, but she had a date later on, so I should consider myself on my own.

I opted for the back door exit. After faking pain so long, my stomach actually hurt. Maybe I deserved it for lying to the ladies, lying to them when they were so sweet.

# TWENTY-FIVE

It wasn't just my stomach. My forehead throbbed with the combination of alcohol and pool-cue clatter. Inhaling, I caught a whiff of forbidden cigarettes before the breeze could snatch the smell. I used to smoke pack after pack of Kools, lighting the next from the stub of the latest. No matter that it's been ten years since I last slipped one between my lips with a gesture borrowed from an old Lauren Bacall movie, I still lust after them. I was a true addict; one puff today and I'd be sucking down smoke like a chimney tomorrow.

My hand formed an automatic fist around my keys. I recommend it: Car keys make great brass knuckles. It's become one of my Pavlovian responses to darkness. Perhaps I ought to relocate to a cabin on Silver Pond, New Hampshire, get over my knee-jerk attack-prevention routines. I don't carry unless I anticipate the need.

The car, locked tight, was parked under a streetlamp. Late as it was, the neighborhood was noisy, sound spilling from curtained windows, the beat of salsa music, a sudden burst of muffled laughter. Night like this, I could drop by an after-hours joint, a cop hangout, relax, forget finding Marta and freeing Gwen, hear some blues.

I yanked my mind away from the laughter, turned the key to start the engine. I love cruising the late-night streets, calm and hushed under the yellow cast of sodium vapor lamps, studded with shadowy glimpses of hurrying night people. The engine and I hummed along with Chris Smither, on tape, while he sang the hell out of Chuck Berry's "Maybelline." I realized I was heading home.

I found Paolina curled in bed, surrounded by Beanie Babies and the stuffed shark she'd bought on her journey to Bogotá, souvenir of Miami International Airport and the trip during which she'd learned her father's true identity. Sometimes I almost convince myself she is my child. Would it be so bad if Marta disappeared forever? Would Paolina's self-esteem bear up under the double burden of abandonment, first by father, then mother?

I told myself Marta would turn up. Inevitably. You don't abandon your kids, not even for a last-chance romance.

When do you get your last chance?

The question echoed as if I'd spoken the words aloud. I imagined I could hear them reverberate in the drain as I soaped and rinsed my face. They surfaced in the shuffle of my slippers as I crossed the hall and crawled into bed.

*What muck would Peter Breeze rake in his column tomorrow?* I mused as I drifted out of consciousness. . . .

I was angry at the sound that woke me, my mouth stale with the taste of beer. Damn that noise, that annoyingly repetitive *beep, beep, beep,* and the voice as well, a ragged bass, calling, yelling, louder, and the word took shape in my mind and my body responded and I realized suddenly that I was upright, awake, no longer lying asleep, and the word was "Fire!"

If the flickering light were merely the lingering backdrop of a dream, I intended to strangle the screamer. I blinked furiously, and the dim glow pulsed. Flickering meant fire, not a malfunctioning smoke detector, not a dream: Fire!

Paolina's image, sharp as an etching, acid on stone, rooted my feet to the floor. I can clamber from my bedroom window to the front yard oak. Outside in twenty seconds; move! But Paolina slept across the hall. I slapped my right palm flat against the door. The heat made me wince and drop my hand.

I know you never open a hot door, I know it like I know my name, but I needed to go through that door, against knowledge, against gut instinct, because it led to Paolina.

Cover your mouth and nose. Fine, except that towels and water, both located in the bathroom, may as well have existed on Jupiter. Stay low. Facts and warnings tumbled over each other in a rush, but what good was advice I couldn't translate into action?

"Don't be a fool," I lectured myself sternly, and my frog-croak voice shocked me into movement.

A glass of water stood on my bedside table. I tipped it onto one of the men's undershirts I substitute for nightgowns, tied the damp rag over my face like a bandit. This time I didn't bother placing my hand on the door. I knelt and inched it ajar, terrified that a sudden surge of oxygen might cause a rush of flame.

An eerie light rose from the stairwell. I forced air into my lungs, and yelled Paolina's name as I charged to my left down the hall, dodged to the right through her door. *Fire moves fast*, I thought. Fire spreads fast, fire races through floors, shoots through walls, creates its own path.

She'd burrowed into the pillows with the quilt over her head. I grabbed the bedclothes, flung them to the floor, sneezed, and in the instant my eyes were shut it seemed the air grew gray and hazy. Realizing the girl could be unconscious from inhaled smoke, I bent to lift her from the bed.

She murmured, sat abruptly, hair tangled, eyes wild. Struggling under my grasp, she flung out a fist that caught me solidly on the cheekbone. With the undershirt masking my nose and mouth, I must have seemed like a nightmare apparition, a phantom kidnapper summoned from her father's world of drugs and intrigue.

"It's me. Up." Any nightmare, I thought, rather than this too real acrid stink, the suffocating need to swallow, cough, and choke, the knowledge that breath was an enemy. My throat closed and I felt as if I were drowning in air.

With adrenaline pumping the message *flee, flee, flee!* through my veins, Paolina's responses seemed absurdly languorous, as though she were stuck in slow motion, playing at the wrong speed.

"Move!" I grabbed her roughly and started hauling her toward the door.

She pulled away, yelling, "No! I need—"

For a moment her dark hair was pressed against my mouth, then I shoved her off her feet, half dragging, half carrying her, deciding that if she struggled I'd knock her out, then realizing that she'd need to cling to the drainage pipe, reach for the tree, that I'd need to rely on her agility and strength. She behaved as though she understood, as though I'd managed to transfer my urgency to her feet. We made it to the hallway. Then she stumbled, stopped, and a noise issued from her throat.

On the landing a large mirror reflected the foyer below. Yellow tongues licked the wall greedily as a dark figure yanked at the heavy draperies covering the two windows beside the front door and brought them crashing down on a yellow tongue, smothering it in a cloud of dense gray smoke.

Aghast, I yelled, "Get out!"

Paolina moaned and pointed, hypnotized by the reflected flames. She stumbled and I followed her heavily to the floor.

Stay low. Yes, the air was marginally better here. I heard pounding footsteps, turned my head to see K-Rob ascending from the foyer. I wanted to tell him he was crazy, nuts, pulling down drapes, fighting flames, heading upstairs, instead of down. I pointed toward the front door.

"Blocked," he yelled.

"Where's Roz?"

K-Rob mumbled something. He could have shouted it.

Then I saw her, muffled in a wet black sheet, dripping water that felt like rain. I could see her mouth move, then K-Rob's, but none of the sounds registered as words that made sense. I gestured toward my bedroom with its window-to-tree escape route, and Roz broke away in that direction. Expertly, K-Rob, sheeted as well, grabbed Paolina's arm. Between us, we moved her as if she weighed twenty pounds.

We gained the door, and I heard the strain of creaking wood, and then K-Rob, coughing and choking, his thin face smudged with soot, motioned me to the open window. Roz was calling out to some-one below that there were four here, buddy, and all accounted for, except the cat and the bird. K-Rob and Roz pulled Paolina from my rigid grasp, and she seemed able to help herself, to cooperate. Roz flashed me a smile, dipped her head, abandoned her sheet, and plunged out the window. Paolina followed as Roz stayed close to guide her, and there was light suddenly, a huge beam, a beacon, illuminating the oak.

I could hear blaring sirens, but I wasn't sure if they'd just arrived on the scene or if my ears had been deaf to them previously, all my senses tuned to survival.

I'd inhaled smoke, yes, but I know I didn't hallucinate what I saw next. Before he exited the window, before the lunge from drain-pipe to branch, the long climb down the quivering tree, K-Rob shed his dripping sheet to reveal a bare-chested torso, khaki pants. He ducked his head, lifted his left foot, smoothly reached to pat the small of his back in a gesture with which I'm all too familiar, a move-ment designed to steady a pistol tucked hastily into a waistband. I saw it all: move, waistband, the handle of the silver-plated automatic. He saw me notice, and our eyes met before I could shift my gaze to the floor.

Then I was clinging to the drainpipe while voices yelled en-couragement from below, urging me to keep going, move faster. I felt for the tree with my bare right foot, for the familiar branch leading to the wide crook, and soon I was lowering myself through scratchy twigs, choking and gasping. Gloved hands grabbed me as I neared the ground.

# TWENTY-SIX

When I was a cop, if a witness complained that his memory of an event was a blur, I took it as a fanciful remark, and impatiently reminded him that he must have done one thing, then another, like placing one foot in front of the next in order to walk. I began to appreciate what "blur" truly meant in the minutes after I breathed fresh night air: bulky shapes and overbright colors; voices, overlapping and coming from every direction; noise, spiraling out of control. Details escape me even now.

I know the fire department was present in force when I lost my grip and crashed from tree to grass. Men in yellow slickers and cavernous hats loomed above me, oxygen masks obscuring their faces. In the glare of searchlights, they looked like space creatures. I was shocked when one removed his mask and became a neighbor I often saw at the drugstore.

Wet grass stuck to my back. Water hissed from huge hoses snaking across the lawn, punctuated by shouted instructions to "Raise it up!" or "Hold it steady!" A spaceman gave me a drink that tasted like water, then like lemonade, wonderful and soothing and better than any liquor. I sipped and gagged and tried to pass the container to Paolina, who was kneeling nearby, coughing and vomiting. I lost track of Roz and K-Rob. Why had he been downstairs? Should I warn the firemen that K-Rob carried a pistol? A man in orange fatigues slipped a mask over Paolina's face. When I tried to protest, a woman in orange slapped the same sort of gizmo over my nose and mouth, and for a moment I was newly terrified of suffocation.

I have no idea who grabbed my hand, squeezing it in a reassuring grip, but I'd like to thank whoever extended that particular lifeline.

Did I stumble to the ambulance on my own, or was I carried? The journey to Mount Auburn Hospital was frantic with sirens. I protested loudly that I was fine, fine, let me up, where was Paolina? as more orange people strapped me to a gurney. Hey, all that was wrong with me were scratches from tree branches and a purpling bruise where Paolina had landed her haymaker. I tried to impress upon an impassive orange man that I was only agreeing to ambulance transport in order to accompany Paolina. Dammit, I was not some incoming patient.

I must have been doing a good imitation of a patient, because I was wrist-tagged and treated as one, and such was the rush and authority of hospital personnel that I was unable to resist their ministrations. The bright pinpoints of lights in the hallway hurt my eyes. I felt split and unfocused with the desire to be two places at once. I needed to suit up and rescue my home, and I had to comfort Paolina, the child who'd been abandoned too often. Then exhaustion hit like a freight train, and I was grateful for a cot near Paolina's bed. I slept though I would have bet money five minutes earlier that I would never relinquish consciousness again for fear of waking to that smell and that cry: "Fire!"

A murmur tugged at my ears, and yes, for half a second I did consider saying "Who am I?" but I halted the words on the tip of my tongue.

"Yeah," the low voice continued, "I saw it, I know, I know." Its soothing familiarity comforted me and lulled me back to sleep.

Later, when I surfaced again, the same voice was saying, in gentler tones, "Thanks, Teri. Yeah, maybe five o'clock. Sure."

When I finally woke, Mooney, seated on a metal chair by the door, was holding a cell phone to his ear. I tried to sit, which made me aware that I wore a hospital johnny minus underwear. Last night's sweatshirt cum nightgown, ripped and stinking of smoke, had disappeared.

"Paolina?" I said, staring disbelievingly at the empty bed nearby. Hoarse didn't begin to describe the sorry croak that came out of my mouth. I poured water from a metal carafe into a paper cup, swallowed greedily.

"They took her for tests," Mooney said.

"What the hell kind of tests?"

"Something about oxygen levels in her blood, and she'll be back soon, and it's not serious."

"Then why the hell did they admit her?"

He shrugged. "She made me swear I'd stay in case you woke. She said she'd kill me if I woke you, and to tell you she's sorry, but she wouldn't say what for."

"Moon, I'm worried they'll find out she's not my kid. I haven't got her insurance card. I don't even know if she *has* insurance."

"Where's Marta?"

"It's a story." I paused and inhaled. "Moon, what about my house?"

The look in his eyes made me certain he was going to blurt words like *unsalvageable*. I sucked another breath and steeled myself.

"Not bad." He seemed to be looking at me, but I thought he might be staring just over my head, at the grim life-charting machinery on the walls.

"How bad?" I demanded, recalling the flickering light in the foyer. I experienced an eerie flashback—K-Rob with the gun—but I swallowed and said nothing. K-Rob's shout had woken me. He'd smothered flames with heavy draperies, helped me walk Paolina down that long corridor. I wasn't about to repay him by discussing his firearms in front of a cop, not even Mooney.

"Take it easy. I'm not trying to smooth it over. The fire-jocks got there fast and soaked the place. You're going to be squishing around; anything that water could ruin is history."

"It's livable?"

"You were damned lucky."

"My cat?"

"Survived. Even the parakeet's okay. Some softhearted fireman snatched the cage out a broken window."

"The truth?"

"The truth. Your bird called the fireman an asshole. He said he almost let it fry."

Red Emma has no manners. I wanted to leap out of bed, race home, assess the damage. Minus clothing and Paolina, I felt as caged as the parakeet, trapped.

Moon touched his face. "How'd you get the shiner?"

I mirrored his gesture, placing tentative fingers high on my left cheekbone where the flesh felt puffy.

"Don't ever startle Paolina when she's sleeping," I advised, wincing. "I ought to warn the nurses."

"She smacked you?"

"She was disoriented. Do they know how the fire started?" My throat felt like it had been scoured with steel wool. I poured another cup of water, spilling a few drops down the front of the johnny.

"What other cases are you working?"

Very softly I asked, "Why?"

"Do any of your clients seem odd? Unbalanced? Angry at you?"

"Oh, shit." I repeated myself and then I used other curses of which Mooney highly disapproves.

Moon said, "The fire marshal wants to talk to you."

"The fire marshal can't think—what? He thinks some—some *enemy*—burned my fucking house down?"

Roz had been my first guess—not that she'd torched the place but that flammable gunk from her "studio" would ultimately be declared the cause of the blaze. Second place had gone to faulty electrical wiring. Dammit, a buildup of drier lint had placed higher on my list than arson. Fire's a dicey way to kill someone. It speaks more to destructive hatred than a desire to kill.

I found my hand at my throat, although I couldn't remember

moving it, and I licked my dry lips. An unknown creep could have killed me. Killed Paolina. Gulping one deep breath after another, I gripped the water container, stifling an impulse to fling it at the wall. One, one thousand, two, one thousand—I counted seconds and waited for my pulse to quiet.

"It's been a hell of a morning," Moon observed.

My throat wasn't cooperating. I couldn't respond.

He went on. "I don't suppose you watched any TV last night?"

I shook my head.

"You missed some inspiring coverage of church rallies for Gwen Taymore. Earned me three calls from the mayor's special assistant on civil liberties. He'd like to know exactly when I quit being a racist."

"You can hide out here," I managed. "Ditch the phone." I sounded like I'd gargled a quart of whiskey and smoked two packs of Camels. The word *arson* kept hammering in my ears.

"It's gonna get worse this morning."

"Why?" *Arson.* Someone had lit a match, with forethought, with intent, seeking my death.

Moon lifted a newspaper from a metal rollaway cart and offered it to me. He said, "I'll see if I can find some coffee while you read Breeze's column."

"It's not about me, is it?" I asked quickly.

Moon's eyes flickered. "Did you talk to him?"

"Briefly," I admitted.

"About the mayor?"

I stared at Moon with blank incomprehension. "The mayor?" I was focused on arson. Fire.

"Breeze accuses the mayor of complicity in Valentine Phipps's death, blames His Honor for killing not just the old lady, but the whole damn Fenway neighborhood. Enjoy." He handed me the paper and walked out the door.

Underneath the familiar caricature on the front page, left-hand column, the piece was headlined SABOTAGE CITY.

I couldn't fix my mind on it at first. *Arson.* I've done a ton of investigative work, handled my share of sensitive inquiries. I don't always ferret out the desired results, but who had I enraged?

I read:

"In Manhattan, fashionable addresses edge their way uptown till they crunch against Harlem and coil back. Boston's neighborhoods rise and fall in a more erratic pattern. Jamaica Plain, Charlestown, the South End, Hyde Park slide in and out of style, following some unheard natural beat, an idiosyncratic rhythm.

"That is, until now. Is it just me, or is City Hall fooling with the Fenway?

"The callous murder of Valentine Phipps is focusing attention on a neighborhood poised at the brink. Valentine Phipps's death can be seen as a tragic symptom of a social disease. Let's try to name the disease. We could call it Abuse of Power. We might call it Greed.

"In the Fenway, city services haven't declined, they've plummeted. According to the Department of Sanitation, seventeen major sewer backups were reported in the past six months. The Department of Public Works sent out crews to deal with water-main leaks twelve times in the same six months, a record for any Boston neighborhood. Boston Edison counts eight big power blackouts, eight times as many as in neighboring Back Bay. Valentine Phipps's neighbors voice additional complaints: Crossing guards have vanished from busy corners near schools; there's an epidemic of vandalized parked cars. It took three days, count 'em, three, for neighborhood streets to get plowed after the April snowstorm. Potholes multiply unfilled. Rats roam the alleys. Police response time is higher in the Fenway than in any other part of the city, and the cops defend themselves by saying that Fenway nuisance calls have hit an all-time peak.

"Say I'm the mayor, say I want to boast of new construction and enrich my campaign coffers with political contributions from key real estate developers. Say I'm stymied in Southie by environmental committees concerned about the waterfront. No problem: a few strategic memos to department heads, and I've got a neighborhood on the run, empty space galore. Taken separately, it's just the day-to-day hassle of living in the city. Taken together, the evidence points to the systematic destruction of a neighborhood.

"The exodus of tenants began with the fall of rent control,

which our mayor fought long and hard to repeal. Where will it end? This reporter doubts that Valentine Phipps will be the last victim of the mayor's high-stakes real estate grab."

"Whoo-ee," I muttered under my breath. Breeze had drawn a sharp line, but I'd pointed him to the dots along the way.

Inhaling through my nose felt slightly better than breathing through my mouth. I scanned the column again. No mention of Peritti. Nothing about Millennium Towers. Was Breeze still working that angle? Was this an opening salvo?

If Roz had done a computer search on Millennium the fruits of her labor might have been destroyed in the fire. It occurred to me that one of the Millennium principals might be named Hohen.

Bronson Hohen was interested in music, not land, but wealthy companies tend to diversify their holdings.

"Interesting" was all I offered when Mooney kneed the door open, a coffee cup in each hand.

"Hot," he warned, speaking about the coffee. "The whole thing's speculative as hell."

"Breeze doesn't name any developers."

"Developers sue; mayors take it on the chin. No, take that back. Mayors pass the pain on to their subordinates."

"The bigger the stink, the more papers Breeze sells."

*Should I tell Moon that the church rallies were a ploy designed to further a plea-bargain attempt?* Henry Fine and Peter Breeze . . . Both stood to gain from this case—in political pull, in prestige.

Coffee burned a path down my raw throat. Valentine was dead. What had Gwen stood to gain from her death? I wished I'd clapped new locks on the old woman's doors the same day I'd met her. But if Gwen had done the killing, new locks wouldn't have prevented the crime, right? Or did Mrs. Phipps want new locks precisely to keep out Gwen? She'd given Gwen a key. Or so Gwen said.

Valentine could have altered her view of Gwen's trustworthiness. If she saw her with Peritti . . .

"What was in the will?" I asked Moon.

"Huh?"

"Sorry. Valentine Phipps's will. Were there other legatees? Besides Gwen?"

"No."

"Was the estate valued? Itemized?"

"Simple will, handwritten, the kind you copy from a book. Everything to Gwen. Everything of which I die possessed."

No description of a specific valuable item. No new suspect. No mention of Bronson Hohen.

The cell phone chirped. The noise reminded me of Red Emma's squawk. I advised Moon to use the bird's tried-and-true technique: Shout "Asshole," and hang up.

With a sigh of regret, he pushed a button, spoke his name.

He was annoyed at the message but not the messenger. I watched his eyes. I deduced that the speaker on the other end was Teri Kiley. He called her Theresa, and I felt like echoing his regretful sigh.

They were less unlikely a couple than Peritti and Gwen. Would Moon's dragon-lady mother approve? She despised me: I was divorced, half Jewish, "wild." She wouldn't adore Teri, either, unless Teri proved willing to abandon this cop nonsense, stay home, sew, cook healthy meals for the inevitable add-one-per-year brood.

"I have to go." Moon pushed a button to end the call.

"Trouble?"

"Same old. Aggravation. Politics."

An evasion.

I straightened the thin blanket. "Teri's working out on Homicide, huh?"

I've seen Moon face an armed IRA terrorist with aplomb, so his sudden loss of equilibrium was disconcerting. Muttering "Yes, no, I don't know," he sank into a nearby chair, lifted his arm, started to shove his hair off his forehead, stopped halfway through the familiar gesture, as though his hand had lost its way.

"Mooney—," I began.

"Dammit," he responded, "don't ask me to talk about it."

"Okay."

His hand resumed its movement, settling at the back of his

neck, just above the collar of his pale blue shirt. His elbow blocked his face so I couldn't see his eyes.

"Sure you don't want to talk about it?" I ventured hesitantly.

"I'm screwed."

The second hand circled twice around the aluminum clock over the door. I sipped coffee dregs, held them in my mouth.

He sighed. "If I add her to the squad, which she damned well deserves, which she absolutely wants, I'm going to get blasted for promoting a woman I'm . . . seeing outside the office."

They couldn't keep an affair quiet. The minute Teri entered Moon's office and closed the door, some busybody would consult his watch, time the interlude. How could they hope, surrounded by nosy cops who mainlined gossip, to keep their infatuation secret?

"If I don't give her a shot it's so damned unfair. She *wants* Homicide, the same way I did, the same way you did. She's ambitious and smart, always asking questions, then asking more. Hell, she could be my boss in five years. But if I hire her, that's the end of us, of me and her together, right? I can hear 'em now: I can't judge her work impartially. And how would it look? Remember what happened to—"

I carefully swallowed the coffee before I finished his sentence. "To us?"

He stared at his sneakers. "You built a wall against me."

"Teri's not me." *Maybe she's braver,* I thought. *Maybe she won't notice the raised eyebrows and elbowed ribs whenever she enters a squad room. Maybe the scornful comments won't eat at her pride.*

I could have mouthed comforting words, but to tell the truth, I thought Moon had the situation nailed. Unless Teri left the force the romance was dead. . . . Unless he left the force . . .

He shifted his weight uncomfortably. "I'm late. Make sure you see the fire marshal." ·

"Will do."

He leaned over and brushed a strand of hair off my forehead, so briefly and gently I barely felt his fingertips. Then he was through the doorway and gone.

I considered calling after him, lying. Hell, I wasn't an upbeat rookie, couldn't simulate the required rosy innocence. I didn't believe it would all work out for the best. I wasn't sure I wanted it to work out, not for Moon and Teri.

For an instant when he'd leaned toward me, my lips had responded, and now I wished he'd kissed me good-bye. When I'd bricked that wall between us I should have used stronger mortar.

"Asshole," I muttered to myself.

# TWENTY-SEVEN

"If somebody'd burned a cross on your front lawn, it would have been national coverage." Peter Breeze sighed wistfully. One of his hands rested in the pocket of his corduroy slacks. The other held a spiral notebook. I couldn't see a pen.

"You are a very sick man," I replied, gazing at the wreckage.

Hoses had flattened the yew hedge; the lawn had been trampled by dinosaurs. Over the foyer the roof gaped like a toothless mouth. The living room's bay window was gone, not shattered or broken, but gone, and the iron curtain rod hung crazily down one side of the gap, heavy with sodden cloth. Water and the firemen's smashing axes had done more damage than the flames.

"A sick man? Can I quote you on that?" A stubby pencil butt emerged from his pocket along with his hand.

"Anytime."

After reading his attention-grabbing morning column, I was surprised to find him in front of my damaged house instead of holding a self-congratulatory press conference, busily pouring gasoline on the political blaze he'd kindled. Before I could ask what he wanted, Roz, in black bike shorts and skimpy halter, hurried down the front walk, T.C. in her arms. I greeted the foul-smelling cat with a hug. He purred and tried to crawl under my sweater.

"The murals are fine," she assured me.

Breeze quickly introduced himself and seemed disappointed when Roz didn't react to his name. I didn't find it odd, since I doubt she's ever read a newspaper. When I asked her to take T.C. inside and feed him, Breeze watched her swaying hips depart with regret.

I'd just spent a less-than-fruitful hour with the fire marshal. Captain Ed Flowers, a pinch-faced man who looked born to wear a uniform, had quickly disclosed his thoughts on the blaze: A shameless publicity hound like me would be his number-one suspect. The arson squad would immediately initiate a financial records check, relating to ownership, outstanding mortgages, and insurance benefits.

"You know Ed Flowers?" I asked.

"Sure." Breeze nodded. "I always praise our men in rubber."

Flowers's crew had finished photographing the scene. He'd admitted that the back entrance was serviceable, warned me to stay out of the foyer and off the stairs till the fire-and-water-damage agency I'd hired gave the okay.

"Flowers." Breeze repeated the name, furrowing his brow.

"Yeah."

"Who knows you're working for Taymore's attorney?" the reporter demanded sharply.

"You do."

"Who else?"

"It's not a secret, who I work for. I didn't sneak into Fine's office through the ventilator."

"If it's Flowers, it's arson, right?"

For a relatively new kid in town, he was good.

"Somebody sets a fire at your house while you're working a case like this, you have to figure the two things are connected." His voice was eager, animated.

"Here's another connection: some nutcase reads my name in your column; my house burns down."

When Flowers requested, merely as a formality, a list of potential firebugs of my acquaintance—dissatisfied former clients, ex-spouses, and neighbors who didn't like the wild parties I threw were among his suggestions—the image of Diego came to mind. I'd humiliated him, denied him a place to crash as well as an easy conquest. He could have followed me home or discovered where I lived from Paolina's careless chatter.

She remained at Mount Auburn, where a sweet-faced nurse seemed to have temporarily adopted her. "*No peligro, no peligro,*" the nurse had assured me. *No danger.* Just a persistent cough, a few more hours of observation.

"Don't you have someplace else to go?" I asked Breeze.

"I'm soaking up atmosphere. No need to be rude."

The cleanup experts were nowhere in sight and I couldn't exactly dial them on the nonfunctioning phone to inquire about the holdup. I excused myself, deciding my time could be better spent in checking the contents of my desk, particularly the contents of my locked gun drawer. Breeze stayed on the lawn, scribbling in his notebook.

My desk lay on its side, shifted by firefighters or heavy streams of water. Only one corner was blackened but it was effectively destroyed. Drawers had been yanked and flung. One had no bottom, one was smashed. Soggy lumps of paper lined another. I isolated the locked drawer; it remained in the backless frame, one side shattered. I used a broken board to poke through it. My Smith & Wesson forty was safe in its case.

K-Rob hadn't stolen it.

Had the drawers been removed by the first firefighters on the scene? Was this the work of Captain Flowers's arson team?

Valentine Phipps had asked where I'd hide something of value. She was dead, the victim of apparent heart failure, and her apartment had been searched after her death. Gwen was in prison, and her attic room had been ransacked after her arrest. If Valentine's killer hadn't found "something of value" on Kilmarnock Street, hadn't located it at Gwen's . . .

I squatted on my heels, feeling the weight of the gun in my hand. If a killer had searched for "something of value" here, in my home, why the fire? Spite? Frustration? Valentine Phipps had given me nothing for safekeeping. Gwen had given me nothing. I closed my eyes to block out the damage, to concentrate.

I could still hear Flowers's tight tenor: "This blaze had several flashpoints, points of origin, making it indisputably arson. And an amateur job at that, poorly set."

"Set how?"

He'd stared at me as if I ought to know the answer to that particular question better than anyone.

"Books of matches and plastic bags filled with Coleman fuel—not nearly enough of it, which is why I can give you the details."

Books of matches. Plastic bags filled with Coleman fuel. A faint chime sounded in my memory.

Breeze, poking his head in the window hole, had to clear his throat loudly to command my attention. "Um, anything I can do to help?" His notebook was nowhere in sight.

"Yes."

He seemed surprised at my agreement. "What?"

"Have you written a story about fires? Lately?"

"Why?"

"I'm looking for somebody who knows local fires. Everything about them, the history, the—"

"Frank Hennessee. That's who you want. Hands down, he's the best."

"Put me in touch with him."

"When?"

"How about now?"

# TWENTY-EIGHT

The reporter piloted a boxy gray Ford with dark red leather seats. I usually prefer to drive myself, in my own car, but nights in hospitals mean fluorescent lights and repetitive beeps and periodic code calls rather than sleep. My head throbbed with a threatening ache, and swallowing, a task I used to perform on automatic pilot, required both thought and effort. I asked permission to appropriate Breeze's car phone, got through to Paolina, who declared herself fine with telltale huskiness. Enthusiastically, she inquired whether nurses needed to go to a four-year college.

"You bet. Nurse-practitioners are almost like doctors. Some nurses have Ph.D.s." I mentally worded the letter of commendation I'd write to the hospital praising Paolina's new mentor.

My Little Sister responded with a thoughtful hum.

"Pick you up soon," I promised.

In quick succession I phoned my insurance agent, who'd already swung into action, and located the emergency response team over-due to board my windows and tie a tarp over the wounded roof. I relayed information from my insurance agent to their secretary, was informed that the house could be evaluated and cared for without requiring my on-the-spot presence.

After a moment's hesitation, I dialed my friend Gloria, former owner of the Green & White Cab Company, certain that she'd already heard through the grapevine that I was fine. Not only does Gloria tend the best grapevine in town, but it's always soothing to hear her gospel-singer's contralto. If I needed anyone to coddle Paolina, she announced, she'd be happy to volunteer. Plus she knew everybody in the construction trade, and would see what she could do about discount materials, and reliable low-cost labor. Anything else?

The woman's a blessing. I thanked her, feeling my headache subside under the rush of her friendly concern, signed off, and finally took note of my surroundings. I'd assumed we were aiming for inbound Storrow Drive, on our way to the suburbs via the Central Artery. When we bypassed Storrow, I reevaluated.

"He lives in the Fenway?"

"Scene of the crime." Breeze honked at a slow VW and eased left to pass.

"Writer? Researcher?"

"Used to be a fireman. Now he's a spark."

"A what?"

"A fan, an enthusiast, a buff, a guy who can give you the stats on the fire department the way some guys can rattle off the Red Sox batting averages."

"Right. A buff." Cops have buffs.

"There are three clubs in Boston especially for joes who like to wear slickers and race to fires, the Bucket Brigade, the Tappers, and the Fifty-twos."

He parked in a tow zone, slapping a rectangular placard emblazoned with the word *Press* on the dashboard.

"That works?"

"Often."

I'd have Roz make me one just like it.

Breeze identified himself via speaker in the foyer of a brick building on Westland Avenue and we were swiftly buzzed inside.

The hallway smelled of lemon-scented furniture polish. I heard a door creak, shuffling footsteps followed by a loud bellow.

"That you, news hack?"

The reporter led the way up narrow stairs to the second floor. The door to the third apartment on the left stood ajar.

"Damn those false alarms," a man yelled as we entered. He wore a firefighter's uniform shirt that hung unbuttoned over a dingy white tee and raggy jeans. A police officer's billed hat kept a shock of white hair under control. A scar ran from the outside corner of his left eye down to the edge of his jaw, puckering the side of his face. He was out of breath, as though he'd been running. I pegged him at retirement age.

"That makes eleven—nope, I'm a lying bastard—twelve this week," he continued, "each one a potential disaster."

If Boston Fire Department headquarters ever burns, the troops can move right into Frank Hennessee's place and feel at home. Maps, dotted with pins and flags and the occasional word scrawled in colored marker, hung on all four walls of the living room. In one corner, an emergency scanner crackled and spat staccato phrases. The dining-room decor, visible through an archway, consisted of fire-boxes, fire company signs, framed photographs of what appeared to be every ladder company in the state, if not the country.

Staring up at me, the man squinted his blue eyes. "Do I happen to know you?" He was five-eight, maybe five-nine.

"Not yet." I extended a hand. "Carlotta."

"I'm Frank. Just a minute, just a minute, that's an ambulance coming through. Ladder Company Fourteen, Allston's best. Let me make a note of that."

I raised an eyebrow in Breeze's direction.

"Hey." Breeze got Frank Hennessee's attention by the simple expedient of slapping him on the shoulder. "You got any time to talk?"

"What about?"

"Arson," I said. "And history."

"She some kinda professor?" He addressed Breeze as if I weren't even there.

"Sort of," Breeze responded with a shrug.

Hennessee awarded me an appraising stare. With his vein-reddened nose, barrel chest, and skinny legs, he reminded me of one of the old-time Boston Irish cops. He ran a hand across his jowls as if he were checking to see when he'd last shaved, then crossed the room, and plunked his body down on a worn plaid sofa. He patted a nearby sofa cushion by way of invitation, waited till I sat.

Breeze moved a dingy armchair catty-corner to the sofa, lowered himself into it.

"Arson," I repeated.

"What about it?"

"Whatever you can tell me."

"Well, it's sure different than it used to be." He scowled as he removed his hat and fiddled with the brim. "Technology and fuel-sniffing dogs, what the hell did we know about them? In the eighties, then and before, we didn't know so much about arson, so if you wanted to get rid of property and let someone build on the land, a fire was a very profitable thing. Today, computers make it easy to follow a paper trail and find out who stands to profit. So between proving the crime of arson and showing who stands to benefit, the arson boys can do a pretty good job, and arson for profit is way down."

Arson for profit. I stood to break even at best, most likely lose. Who'd profit from my loss?

"Want more?" Hennessee asked.

"Whatever you've got."

"Well, today it's arson for revenge, mostly. Or terrorism, though we don't see much of that, thank God, we're not New York yet. And while it isn't tough to know who did it—the victim usually knows— it's hard to put the friggin' enemy at the site and make it stick. No neat fingerprints because the evidence usually burns."

The victim usually knows.

"Do you remember the Friday fires?" I asked.

"I should. I fought 'em."

"Great. Let's zero in on them."

"Why?"

"Humor her," Breeze interjected. "She's an academic."

The man sighed and glanced longingly at the silent scanner. "Okay, here's the lesson: In eighty-two and eighty-three, two hundred sixty-four fires were set in Boston and the surrounding towns— Revere, Chelsea, the like. That's a lot of blazes—three hundred sixty people were injured—and at first it was blamed on your juvenile delinquency, and then on your gangs, and then on your general breakdown of society, you know? But we firemen knew all along what was going down. There was this gang of sick boys, and they loved nothing better than setting fires, especially on Fridays. They set 'em, and then they'd come to watch afterwards, hollering like cheerleaders—"

"Sparks," Breeze offered.

Hennessee rounded on him, bristling. "Sickos, every one. A spark never interferes with a firefighter and never starts a fire. Sparks are fans, okay, and sometimes they get a little carried away, but where's the harm in that? A lot of fine people think firefighters are just as interesting to watch as football players. Who faults a football fan for going to a game? Firefighting's the last stronghold of real-life heroes, and maybe it's not so bad for people to watch and appreciate what firefighters do. So don't sully the names of the good ones with the names of these freaks. Freaks, that's what they were, and five of 'em are still in prison."

"Sorry," Breeze said quietly. "What I meant to say was they *called* themselves sparks."

Hennessee turned to me. "What those bastards said, after they were caught, mind you, was that they set the fires to protest the firing of firemen. Trust me, people set fires because it's some deep secret thing they need to do, an urge, not a rational business at all."

The scanner let out a *bleep* followed by a flood of numbers. Hennessee listened, eyes closed, then hurried to a map, peering at it with fierce concentration until he triumphantly stuck a yellow-topped pin into an area near the left border.

I gave him time to settle back on the couch. "Wasn't there a link between the Friday fires, matchbooks, and plastic bags of gasoline?"

"You've got the basics. It went like this: Place a lighted cigarette in between the match heads of an open matchbook, cover it with paper, and set it down near a Ziploc bag filled with Coleman fuel. Sometimes used old tires as well. Got a good memory, this girl." He nudged Breeze approvingly. "Bring her by anytime."

"Wait a minute. Wait—Carlotta, is that how your fire was set?" Breeze's notebook appeared in his hand like an ace of spades in a magic act.

Hennessee said, "What do you mean, *her* fire?"

Breeze slapped his pockets, probably searching for a pen. "I think she's got more than an academic interest in this."

"Someone torched my house, using matchbooks and baggies. And, Breeze, if the perp reads it in the paper, I'll never catch the bastard."

"House fire?" Hennessee's back straightened. "Last night, Friday night, the Cambridge blaze?"

"Yeah." I was impressed.

"Ladder Number Four," he said. "Those boys really moved ass."

I said, "Peter, I'm not talking for your column."

"Will I get it eventually? Exclusively?"

I nodded, waited till the notebook disappeared. "Frank, do you remember the names of the firebugs? The guys in jail?"

Without visible effort or notes, Hennessee rattled off five names that rang no bells.

"They were joy fires, right? Not property scams?" I asked.

He wiggled his backside into the saggy sofa cushions. "Well, I had a theory," he admitted, "but I couldn't prove it."

"Run it by me."

"Idle speculation."

"I'd love to hear it."

"With so many fires following a pattern and all, it could be these firebugs got an idea started in the minds of a few semi-shady folks who wanted to get rid of unprofitable buildings. What with the town burning every Friday night, it must have been a temptation. You might say—as a joke at first—that you wished the firebugs would choose your place. You couldn't exactly hang a welcome sign and offer free beer, but you might be tempted to copy their bad example, especially if you were interested in fires yourself, and knew how the fires were set, and what the arson squad would watch for, to tie one fire to another. There were a few blazes the sickos never copped to."

"In the Fens," I said quietly.

"You got it."

"Who owned those buildings?" I was sure I could name him, but I didn't want to lead the witness. With a glance I cautioned Breeze to keep silent. Hennessee noticed and his eyes grew wary.

"You're not a lawyer planning to slap me with a defamation of character lawsuit?"

"No."

"It's bad enough, blabbing in front of a newsman, but I have to watch my reputation."

"I'm no lawyer," I repeated.

"Well, I'm not going to name names. Theories don't get you in half so much trouble."

"Come on," I pleaded. "Give."

He stayed stubborn through my appeals, withstood Breeze's as well. I listened raptly to his explanation of the yellow, red, and blue pins on the wall maps, admired his collection of authentic antique fireboxes, nodded my head through three long tales of the old days to no avail. Every time I tried to steer the conversation back to the Friday fires and the Fenway, he met my gaze unflinchingly and changed the subject.

As we were leaving, he loosened up enough to stand on his toes and whisper in my ear. "I'll give you a hint," he murmured. "You're looking for a spark who was with the Tapper Club then, and it's my belief he still belongs. Local man, here in the Fens, former real estate honcho."

Old man Peritti.

"Hey, what did you tell her?" Breeze asked Hennessee.

"Asked her to marry me, ya friggin' moron. I ain't too old to remember."

# TWENY-NINE

Breeze strode toward the car at a velocity intended to leave me struggling far behind. Far from fazing me, his pace proved energizing; I needed to stretch my legs.

He gunned the engine. "So, did you accept the old fart's proposal? Or are you still married to the Mob?"

The edge in his voice didn't catch me by surprise, but the comment did. It shouldn't have; due to circumstances beyond my control, my love life has, from time to time, been chronicled in the press.

"That's ancient history."

He shot me a triumphant glance as if to say, Well, if it's so ancient why does it annoy you?

Guilt, I informed myself, that's why any reference to Sam Gianelli disturbs me. "Mob," used the way Breeze had used it, meant Sam, former co-owner, with Gloria, of Green & White Cab, once my employer—before he became my lover. Gloria imagines Sam and I have a future. Gloria reads trashy romance magazines.

We've started over before; it's not beyond the realm of possibility. I used to imagine us as opposites, cop's daughter, mobster's son. Now it seems we're too similar—detail-driven obsessives, working too hard, playing too hard. I wished I could observe him through one-way glass, study his rehabilitated gait, read his eyes. Did he blame me? Hate me?

What I feel is more complex than guilt, a jumble of emotions stirred and shaken with time, filtered through nostalgia.

I used Breeze's cell phone to call Gloria, who'd set herself up as my message center, anticipating the need. She informed me that Roz had sprung Paolina from the hospital, a trick I'd have liked to witness, that the fire response crew was currently at work, and that she'd chatted personally with the foreman, who happened to be pals with her brother Leroy. None of this astonished me, given Gloria's infinite resourcefulness.

"How can I reach Roz?" I asked.

"She's at Lemon's. You need the number?"

Lemon is Roz's karate instructor and sometime lover. I wondered if he was providing shelter for the new boyfriend as well.

"Got it, thanks."

When Gloria decides to run, we'll all get the chance to vote for the first overweight, wheelchair-bound, black woman president.

Lemon didn't answer his phone.

I stared briefly out the window at the sailboats on the Charles. I knew I was starting to rebound from the fire; I felt the desire to drive. Speeding along Memorial Drive, admiring wild geese and athletic bicyclists, can be pure pleasure as long as you shun rush hour.

Traffic was thickening. I glanced at my watch, impatient to get home, click onto my computer, discover if property owned by Peritti Senior had changed hands during the period covered by the Friday fires.

Click onto my computer . . . Sure. In a house with no electricity, a water-sogged P.C., a dismantled desk. I was off the track and stymied, investigating my fire instead of Valentine's death, stuck minus sophisticated research tools.

Lowering the vanity mirror, I inspected my shiner.

Arson for profit. Arson for revenge. Arson as a blind? Had the fire been set to grab my attention, switch my focus, stop me from clearing Gwen? What path would I have explored today had I passed a peaceful night?

"Peter, turn the car around."

"What?"

"Can you pull clips on the Friday fires? At the *Globe*? I need to see which details the paper publicized."

"Most of the eighties stuff has been transferred to CD-ROM, and somebody else has the key."

"Who?"

"The paper lions, the librarians down in the morgue."

"Open today?"

"Newspapers never sleep."

"Cooperative?"

"As cooperative as I am charming."

"Then what's the problem?"

He hesitated. "No problem, except I might not have the time to hang around."

I was counting on that.

# THRTY

If I have to visit a morgue, I'll take the one at the *Globe* over the one that stinks of formaldehyde. The only smell at the news morgue was due to location; it was dank, as befitted a massive basement room.

Breeze entered with the swagger of a slumming celebrity.

Two guardians, his "paper lions," shared a pair of oak desks built before personal computers were dreamed of; an elderly woman and a pasty-faced man who blanched further when he saw Breeze, quickly mumbling something to the woman before vanishing between filing cabinets into a warren of shelves. She started to protest, to demand her coworker's return. Then, recognizing Breeze, she nervously patted her cloud of graying hair, and aimed her thick glasses in the reporter's direction.

"Afternoon." She may have actually said "Good afternoon, sir," but her voice was so gruff and uncertain that only the single word was audible.

"Yvonne?" Breeze blatantly eyeballed her name placard.

She beamed with pleasure. "What can I do for you, Mr. Breeze?"

*Call him Peter,* I thought. *If he chooses to address you, a woman old enough to be his mother, by your first name when both are adequately displayed, for chrissakes, return the insult.*

Breeze requested any files on arson, specifically the Friday blazes of eighty-two and eighty-three, plus whatever she had on the Perittis, father and son. He spoke loud enough for broadcast and spelled the name, adding, "It's to help out a friend of mine, here. She's doing some research for me."

Not bloody likely.

While Yvonne bustled to do her master's bidding and "just set things up nicely for you, sir," I brooded about security. "I wouldn't want word to get back to Peritti."

Breeze shrugged off my concern. "Hey, security's big here. We run exposés, you know? Somebody at the crosstown paper finds out, it's a fucking disaster."

I waited for him to plead business upstairs. He hung around.

No compilation of Friday Fire clippings was available. Fine with me. Breeze dismissed Yvonne and I played with the P.C., scanning articles tagged "arson" or "fire," dated in appropriate years. The room was cool and quiet. I read each piece slowly, twice through, noting dates, addresses, and names.

Breeze read over my shoulder. I hardly spoke to him, seemingly absorbed in my work. I wondered how much longer he'd hold out.

The high jinks of Mr. Flare and the Friday Firebug had started with Dumpster blazes reported in brief paragraphs, slowly ramped up to hundred-thousand-dollar losses and front-page headlines. Diligently, I searched for mention of Peritti, for a description of the fire-setting technique: the cigarette folded into a matchbook, the plastic bag filled with Coleman fuel.

Finally, after twenty-seven minutes, Breeze glanced at his watch. I flipped a page in my notebook, showed no signs of finishing.

Twelve minutes later he murmured, "I'm running kind of late."

I focused on the screen. "Why don't you go ahead? I've still got a few more articles."

"Sure you'll be okay?"

I gave him my most reassuring smile; it turned triumphant as he exited. Yvonne wouldn't dare throw me out; in her mind I was associated with Breeze. Only problem: Should he inquire, she'd inform him exactly where my research led.

Fortunately, she was busy helping a gentleman in a somber suit thread a microfiche machine. I waited five minutes to make sure Breeze wouldn't return, stretched, and got to my feet.

Shelves housed law directories and alumni directories, atlases and dictionaries, college and business guides. The method of organization wasn't readily apparent. I opened shallow drawers, found tins of microfilm. CD-ROMs were housed in paper sleeves, numbered.

"You work for Breeze?" The pale man who'd disappeared earlier materialized at my side. From the curve of his lip when he mentioned Breeze's name, I decided he was not a charter member of the newspaperman's fan club.

"No."

"Good."

"Would you kick me out if I did?"

"I'd do my best to make your stay unpleasant. Guy's an asshole." His teeth were dismal gray bumps on his gums.

"In what way?"

"Bastard got me in trouble when I couldn't find something."

"Are you good at finding things?" I tossed the challenge out casually.

He shrugged. "If it's here, I can find it. If it's not, I'm not citing any phony journals."

"Breeze expected you to do that?"

"Once."

"How interesting." I scrambled in my backpack for one of my many assorted business cards. "If he does it again, ever, I want you to call me, okay? Anytime."

"Who are you?"

I checked the card to find out. "Mary Chapman," I lied. It gave a fake address for an all-purpose entity called Hazelwood, Inc., as well as a nonexistent 617 area code number. Business cards are cheap, legal unless used to defraud, and people love to collect them. "I'm an outside consultant, fact-checking for the paper."

The young man studied the card. "Does he know who you are?"

"He's supposed to be cooperating." With the media buzzing over fabricated news, I didn't think I'd need to spell it out in greater detail.

He slipped the card into his shirt pocket, looking smug. "Breeze makes things up, right?"

I lowered my conspiratorial whisper. "Could be he just makes mistakes."

"Can I help?"

"Depends. How far back does the archive go?"

"On CD, on microfiche, or in stacks?"

Valentine Phipps had married Bronson Hohen in 1940 and her husband had died two years later. "He did a piece that deals with some stuff that went on in 1942."

"Probably invented the whole thing. You need news articles?"

"I'd like to see a death notice."

"Whose?"

I feigned indecision. "What's your name?"

"Dale Gitlin."

We shook hands. His was warm and moist. "If you tell Breeze, it could screw the whole thing," I said.

"Trust me," he pleaded. "If I could help get that bastard fired, it would be the greatest achievement of my life." Gitlin's animosity seemed sincere.

I gave him the year, spelled the name *Hohen*.

He was bursting with confidence. "I'll find it."

"If it exists." I winked at him slowly. His answering smile was marred by his ghastly teeth. I asked if there was a phone I could use.

He nodded. "Dial nine for an outside line."

The phone was on Yvonne's desk and she wasn't happy that Gitlin had given permission to use it. I checked in with my insurance agent, then dialed Gwen's attorney. Henry Fine offered his sympathy vis-à-vis my fire, blithely assumed I'd need to abandon the case in order to tend to its aftermath.

"I'm not quitting. I need to talk to Gwen again."

His voice lost its warmth. "Talk to me. I'll take a message. She's been moved out to Framingham."

"I can drive."

"If I get you in, you gonna push the plea bargain?"

"Give me the name of the tenant on Kilmarnock, the one who says he saw her." I hung on while he shuffled papers.

"There are two: Evangeline Dexter, she's on the first floor; Gregor Daly, apartment three-A, says he heard the fight."

Three-A. *Directly underneath Valentine's flat,* I thought. Same layout, probably.

"Got it. Now, when can I visit Gwen?"

"You'll talk plea bargain?"

When I didn't respond, he sighed. "I can't get you in on a weekend. It'll have to wait till Monday morning."

"Nine o'clock?"

I rattled off Gloria's number so he could leave me a message confirming the time. "Mr. Breeze is really going to appreciate this," I told Yvonne while dialing my next target. Her smile looked like she'd fixed it in place with hair spray.

"Shotokan Karate, Ninjutsu, and Tiny Tiger." Roz's imitation oriental accent was not helped by tinny background music.

"What's Tiny Tiger?" So Roz played receptionist at Lemon's combination crash pad and dojo. News to me, but then the more I don't know about Roz's life, the better.

Recognizing my voice, she abandoned her front-office persona. "Tiny Tiger is five-year-olds beating the shit out of each other. They'd do it anyway, you know what I mean?"

"Did you get a chance to run Millennium? Peritti?"

"Yeah. Sure. I did 'em from here. Lemon's got awesome computing power. With the insurance money, you ought to upgrade. Hang on."

"Hang on" implied the information was close at hand. I bared my teeth at Yvonne.

When Roz came back on the line, she was chewing gum and cracking it. "Peritti, father and son, have a fifteen percent interest. They're partnered with a whole string of Italians."

"One of them named Hohen?"

"That's not Italian."

"Yeah, but is it in any way associated with Millennium?"

"One of the Italians could be his brother-in-law."

"Run Bronson Hohen and Hohen Music. I want the financials."

"Okay."

I inhaled. "Roz, how exactly did you meet K-Rob?"

Gum cracked.

I tried again. "Do you know his full name?"

"Carlotta—"

"Look, I try to stay out of your private life."

The gum chewing halted ominously.

"Was he in the bar when you entered?" I asked. "Did he follow you in? Did you flirt with him? Did he buy you a drink?"

"None of your fucking business."

On the whole, I agreed with her. Still I persevered. "Okay. Number one: Does he speak Spanish?"

Her tone was icy. "He hasn't. Why would he speak Spanish to me?"

"Number two: Does he have a gun permit?" I lowered my voice and shielded my mouth. Yvonne was observing me with penetrating eyes.

"And what's number three?" Roz asked.

"Keep him away from Paolina."

"Okay."

I advised her not to mess with any Tiny Tigers, then hung up.

Dale Gitlin was hunched over the microfiche reader with several round tin canisters piled in front of him and an obit neatly framed onscreen. I squared my shoulders, recalled that my name was Mary Chapman now.

Gitlin's enthusiasm had waned. "The guy definitely existed. I've got the *Globe*, the *Herald*, the old *Record-American*, remember that? The *New York Times*. From the space he rated in our rag, I figured the notice went national."

"Good job."

"You're not going to catch Breeze on this one." Gitlin's disappointment was severe.

"So maybe he didn't make it up out of whole cloth. But he might have embroidered." I patted the researcher encouragingly on the shoulder. "I'll need copies of these."

Obits were more conventional in 1942. No chatty headline, just name, date of birth, date of death.

Bronson Garrard Hohen, 57.

I scanned the formal phrases. "The death of entrepreneur/collector Bronson Garrard Hohen was mourned throughout the art world." Education: Groton and Harvard. World traveler. Grieving wife, sons, daughter, brothers. No mention of the fact that Giselle Lurie Hohen had been his first wife, not his current wife. No mention of Valentine at all. Had Hohen's family, who sounded like blue bloods all, decided to cut Valentine out of even a mention in the obituary?

The curator of European paintings at the Museum of Fine Art lauded the late Mr. Hohen for his role in arranging several shows featuring works from the great collections of the Kanns, the Rothschilds, and the Rosenbergs. Hohen sat on the board of the Private Reserve Bank and the Citizen's Commercial Bank. Three charitable foundations lamented his passing.

"He's indexed," Gitlin interrupted. "Business section, occasionally. Then a ton of mentions the week before he died. Not in Business. Because of some robbery."

I pretended to check my notebook. A robbery the week before he died. Had the shock of it contributed to the man's death? One obituary termed his end "sudden," another said "heart attack." "Yeah, that pans out. Did you pull the stuff on the robbery?"

"Not yet. I Just scanned the headlines: Fancy Milton mansion burgled. That kind of thing. Breeze wrote about it, huh?"

"Think you could find the articles?"

This time he smiled narrowly, so the bad teeth didn't show.

It took him twenty minutes to unearth the first one. By that time, my mind was racing ahead of the facts. Had Hohen been murdered in 1942? Had Valentine married him to get her hands on his art collection? Had she—and perhaps some secret lover—stolen the Hohen collection? Could her death, over fifty years later, be linked to an unsolved crime?

In a word, no.

The news clips were clear. The morning of November 8, 1942, Milton police had been called to the scene. The *Record-American*'s coverage was the most ambitious; they'd printed a grainy photo of the imposing estate. Valentine hadn't exaggerated its grandness. They'd interviewed Sergeant James Farrell, who estimated the value of the missing paintings at hundreds of thousands of dollars. The stories were front page for two days, then relegated to the inside. No follow-ups during the three days prior to Hohen's death.

After the death notices came a flood of sympathy for the Hohen family, general indignation at the heavy-handedness of police and tabloid press alike. Much was made of the dire effect of publicity on a reclusive man. The family issued a plea for privacy. Letters to the editor scolded reporters. The local police department declared it would patrol the grounds; sightseers were warned away.

Then, two weeks after the death notices, a brief announcement that the artwork had been recovered, that there had been an error, a simple misunderstanding, concerning the loan of paintings to a Worcester museum.

No robbery. The investigating officers were delighted that the "missing" canvases were all accounted for.

I made copies, smiling automatically at Yvonne. If everything had been accounted for, and subsequently sold to pay off Hohen's debts, then nothing "of value" remained for Valentine to hide.

The guy with the awful teeth promised to call me the minute Breeze fudged any further research. Maybe we could have a drink, he hinted. Mary Chapman thanked him gravely.

# THIRY-ONE

I didn't sleep much that night and I didn't sleep well. I'd hoped to stay at home, but the chemical stink, coupled with the whistle of wind through the tarp, drove Paolina and me to a bargain motel on the Arlington line.

I stayed at the Ritz-Carlton with Sam Gianelli once. I forget the occasion—his birthday or mine—but I remember the wine-red carpet we made love on, and a huge marble tub where I shampooed my hair, comfortably seated between his hairy legs. Sam helped massage the gel into my scalp before moving his attentions to my breasts. Our plans for a fancy dinner followed by a Celtics game melted with the foam and we wound up catching the last quarter on TV, naked in the dark. Later, we ate room service, wearing discreet terrycloth robes.

At the White Roof Inn the plumbing belched. The base of the pole lamp in the corner couldn't hide a greasy carpet stain.

While Paolina slept, I dialed New Hampshire Directory Assistance, knowing the front desk would exact a seventy-five-cents-a-call surcharge, reluctant to leave her for a stroll to the lobby pay phone.

There was a listing for a Graves Fishing Camp. A recorded voice answered after five rings. I chose not to leave a message.

I tried to sleep, crawling between the scratchy sheets of the unoccupied double bed, but failed to silence the quarrelsome voices in my head. Why would Peritti torch my house if Gwen were guilty? If Gwen were innocent? Hell, if he'd been nuts enough to burn buildings in the eighties when he couldn't have been more than a teen, he'd hardly need motivation. Was there a way to find out now, years later, whether he'd participated in the Friday Firebugs' blazes? Had he merely watched his dad set fires with matchbooks and bags of Coleman fuel?

Did he know for a solid fact that Gwen was guilty? Believe she was?

Had my house been searched prior to being set aflame? That would change the equation. If Valentine had handed "something of value" to Gwen for safekeeping, would she have passed it along to Peritti? Had "something of value" been found? If not, where was it? What was it? Had the quest ended?

If I'd been home, I'd have played guitar, choosing a blues with complicated fingering that demanded my full attention, to block out the voices. Here, I flicked on the TV, muting it for Paolina's sake, watched a green-tinted sportscaster display his teeth. I channel-surfed, encountering a run of commercials, old black-and-white films. On CNN, political scandal, on public broadcasting, slides of Cubist paintings and British-inflected voices asking whether works of art currently hanging on the walls of France's Pompidou Center should be returned to their prewar owners. My thumb hit the button. MTV, even with the volume low, didn't prove a lullaby. Zap. More commercials, then a familiar face. I backtracked, inched up the volume on Peter Breeze's talking head as he bantered through farewells with a local news personality.

He'd found something of value in Valentine's death: increased visibility, network TV time. I must have fallen asleep curled in the saggy brown wing chair, because that's where I woke up.

I did not enjoy my Sunday "off." I left a string of messages on Bronson Hohen's office and home phones, asking him to get in touch via the motel or Gloria. I carefully reread the articles about his grandfather's "robbery," searching for discrepancies in the various accounts. I called the Milton police, found no one on duty willing to help me, certainly no one with an actual memory of so distant a non-crime.

Sundays, everybody's out. Phones ring unanswered. You can't find a damn thing.

Paolina had a cold. It rained. My house looked dismal, and the fire crew didn't work Sundays unless they got double overtime.

Monday morning, I arrived at the South Middlesex Correctional Center in Framingham while surly guards were drinking their first cups of coffee. It's a minimum-security joint, less daunting than Walpole, and it occurred to me that some of the women prisoners might have been jailed for child abandonment. Marta was on my mind; no one had answered the fishing camp phone all day yesterday or this morning either. I passed through the guard checkpoints, entered a small, chilly room that looked more like a classroom than a cell. The furniture was bolted to the floor.

"I'm glad to s–see you." Gwen was waiting, her body completely still. Her left toe was tapping, but I don't think she heard its nervous repetitive tic.

"I wish I had good news."

Her smile died, first on her mouth, then in her eyes.

"We need to talk about Peritti. Has he been by to visit?"

Her blue plastic shoes clashed with the orange prison jumpsuit. They reminded me of baby booties; her feet were so small. She shook her head no.

"C'mon, Gwen, let's talk. If it's gonna be you or Tony, you've got to make the right choice."

"I t–told you. He wouldn't hurt Mrs. Phipps." Her hair was scraped back from her forehead, held firmly by an elastic band at the nape of her neck. I missed the beads.

"Does he light fires?" I asked. "Smoke a lot of cigarettes?"

"Oh, s–smoke cigarettes, yeah, h–he does that. Why not?"

"Does he burn small pieces of paper? In ashtrays?"

"What? That's a–against the law?" Her wide mouth was set in a stubborn line and a frown creased her brow like an approaching storm front.

"Gwen, setting fires is a compulsion, a sickness. I think your man tried to burn down my house."

She let the sentence sink in for a moment. "Your house? When?"

"Friday night."

She let her breath out slowly. "No. Friday nights he spends with his p–poppa. Sleeps there, at the nursing home. They let him 'cause the old m–man gave them a lot of money."

"And what's wrong with the old man?"

"That Alzheimer's thing."

"Gwen, with Alzheimer's, the old man might not know whether Tony was there or not. That's no alibi."

"He doesn't need an alibi with me, just like I d–don't need one with him. He knows I d–didn't kill Mrs. Phipps, just like I know he didn't."

"And he never mentioned Millennium Towers to you?"

"No."

"Never told you how much it might be worth to him if Mrs. Phipps left?"

"I don't want to t–talk about this. If all you can do is try to put this off on Tony, maybe you better quit."

She no longer wore handcuffs or shackles. She covered her face with her hands, like a kid playing peekaboo, trying to shut out my questions.

"If you argued with Mrs. Phipps, Gwen—smashed her phone, hid her medicine, watched while she suffered a heart attack—tell me now, and I'm out of here."

No response.

"Should I stay? Can I ask more questions?"

I had to concentrate to understand her muffled words. "It's worse here even than I remember, gangs are worse, f–fights worse."

I stayed silent.

"Lawyer says I gotta plead."

"If you did it, go for the plea."

She straightened her shoulders. "Go 'head, ask what you want."

"You got along well with Valentine?"

"I t–told the cops. She was always happy to see me, chattering away like a bird."

"I need to know more about her past, her marriages."

Gwen shrugged impatiently. "I don't remember stuff like that. I nod my head, go uh-huh, uh-huh, and I'm making the beds or vacuuming. I hear stuff, d–don't get me wrong, all about how she had a big house once, and how she had d–dancing dresses and red shoes and silk scarves."

"Jewelry?"

"She never said."

"Paintings? Vases? Statues?"

"Nothing like that. And she didn't talk that much about her p–past."

"Gwen, you just said she never stopped talking."

Abruptly the young woman blushed, color suffusing her dark face with a warm glow. I raised one eyebrow questioningly.

"I d–don't gotta t–tell you." She stared at me defiantly.

"It could help."

"I d–don't see how."

"Let me try," I insisted.

"You'll laugh at me."

"I won't."

She glanced from doorway to window, lowering her voice to a whisper. "She told s–stories."

"Stories?" I repeated. "You mean lies?"

"No. Stories. Kid stories, yeah, but I never learned them. W–when I was coming up, my mom didn't tell me s–stories, the kind everybody knows. Mrs. Phipps loved to tell 'em and I loved to listen."

"You mean like 'Cinderella'?"

"C–Cinderella, I already heard. I liked Rapunzel, with the long, gold hair, and the tin s–soldier who melted into a heart. Those are my f–favorites."

I tried to imagine them, the busy young woman, the striking old woman, sharing Grimm's tales in the cluttered Fenway apartment, the vacuum cleaner hushed.

"And freedom s–stories."

"Like what?"

"Martin King in Birmingham jail when he wrote a letter to the white preachers. And the Jews when they c–came out from Egypt. Now she won't tell 'em to me anymore."

My aunt Bea used to tell me stories of the Old Country. My mom told tales of her union glory days.

"I can bring you books." Then I thought, *Damn, what if she can't read well?* "They're on tape. I can find tapes for you."

"I dunno. I think remembering w–would make me cry. You can't cry in here, don't do no good."

Time to signal the guard. Maybe Hohen had returned my calls.

"Do you think Mrs. Phipps had those s–stories written down in her beautiful book?"

I stopped halfway to the door. "What book?"

"I–I only saw it the one time. She closed it up fast."

"What did it look like?"

"Nothing like a magazine or a comic. All colors. Maybe, if you f–found it, you could bring it to me."

"How big? Thick or thin?"

"I don't know. Medium, but with bright, bright colors, and s–silver, and gold."

"Gwen, this is exactly the sort of thing I need. Why didn't you tell me about it?"

"You asked about jewelry, Carlotta, not some book she stuck under the bed."

"Under the bed?"

"In a kind of wooden box. When I came in, she shoved it under there. You think that's where the stories came from?"

I'd inspected the place carefully, thoroughly, with a cop, after a crime-scene team had done their work. No "beautiful book" rested in a wooden chest under a bed in the Kilmarnock Street apartment.

# THIRTY-TWO

My mom treasured a hardbound book called *Children of Many Lands*, a childhood birthday gift with a green leather binding and colored drawings of "Esquimaux." She made me scrub my hands before I could turn the pages.

Valentine hadn't offered to show Gwen any pictures. She'd quickly closed her beautiful book and hidden it away. *Children of Many Lands* must have measured nine by fourteen; it wouldn't have fit in a safety-deposit box.

I phoned Gloria from a gas station; no messages. I dialed Hohen; he was "unavailable." I drove to Cambridge. The insurance agent had given me his reassurances, so had Gloria and Roz, but I needed to touch base with the construction crew myself.

A battered navy and rust Dumpster blocked the driveway. I parked at the curb, momentarily rested my head on the steering wheel, preparing for the ordeal.

I didn't hear hammering as I exited the car. The stink was still pungent. Maybe the crew was taking a coffee break. They'd been here; the Dumpster was full. In its maw, I recognized remnants of charred foyer drapes, a misshapen throw rug, sections of ruined flooring, a soggy, twisted shape that could have been a closet door.

I coughed, looked away, and noticed the car. If I hadn't been trying not to stare at the house, I'd have seen it sooner. My block tends to old Volvos with a scattering of new sports utility vehicles. A black Lincoln Town Car with Tony Peritti at the wheel stuck out.

I focused on his knuckles, tight against the steering wheel. When he saw me, he leaned forward. I read the movement as aggressive, and my adrenaline kicked into overdrive. I expected him to gun the motor, make a run at crushing me between car and Dumpster. Instead the passenger door burst open and he approached so quickly that I took an involuntary step backward before forcing myself to hold ground.

He was waving something, and his handsome face was beet red. He hadn't bothered with the ponytail. His dark hair looked stringy and dirty, and he'd spilled beer down the front of his shirt.

"Look at this!" he was yelling. "Fucking look what you've done to me. I ought to smack you one, but I'm gonna sue your ass instead. You're gonna be fucking sorry about this."

I planted my feet and thought about where I would hit him first. Then the cop in me took over, and I stepped back, pitching my voice low so he'd need to listen well.

"Is there a problem?" The mildness of my tone surprised me more than it surprised him. I kept my eyes on his eyes, but I was aware of his hands.

"I'm gonna sue your ass," he repeated.

I warily indicated the folded newspaper he was brandishing, taking care that my gesture wouldn't be interpreted as hostile. "What is that?"

His face grew even redder. "That's you shooting your fucking mouth off, about how I burn houses down. That's illegal, that's what it is. Illegal, what you did."

"Let's turn it down a notch, okay? My neighbors hate noise."

He pivoted to face the homes on the opposite side of the street. For the appreciation of people behind locked doors two blocks away, he yelled, "If I'd torched her damned house, it'd be burned to the ground. You hear that, you fuckers?"

"You've been drinking a bit," I observed.

"Yeah, sure, why not? I don't know why the hell they're trying to set me up for this, after all these fucking years, but it's nothing but a stinking frame, and it sucks what they're doing to me."

Now it was "they" who'd set him up, not me. Not much of an improvement, but I might be able to build on it.

"Who's trying to set you up?" I asked.

"Like as if you didn't know." He thrust the newspaper so close to my face I couldn't read a word. "Yeah, like you really didn't know."

"I haven't had much chance to look at the paper today."

"Then you're the only one in the whole fucking city. It's on TV, too. My phone hasn't stopped fucking ringing. I'm going to lose deals over this, but I'll make up the money, no worry about that, when I sue you and this lousy piece-of-shit newspaper—"

"Let me read it, okay?"

NO SMOKE WITHOUT FIRE was the headline, and Peter Breeze had raked up the fiery past and linked it with the fortunes of the Perittis, father and son. He must have driven straight back to Frank Hennessee's, bribed the man to give details. The business with the matchbooks and the Coleman fuel had now been reported in the paper of record. Breeze must have kept the paper's legal team working late. The word *alleged* was given a healthy workout.

"It doesn't exactly say you set the fire," I pointed out.

"Might as well. Nothing was ever proved against me or my dad, but what's this Breeze creep care, he's ruining my life?"

When I handed him back the paper, he started shredding it and tossing the pieces in the air like confetti. I tried to grab it, stick it in the Dumpster, but he danced around like a kid playing keep-away.

"He's repeating old gossip," I said soothingly. "It's the kind of stuff he writes. Take it up with him, not me."

"Yeah, sure. Where'd he get the idea?"

"Maybe from the police, maybe the fire department."

"Sure. I don't need you raking this shit up for everybody to gloat over. My dad doesn't deserve this. I don't. I've worked real hard—Hey, you could fucking care less, right?"

I found it hard to imagine him behind the desk in his office, with polished shoes and pressed pants. The man had come seriously unglued.

I said, "I care about my house. I care about your girlfriend."

"You think I'm some kind of Mob creep, some asshole Mafioso, don't you? That's all you see when you look at me, right? I got a vowel at the end of my name, so I'm a torch, right? I know your kind."

"How did the Mafia get in here?" I asked. "I didn't start ranting about the Mafia."

"You know, the reason I'm getting screwed here is because of Gwen, because she's black and this is fucking Boston, so all the Irish cops and the Irish reporters are bent outta shape on accounta first, I bring in undesirable tenants, that's one count I'm guilty on: I rent to Haitians and guys from Santo Domingo, I even sell property to black firms, and I'm dating a black girl, and so they're gonna take me down—"

"Cool it. My neighbors are gonna call the cops. Guy lives over there, plays the viola, very sensitive ears."

"I didn't do this shit." He waved his hand at my house.

"You did plenty." Since my sympathy hadn't urged him back to his car, I hardened my voice and went on the attack. "The same kind of people who set fires when they're young pull dirty tricks when they're older. Like breaking car windows, sabotaging elevators, turning rats loose, routing cops to phony crime scenes—"

"Okay, okay." He held up his hands to stop the flood of my words. "So what? So fucking what if I did?"

"You wanted Gwen to help."

"Who says?"

"It's why you made a play for her."

"But I didn't burn your fucking house down!"

"Then where were you when it burned?" I snapped quickly. He was overwrought, on a liquor-induced talking jag, possibly even telling the truth. I might as well take advantage of his candor. My question brought him up short.

"Huh?"

"It's simple. Where were you Friday night?"

"I don't have to tell you."

"According to Gwen, you visit your father most Friday nights. Let's dial the nursing home."

"I wasn't there."

"Too bad."

"A friend of mine's in town. We took him out for dinner, me and some other guys."

I was disappointed. It had the smell of prearranged alibi. If he *were* Mafia, a "couple of guys" was exactly the sort of tale he'd trot out, along with a pet restaurateur who'd back him one hundred percent.

"You might believe the guy." He looked at me with something behind his eyes.

"Yeah?"

"Gianelli."

The sound of Sam's name on Peritti's drunken lips hit me like cold water. I sucked in a deep breath.

Peritti tossed the remaining ripped newsprint on the grass, tried to grind it under his heel. He tilted unsteadily on his feet. Behind me, a window sash creaked, and a voice belatedly called, "Is everything okay?"

"Yes." I didn't turn. "Sorry."

Peritti was staring at me like he expected me to apologize to him as well. Maybe I'd need to. If Sam Gianelli vouched for him . . .

To my amazement, he beat me to the apology. "Hey, I'm sorry about this shit. Sorry I yelled. Man, I don't fucking drink either, most of the time. Look at me, dammit, what the hell am I doing?"

"It's okay," I said.

"No, it fucking isn't. Fuck, look at me."

"It's okay." I felt exhausted, limp and wilted as an unwatered plant.

"If you see Gwen, don't tell her I was drinking."

"Okay."

"I'm fucking sorry."

My neighbor had dialed 911, but the cops didn't come till after he'd squealed away in the Town Car. To an audience of skeptical faces, I explained that it was merely a misunderstanding. Then I gathered all the bits of newsprint from where the wind had dropped them and tossed them in the Dumpster. I weighted the paper with burnt wood that left black carbon on my hands.

The construction crew reassembled after their break. I wondered if they'd heard the argument from my backyard, decided not to interrupt, to observe as though it were some kind of TV soap opera, not an altercation that might have turned violent.

The corner drugstore phone booth is a genuine relic with a bifold door and a round cushioned seat. I fed the phone a quarter and punched in Sam's number from memory. His father kept up the payments on the Charles River Park apartment; he uses it as a hideout when he spars with his fourth wife. Five long rings, six, then Sam said hello, low and deep and easy. I'm such a sucker for voices, always have been. It took me a long beat to realize the hello was only a recording, frame a sentence to blurt at the beep.

"Hey, Sam, it's Carlotta. A friend of yours told me—"

"Hello." He must have been monitoring his calls.

"Sam."

"Hey."

"Welcome home." I was smiling so broadly that anyone who'd glanced in the booth might have debated whether I'd lost my senses or won the lottery. He didn't respond, but it seemed to me that an electric charge pulsed through my hand where it grasped the receiver, tingled up my arm to my shoulder.

"What can I do for you?" The stiffly formal phrase was far more businesslike than the recording.

I answered formality with formality. "You can tell me if Tony Peritti took you out to dinner Friday night."

"You're checking an alibi?"

"Yes."

"Friday?"

"Yes."

"I ate dinner with Tony. Mamma Maria's. Veal."

"Thank you."

"That's why you called?"

"No," I said hurriedly, but he'd already hung up. I gripped the receiver for a full minute, maybe two. It was molded black plastic, with no warmth at all.

When I regained my composure, I dialed Hohen. This time his secretary told me he was out of town.

# THIRTY-THREE

"Hungry?"

I was about to repeat the inquiry when a single word came out of Paolina's mouth.

"No."

"Well, I sure am. How about crab Rangoon at Mary Chung's?" I prefer the Suan La Chow Show, but Paolina can't tolerate the spicy heat.

"No." That syllable again.

"C'mon."

"We always go there." Her voice wasn't exactly a whine, but it threatened to escalate.

"C'mon," I repeated.

"I'm not going there."

"Fine. We'll go somewhere else. My stomach's making weird noises and I can't recall eating in the recent past."

I waited for her to ask if my house was still standing. She continued lying on the living-room couch in her East Cambridge apartment, staring at the TV as if she were having a vision of the Holy

Virgin. Roz had dropped her there after school, with instructions to wait for me, to pack more clothes.

"Paolina," I said.

"This is almost over."

"Paolina, please."

Marta's stove didn't function but wouldn't you know her TV got fifty-some channels?

"Jeez," my Little Sister muttered, angrily switching off the show.

"It's cold. Grab your coat."

"I know how to dress myself."

My lips formed a circle, but I didn't let the whistle escape. She reappeared three minutes later, an oversized sweatshirt pulled carelessly over tight jeans.

"Paolina, it's cold out, really. Wind. Major chill. For October, it's a lot like November."

She shot me a look, spun on her heel, reappeared reluctantly zipping her old red parka. I wondered if it was no longer fashionable, or never had been fashionable. Fashion, I'm told, is ultra-important in the age of mallcrawlers and designer togs for babes in arms.

Cars had sandwiched my Toyota in so tightly that it took three tries and a prayer to the goddess of power steering in order to exit my parking space.

"Where to?" I asked cheerfully.

"McDonald's."

"There's a new Szechuan place in the Square. Or—"

"McDonald's, really."

"You in a hurry? I thought it was a no-homework night."

"That's where I want to go." Her lips were a thin line of assertive red.

If I'd known, I'd have left the car and walked. The hamburger joint across from Mary's in Central Square is within easy strolling range. I don't mind McD's, but I do tend to think of it as a provider of food appropriate for stakeout, rations to gulp while crouched behind the steering wheel, camera poised, waiting for a supposedly disabled man to lift heavy weights. Given time, I like to order from a menu in a foreign language written in utterly baffling script. I like to go to strange corner dives and ask the waitress to get me what's good. I'd had my eye on a couple of Vietnamese places in Allston.

Paolina wanted McD's. I pulled into the lot.

Under the too-bright glare of pin spots, I ordered a Big Mac, large fries, a vanilla shake, and turned to Paolina, who was studying the menu board with the same concentration she'd lavished on the TV screen. Her tongue was trapped between her teeth and she looked troubled beyond the difficulty of choosing between Mc-Nuggets and McRibs.

"A hamburger." She frowned slightly.

"Quarter Pounder?"

"Just a hamburger."

"To drink?"

"Just a hamburger, okay?" Her voice got slightly louder with each repetition.

I shrugged and paid the anxious young server, who seemed terrified that a line might materialize behind me.

"If you want to find a table, I'll wait for the food," Paolina offered grudgingly, as though I'd accused her of standing around and doing nothing, not pulling her weight. It didn't seem like a good time to remonstrate, so I went to search out a likely spot.

The only available table was wedged into a corner. The seats should have come with a warning label: If your legs are longer than an eight-year-old's, forget it.

I sat and pondered Paolina's order, one lone, puny hamburger.

My Little Sister has never dieted. She's not skinny, not heavy. Far as I know, she doesn't brood about her weight. I considered her TV viewing. How could she avoid brooding after observing the wraithlike females on TV?

She joined me and I watched her eat her burger, nibbling so slowly that I seemed to wolf my food by comparison. When I offered her ketchup-soaked fries, she demurred.

"Hey, Paolina, either you missed Lent, or you're too early for it. I know that for a fact. Wrong season of the year."

She didn't respond.

"Seriously, are you on some kind of diet? Because you don't need to lose weight. You look fine."

"I'm not on a diet."

"Then, what?"

She gave me a withering glance, opened her mouth, then clamped it shut.

"Tell me."

"It's the money." She lowered her voice so the leather-clad teens at the next table wouldn't overhear. "Food costs money, and I don't have much, just what Marta left, and I'm going to have to get used to it. One hamburger's plenty."

It was my turn to say nothing.

"Until I get a job," she added.

"You're in school."

"Who knows how long that's gonna last?"

"Paolina, that's going to last quite a long time."

"Things are sort of different now. If Marta doesn't come back, they're way different."

*Marta*, not *Mom*. As though it were okay for Marta to desert, not Mom. I hated this, despised every second spent watching the scar tissue form and spread. Damn Marta, anyway.

I said, "I have money for you."

"I'm not taking your money, Carlotta."

I took a deep breath. "It's your money."

"Thanks, but no thanks."

"It's not my money and it never was my money, Paolina. Your dad sent it."

Her chocolate eyes stared at me and her lips parted. "He did?"

With a sentence I'd turned her absentee father into a hero who'd leapt into the breach at her time of need, surfaced like a god on the halfshell as soon as her mother deserted. The timing was all wrong. I'd spoken without sufficient thought, dammit, offered her a father like a candy bar, a father who loved her as demonstrated by his gift of cash. In my haste to reassure her, I'd opened a can of wriggling nightcrawlers.

I scooped my coat off the back of my chair. "Are you done? Let's go."

"How did he send you money? How did he know about you? Does he want to see me? Can I call him? How much money?"

"Paolina, your dad—you know, it's an uncomfortable situation. He can't be a real father to you. He doesn't even want anyone to know he's your father. It could be dangerous, for you."

"But—"

"Let's not talk about it here."

She bit her lip, rose and flung her parka around her shoulders, stuck her hands deep in her pockets. A strange expression came over her face, a compound of consternation and regret.

"Oh, no. Oh, hell."

"What?" I asked.

"I forgot."

"Forgot?" I repeated.

"I jammed it in my pocket—and then I wore my windbreaker or my sweatshirt. I didn't feel like wearing this."

"What?"

"Nothing."

"What?"

"That crazy old lady asked me to mail this, and I forgot."

I grabbed her wrist. "What crazy old lady?"

"Carlotta, stop it. The one you made me go see. She gave me this, told me to just slip it in the mail—"

"Give it to me," I barked.

"Hey."

I snatched it. Holding the envelope between tense fingers, I envisioned Gwen's ransacked apartment and the burned timbers of my foyer, the spoiled carpet, the Dumpster filled with my aunt's past.

Paolina said, "I'm sorry, okay?"

The envelope was plain white, check-sized, lumpy. In addition to the address, she'd scrawled "Please Hand Cancel" front and back.

It wasn't heavy.

Addressed to herself.

I debated only a second, slit the top.

Paolina looked outraged. "It's not yours."

"Sit down," I ordered.

She obeyed without protest.

"This woman is dead, honey."

She bit her lip.

"It's not . . . it's not because of me? It's not—"

"No," I said.

"People around me die or disappear. What is it with me?"

"It's not you, honey."

She turned her face away. Her hair swept down at a slant so I couldn't see her eyes.

The envelope was addressed to Mrs. V. Phipps. Her shaky hand had wielded a blue ballpoint.

*"Where would you hide something?"* I could almost hear her querulous voice.

*"You could mail it to yourself,"* I'd said.

She'd taken my advice.

I tipped the envelope out onto the table. Nothing. I stuck my fingers in and grabbed a rough sheet of paper. Fumbling, almost dropping it in my eagerness, I unwrapped a key from its paper towel swaddling.

*"Rent a safety-deposit box,"* I'd suggested.

For a moment my hopes soared.

It didn't look like any safety-deposit key I'd ever seen.

"Carlotta?" Paolina's voice broke in.

"What?"

"Is it okay if I order a chocolate shake and some fries? And a Quarter Pounder?"

"Fine."

# THIRTY-FOUR

Back at the motel, Paolina was too fidgety and excited to sleep. The child I'd known was almost grown, no longer easily placated with a casual "Trust me; I'll handle the details." That was as it should be, I supposed, quelling a pang of regret. On her own she'd realized that Marta's continuing absence would have far-reaching ramifications, taken it on herself to begin planning her motherless future. I was proud of her for that, and told her so. But now she wanted answers to a hundred questions, and I wasn't ready with responses.

What I try to do with Paolina is simple: I try to tell her the truth. I didn't know the truth about her father's money, whether he sent it out of guilt, love, duty, or for some obscure reason I had yet to fathom.

So I told her how Roldan Gonzales had broached the subject, sent the cash, the unembroidered facts. I explained that gifts often come with strings attached, that this one was tied in ribbon that said "college." That, in order to assure her graduation from high school, I was certain an arrangement could be worked out. That while she wasn't a wealthy heiress, she didn't have to restrain her appetite to small burgers.

I agreed that it was a fine gesture on her father's part. I didn't say that his love and his time might have been better gifts. Finally, she let me sing her to sleep with an old lullaby, like I used to when she was small. She joined in on the chorus, piping a high, true harmony.

In the yellow glow of the desk lamp, the inch-long key looked fragile. It hung from a plain circle of metal, the size of a pinkie ring. The manufacturer's name, Mosler, was inscribed on the key's shaft. I slept with it under my pillow, like wedding cake, but I don't remember whether I dreamed of Valentine Phipps.

The next morning I checked in with Henry Fine, who told me he thought Gwen might be wavering on the plea bargain. Had I interviewed the Kilmarnock tenants?

I promised to take care of it today.

On a map I penciled concentric circles around the Phipps apartment. If Valentine had obtained her hidey-hole recently, frightened by her landlord's intrusion or her Breeze-induced celebrity, perhaps she'd stuck to her immediate neighborhood, her safety zone, the places she knew best.

Since it was only an assumption, I dialed Gloria, requesting information on jockeys who'd picked up elderly women on Kilmarnock. Phipps hadn't driven a car; perhaps she'd frequented cabs. I asked Gloria to concentrate on the days preceding Valentine's death. I didn't wait for the data. She's fast, but there are quite a few Boston garages, and Mrs. Phipps's tight-fisted grip on twenty-dollar bills, her insistence on keeping my photograph of Paolina in exchange, made me doubt the existence of a favorite cabbie.

I drove to Kilmarnock Street. In Mrs. Phipps's vestibule, I buzzed Daly, G. in apartment 3A. No response. I tried Daniels, E., in 1C. Nothing. Which left me with a key and no lock.

The drizzle that had started during the night showed signs of increasing to a downpour. I keep a hooded slicker in the trunk of my car. I didn't bother with an umbrella; the northeast wind was fierce and uncertain.

I turned left into the driving rain, legging it down Peterborough to Park Drive. There I chose a right-hand turn, the path of least resistance to a heavy stream of traffic. On the corner of Park and Boylston, I entered a gas station. No, the Haitian attendant didn't recall an elderly woman coming by last week. He then hastily excused himself to answer the phone, a man of little or no apparent curiosity. No lockers or lockboxes were in evidence.

I crossed Boylston Street, entered a restaurant, chatted to no avail with the black-and-white–clad wait staff. A bank farther up Brookline Avenue denied the key. A Thai restaurant owner and chef declared Mrs. Phipps not a regular customer. The key stirred no recognition on his broad face. I plodded on, stopping at laundromats and drugstores, asking about Valentine Phipps, garnering smiles, rude stares, disinterested shrugs, and a frustrating chorus of negatives.

From a pay phone, I dialed Gloria, even though I had no right to expect a response yet, just to stay out of the rain a moment longer, just to listen to her mellow voice. She'd spoken to dispatchers at three top garages. No luck.

I pressed on. My shoes felt soggy, and I wriggled my toes inside my damp socks and pondered dire visions of frostbite-blackened toes and toenails that fell off. I soaked my right leg in a gutter swell of massive proportion when I underestimated its width and came up short on a leap. A speeding VW wagon plunged through a puddle, shooting a tower of spray that caught my left side and evened up the soaking.

Heading down Boylston toward the Victory Gardens, I assessed my chances of finding the right keyhole at the Star Market as extremely remote, but I stepped on the open-the-door mat to escape the weather. No one seemed to know Valentine Phipps; no one seemed eager to help. Every so often I feel the need to eat something healthy to counter the effects of junk food, so I purchased a carton of yogurt, and requested a plastic spoon. The checkout clerk offered a little wooden paddle that made me recall the Dixie cups of childhood. I bought an apple as well, added a crunch to the slip-slop of my feet on the slippery pavement.

I learned that there are no employee lockers at either Staples or at the nearby office-furniture store (which is about to go belly-up because of chain discount pricing). I had a minor brainstorm and sped over to the Ipswich Street garage that houses the Town Taxi Fleet. At Green & White Cab, where I used to do my driving, the hacks hung out in a back room complete with lockers. At Town all the locks were combination jobs hung through the locker handles, and no one remembered Valentine Phipps, although one cigar-puffing driver said she sounded like his late mother-in-law.

My next soggy burst of inspiration involved Fenway Park. Surely there had to be lockers in the vast caverns under the stands, lockers in which vendors stashed their wares between homestands.

"Lady, they ain't giving no autographs today." The dour guard had me pegged as an obsessed fan, and I got no further.

I was so wet I approached Harry's Hardware with mingled delight and relief, imagining the always-offered coffee, forgetting both its quality and my irritation with the proprietor who'd identified me to Peter Breeze, branding me as a woman who offered security to dead clients.

I headed around the corner with a burst of speed. Maybe he'd even know something about the key.

Better, he owned the lock.

# THIRTY-FIVE

The bell jangled softly when I came in out of the rain. I pushed back the hood of my slicker and stood dripping in the doorway.

The nine-inch-square lockbox on the counter near the old-fashioned cash register was backlit like a haloed saint in a faded church painting. If Harry'd been away from his post, I'd have snatched it and run like a thief.

He was punching the register, toting numbers, a fierce scowl on his face, eyeglasses low on the bridge of his nose. I kept my voice matter-of-fact level, inquired how he was doing.

"Not many customers in this muck, so I'm figuring my shut-down costs. Found some fool wants to buy my bins, would you believe it, those old relics? For decor? He's gotta be one dumb S.O.B., right?"

"Remember the last time I was in, Harry?"

He glanced up. "Yeah?"

My voice was no longer so matter-of-fact. "You didn't mention you'd just seen Valentine Phipps."

He shrugged.

"Why is that?" I asked intently. "I was working for her. I told you that. You remembered the details for Breeze's column."

"Hey, okay, no hard feelings?"

I didn't respond.

His fingers clicked on the register keys. "Look, I thought she was checking up on you—she was like that—first, she checks out the prices, then she sends you over to buy for her. You charge her twenty cents too much, or buy the most expensive item, she's right on your case. She didn't like being cheated, you know? That's why she got so hot about the rent hikes."

"When did she come in?"

"Day before you did. Late afternoon. With you, she was talking home security, right? With me she talked home safes, asked if she could try one out, a good strongbox, like a fire safe."

"Like this one." I patted it, noting the Mosler insignia. If I had to, I'd buy it. God knows I could use a good fire safe.

"She asked me to show her a couple, bring 'em to the counter. Honest to God, she was wearing a hat, you know, with a little veil, like I haven't seen a woman wear in years. My wife had one back in—"

"Go on."

"Yeah, yeah, so I fetch a few for her to eyeball, but nothing's good enough. This one here was way up on the top shelf. I had to climb a ladder, coulda broke my neck, and then where'd we be? Then, while I'm still huffing and puffing like an old fart, you should excuse the term, she locks the box, bing-bang, and drops the key, my key, into that big handbag of hers, like a bottomless pit that bag is, and says she wants to see does the lock really work, and do I happen to have another key for it?

"Well, I don't have another key. I mean, this is a good box; it's not like every key fits, one model to the next. She gives me a little laugh, and says she can't find the key right now, and she doesn't want to buy it either, not right now. I ask you! I'm gonna empty that handbag right out on the counter, that's what I tell her. But she says, What's the big hurry? She'll sort it out at home, she's feeling tired, and she doesn't want me pawing through her stuff. She'll come back in a day or two. I mean, what's a guy to do? I'm gonna have a fistfight with a lady wearing a little scrap of a hat with a veil?"

My pent-up breath escaped in a rush. "It's okay, Harry. I brought you back the key."

"Terrific," he boomed, "I thought I was gonna have to write to the manufacturer."

The first time I tried to insert it in the lock, I dropped the key on the floor.

"Let me," offered Harry.

"No."

It slid in easily, turned with the slightest rotating pressure. The small handle gave a sigh when it opened.

The two small sealed envelopes made Harry's eyes narrow suspiciously. "Hey, I didn't see her put anything in."

"It's okay, Harry."

"It is?"

"Yeah." I removed them, handling them carefully by the edges. "Because you didn't see me take anything out."

# THIRTY-SIX

"My darling Val."

The yellowed paper was thin as a moth's wing, covered with a looping scrawl in faded indigo ink. Beneath Bronson Garrard Hohen's crabbed signature, he'd penned "November 5, 1942." According to the obit in the *Record-American*, ten days before he'd died. Two days before the robbery.

"Don't worry, little one. I know things seem hard, but trust me to do what's best for us." The handwriting was difficult to decipher, each letter cramped and elongated.

"I promise to make everything right again, I swear it. As to the package, stick it in your closet behind a few dresses, or in a drawer under your lace nightgowns—and don't mention it to a soul. I'll require it in a few weeks, but for now I wish to truthfully swear I have no idea where it is. (You know what an unconvincing liar I am!) Believe me when I say that these bad times will be behind us soon, and forever.

"Would you prefer France to London? When all this is past, this silly business of money, and has proved nothing more than a temporary embarrassment, we'll choose between a cottage in Provence and a flat near Harrods. Only keep this for me, darling Val, and keep your exquisite lips sealed."

My hands, sweating inside plastic gloves, felt so damp that I thought moisture must have seeped down from the rain-spattered windshield. I sat in the passenger seat with the dome light on, peering at the harshly illuminated past.

Two days before a dubious robbery had stripped his gallery of a collection containing works by Italian masters as well as samples of the then-shocking French Impressionist School, Hohen the elder had given his wife a package to conceal. A pulse thudded in my right temple, deep and regular as the tick of a clock.

Hohen had died, suddenly, unexpectedly, before reclaiming his package. Surely his penniless widow would have sold anything of value.

*"Only keep this for me, darling Val, and keep your exquisite lips sealed."*

For how long? For what reason? I gnawed my lower lip while rereading the letter, staring hard at each word as if close scrutiny could force extra meaning from the spidery letters.

The rain hammered against the windshield. The headlights of passing cars tried to penetrate the gloom. Tires hissed on the wet pavement.

I held the second envelope up to the dome light. In appearance, it was identical to the first, a check-size security envelope. It felt stiffer, heavier.

For a moment, as I stared at the partially revealed contents, I assumed it was my lost photograph of Paolina. It was the right size and shape, and I was delighted until I realized it couldn't be. The timing was off, wrong. Valentine Phipps had handed Paolina the lockbox key only moments after snatching the girl's photo from my wallet.

I removed the glossy wallet-size shot from the envelope. My gloved hands felt too large for the task, ungainly. There was a single penciled sentence on the back. It didn't make sense to me. I turned the photo face up.

*I never forget eyes I meet over the barrel of a gun.*

Teri Kiley's gray eyes stared levelly from underneath a regulation blue cap. Teri Kiley's Police Academy graduation photograph . . . sharing a lockbox with Bronson Hohen's letter.

The scratchy writing on the back said "October 2, 1998. Gave it to Teri for valu."

The beginning of this month. Gave it. Gave what? To Teri for valu. For value? For value received?

I muttered the inscription aloud. When she'd appropriated my photo of Paolina, Valentine had already been holding Teri Kiley's. She'd siezed Paolina's photo, calling it "collateral," to keep till I installed the locks that she'd given me cash to buy. Was Kiley's photo also "collateral," for a package given by Bronson Hohen to his young bride long ago, "something of value," to be kept safe?

"Gave it to Teri for valu." For valuation? For appraisal? Valentine had been worried about money. Her rent was poised to skyrocket.

Through the rain it seemed that I could hear the echo of whispery voices: Peritti, mentioning the do-gooder lady cop who attended Fenway tenant meetings; Harry, joking about how well he got on with the new lady cop.

Teri, who'd arrived so quickly at the scene of Valentine's death, had later insisted on accompanying me to search the dead woman's apartment. She'd found the pill bottle underneath the sofa cushion.

Gave *what* to Teri for valu?

I tried to find reasons that Valentine Phipps might conceal a cop's photo, innocent reasons that would mean Kiley had nothing to do with the old woman's death. Why would a cop conceal the simple fact that she'd known the old woman? "Gave it to Teri," not "Gave it to to Officer Kiley."

A raindrop trickled down the windshield and deflected off the motionless wipers. I closed my eyes. Rubbed them with my fists.

I could use a damned cell phone in the car.

# THIRTY-SEVEN

It took three minutes to sprint to the gas station at the corner of Park and Boylston. Six variations of Frank Hennessee's name were listed in the book; only one lived on Westland Avenue. I borrowed a ballpoint from a mechanic to scribble the number on my wrist.

"Hey now, darlin', I was hoping you'd call."

I made sure he remembered exactly who I was and why I'd spoken to him previously before I went on. "Mr. Hennessee, you had the lowdown on the Friday fires, numbers, everything, at your fingertips. Why?"

" 'Cause I'm a friggin' genius is why. Didn't I bedazzle you with my brilliance?"

"Why?" I repeated.

He hesitated so long I was afraid he might have hung up. "Because they were fresh in my head."

"Someone asked about them?"

"Yes."

"Who?"

"Didn't get a name."

"What are you telling me? You spout off to a voice on the phone, you don't even ask who's calling?"

"It was official." He sounded indignant. "Boston Police business."

"A woman," I said.

"A lady," he corrected. "Sweet voice and full of proper respect."

A cop in the Fenway, Teri had probably heard locker-room tales of the Friday fires. She'd mimicked the details, setting fire to my house, threatening Paolina's life and my own, to distract me, to point me in the wrong direction, toward Tony Peritti.

I think I thanked the man, know I hung up and stared at the receiver.

I didn't call Mooney.

If the wind hadn't been gusting to thirty-five miles per hour, my slicker might have done its job. As I hurried toward Kilmarnock Street, my hood kept blowing off, sending streams of chilly droplets down my neck.

Daniels, E., was still not answering her buzzer, but Gregor Daly, the man who'd heard a fight from one floor below, responded to my ring.

A surly white man in his fifties, he was busily sipping a Michelob, eager to inform me that he wasn't some pushover whose testimony a wily defense attorney could twist at will. He wouldn't invite me over the threshold till I promised to remove my slicker and leave it on the doormat. I didn't blame him.

I accepted his offer of a beer, chose a seat at the kitchen table where the radiator would pump heat at the backs of my legs.

I started with the night of Valentine's death. That's where the cops had probably begun their inquiries; that's where he'd expect me to focus.

"Were you asleep when you heard the voices?"

"Drifting off," he replied calmly. "I'd watched the eleven o'clock news, and a few innings of a ball game. Started getting ready for bed about the fifth, sixth inning."

"Who was playing?"

"Yankees at the Angels."

"Score?"

"Seven–two Yanks when I turned it off. Wells was pitching, but they brought in a reliever with two on base, one out, and I decided to pack it in. I set my alarm like I always do."

He'd be a hell of a witness, remembering details like that. At first, he told me, he'd thought the argument was televised. Only when steps had shaken the light fixture in his bedroom had he realized the high-pitched angry voices were live.

"Could you be sure it was Mrs. Phipps?" I demanded, like it was the key question in the defense strategy.

"No. Not really. But there were two voices, I can say that. Both women's, I can swear that."

I asked if he'd heard any specific words or phrases.

"No—I don't mean no, I didn't hear any. I mean I heard someone shouting 'No.' And then something hard crashing to the floor."

The cracked telephone.

Gently I led him back in time, probing earlier events under the guise of examining Gwen's possible motives. We were chatting like casual drinking buddies by the time he mentioned that an attractive female police officer had visited some six months earlier, advising him, in the wake of a burglary, to take greater care of his possessions.

"I used to keep my dad's gold watch in my sock drawer," he said, "but I took her advice, put it in the bank."

It was too warm in the kitchen. Stifling. The business card in my pocket was curled at the edges with damp, but it was genuine, one of my own. I asked him to call if he remembered any more details about the argument.

"Static," he said abruptly as he escorted me through the front room to the door.

"What?"

He shrugged and repeated himself. Then he elaborated, "As I was dozing off that night, seems to me I heard static."

The rain was falling steadily but no longer bouncing back from the pavement. Back at the pay phone, I could still read Hennessee's number on my wrist. Sure, he'd been monitoring police and fire that Monday night as usual. I hung on while he fetched his logbook.

Yankees at the Angels. A night game on the West Coast would have started at seven—ten o'clock Boston time.

"Okay," I told Hennessee. "Around midnight."

He read the entries from eleven o'clock on, but I stopped listening after the oh-five-ten from Area Four.

Area Four is the Fens. Oh-five-ten is police radio code for forcible entry in a nonresidential building. It's a top-priority call. An on-duty cop has to move on it—quickly, or she'll find herself answering hostile questions in a sergeant's office.

I could see Teri in my mind's eye, tap-tapping at the keyboard, explaining that she hadn't been able to finish the paperwork on a burglary call, a lone copy of *Arts and Antiques* magazine on a shelf in her barren cubicle.

Gregor Daly had heard static all right, static from her two-way radio. Because she'd had to answer its summons, she hadn't had time to tidy up Valentine's apartment, make her death look like a suicide. And before she'd had a chance to get back to Kilmarnock Street, I'd discovered the body.

# THIRTY-EIGHT

The same skinny mechanic who'd lent me the ballpoint pen handed me four quarters in exchange for a damp dollar bill, pointedly ignoring the ABSOLUTELY NO CHANGE sign over the register, even though ABSOLUTELY was underscored in red. Maybe he was afraid I'd pull a stickup if he refused. One can only expect irrational behavior from a red-haired Amazon bent on monopolizing an unsheltered pay phone in the middle of a deluge.

My shoes were ruined, every scrap of clothing drenched. I squished back to the phone, left an emphatic message for Henry Fine: No plea bargain.

I should have called Mooney. I knew that. Instead, I shook the rain out of my hood and dialed Roz for a report on music mogul Bronson Hohen. Then I got in the car and drove rapidly downtown while the rain continued to fall in wind-whipped sheets. I parked at the base of Beacon Hill in a slot reserved for government employees, trudged half a block. When Hohen's secretary saw me, she lifted a manicured hand to protest my sopping jeans and drowned-rat hair. Ignoring her, I marched down the hall.

Hohen's concentration was riveted on a white golf ball. As I entered, he flexed his fingers on the grip of the club, and sank the putt.

I said, "You haven't been exactly frank with me."

He lined up another shot.

"You haven't returned my calls," I continued prodding.

"It's okay, Yale, I'll handle this." His crisp tone stopped the secretary at the door. She retreated quickly. "I'm not sure what you're talking about, Miss Carlyle."

While he was dealing with the secretary I'd removed his grandfather's letter from from my backpack. Now I held it aloft, encased in a plastic evidence bag.

"I think I know where," I said, "and since you know what, isn't it time we worked together?"

"Go on." He readjusted his putting stance.

"When you hired me, you expressed an interest in your namesake's correspondence."

"Yes. I did."

"You also said your interest in Valentine Phipps began with a newspaper article."

"Have you found something?"

"What really brought Valentine to your attention?"

He balanced the shaft of the putter carefully against the wall. "What if I told you that a man mentioned her name?"

"I want to know who."

When Hohen failed to respond, I unzipped my backpack and began to replace the plastic-encased letter. I could feel drops trickling from my hair down my back, that's how wet I was.

"Whatever the police find," Hohen said firmly, "will come to me. That will's invalid. Undue influence. Anyone can see that."

"Possibly." I stretched out the word. "Eventually. If they find it. In due course. But by that time, Hohen Music will be a subsidiary of a larger company, and you'll be out on your ear."

"Not necessarily."

"A takeover attempt—"

"An attempt, that's all it is, right now. It's true, if I didn't need the money—"

"You wouldn't have called me. You'd have waited it out."

"Perhaps."

"Tell me about the man who mentioned Valentine."

"Tell me what you've found."

We had a five-second staring contest. He looked exhausted. The web of lines surrounding his eyes had spread and darkened. When he sank into the chair behind his exotic wooden desk, I took it as capitulation, and an invitation to sit as well. I hoped the visitor's chair was waterproof.

"Eight months ago," he said, "a well-dressed man with an accent made an appointment to see me. He inquired if I was descended from Bronson Hohen, the connoisseur, the collector. I imagined I'd be sitting down to a few choice reminiscences leading up to the fact that his father had known my grandpa at Groton—and that his son played in a rock band. You wouldn't believe the forgotten acquaintances and distant relations who approach me clutching demo tapes."

"His kid didn't play?"

"He thought I had something that belonged to him. He got argumentative, belligerent. I almost buzzed and had him tossed out. I had a male receptionist then; Yale came later. I asked what I was supposed to have that belonged to him. He said it wasn't so much a personal debt, but that my grandfather had borrowed something, or been given something—I wasn't sure which—and not returned it. I said that, whatever it was, it was gone forever because my grandfather lost everything. There was no estate. Period. Simple as that. Good-bye. That's when the man asked if I'd stayed in touch with Valentine."

"That's all?"

When Hohen didn't answer, I peeled off my slicker, and hung it on the back of my chair. "Why did you tell him there was no estate?"

"There was none."

"Why? All your grandfather's paintings were recovered after the robbery."

Hohen inhaled sharply. "Would you like coffee?" he asked.

Just the idea of hot liquid was reviving.

He buzzed Yale—coffee, two cups—released the intercom button. Then, taking his time, he chose a Slinky from an arrangement of toys on one corner of the desk, shifted the metal coil from palm to palm, as though he were weighing it. "You know about the robbery."

"It made the papers."

"My mother wanted to change her name afterward. The shame of it would kill her."

"The shame of what?"

He put down the toy, twisted a signet ring on his right hand. Silence.

"Look," I said, "I have a call in to the Milton police. It might take me a while longer if you don't tell me now, but believe me, I'll find out."

He clasped his hands. His knuckles were white.

"You can trust in my discretion," I said.

The secretary knocked. We listened to her heels click across the floor, then to the clatter of spoons against china. I held my cup between my hands, ignoring the handle, warming my chilled fingers.

Hohen waited until she shut the door. "My grandfather owed everyone money. The insurance policy was recent, extensive coverage on the art. The investigators were skeptical from the beginning."

In his letter to Valentine, he'd admitted he was a poor liar.

"If he hadn't died, he'd probably have spent the rest of his life in a cell. As it happened, doctors found a key in his pocket, and the key opened a self-storage locker filled with the 'stolen' artwork. It wasn't clear if he'd planned the theft alone or with an accomplice. Valentine was suspected, of course."

I sipped coffee, holding the warmth in my mouth before swallowing. Of course. The family hated her—the interloper, the child bride. They must have relayed their suspicions to the police.

"My grandfather had overinsured, overvalued the art. The recovered works were auctioned, but the prices were low. There wasn't even enough to pay his debts."

If Valentine had produced the item her husband had given her to hide, would the family or the police have believed in her innocence?

"I'd appreciate it if my grandfather's larceny could remain a family secret." Hohen's frown etched new lines near the corners of his eyes.

"Tell me more about your visitor."

He shook his head. "It's your turn. What's in the bag?"

I probably should have used my plastic gloves again, but I didn't. Rain spattered the office windows in rhythmic bursts as I read the letter aloud.

"My God," he whispered when I finished, his coffee steaming and untouched in front of him.

"You know what he's talking about. Don't you?"

He picked the cup up, replaced it in the saucer without taking a sip. "My God."

"Why would your grandfather keep one item separate?"

"What was the date on the letter?"

"November eighth, 1942."

"Suppose he'd received something very recently, suppose he was holding it for someone else—"

I said, "That's it. It wasn't insured. He didn't have time to insure it, or else it wasn't his, so he couldn't insure it and then steal it—"

"Will you help me get it back?"

"If I don't know what it is, I can't help you at all."

Shoving back his chair, he rose, walked to the window, and pretended to adjust the blinds. The sky was gray; there was no sunlight to bar or admit. I sipped coffee and waited for him to decide.

When he began speaking, his back was turned. "My grandfather had many friends among European art dealers."

Bronson Hohen, the elder, had arranged exhibits at the MFA. I'd read it in his obituary.

"In 1940, when France fell to the Germans, Paris was the center of the international art market. That's where all the great art dealers lived. Many of them were also great collectors."

Hohen glanced at me and I bobbed my head to show that I was following.

"My grandfather was particularly close to a man named Étiènne Rosenblum. Rosenblum was part of a circle of Jewish collectors, along with the David-Weills, the Rothschilds, the Schlosses, the Kanns. All of them knew bad times were coming, but none of them realized how bad it would get. Some sent their possessions to the countryside, to the family chateau, had them crated and stored in the cellars."

I drank coffee without tasting it, thinking that Gwen would have enjoyed this story, wondering if Valentine had ever held her spellbound, her vacuuming suspended, with this particular tale. Wondering if Valentine had even known the tale.

"Étiènne Rosenblum corresponded regularly with my grandfather. I reexamined his letters after the man's visit."

"Was the man named Rosenblum?"

Hohen didn't respond; he stared out at the rain.

"Go on," I prompted.

"The Rothschilds owned a fabulous collection of Judaica, which could have been destroyed—or more likely sent to Poland to become part of the museum Hitler had planned to house the last traces of an extinct Jewish people. They hid it in a storeroom, bricked up the doorway, hung a tapestry over it, redecorating so that it looked as if the tapestry had always hung there. Troops of German soldiers billeted at the Rothschild chateau never discovered the room; the servants took great pride in keeping the secret."

"Was that in Rosenblum's letters?"

"Rosenblum planned to send his Judaica to the Rothschilds. Then, when he heard the room was already sealed, he panicked. In one of the last notes he sent my grandfather he said he had a chance, through a family friend, to send something out in a diplomatic pouch, to get one item safely to America."

"Yes?"

"I can only assume he sent it to my grandfather."

"To hold for him until after the war ended."

"The war ended for him in Auschwitz."

I almost flinched at the word of childhood terror, the word, according to my mother, that my grandmother would mumble in her sleep, waking drenched with sweat and anguish, inconsolable for days.

"What was it?" I kept my voice low. The steady patter of rain had turned to an almost hypnotic murmur.

"The letters that survive don't specify. I've researched the archives, the lists, the books, the catalogues—the French Foreign Ministry publishes catalogues of stolen works, works that were never recovered or claimed. The Rosenblums owned a remarkable kiddush cup, ancient and beautiful. There's a photograph of it in—"

"What else did they own?"

"A collection of prayer shawls."

"How about a book?" I said.

"A book?" He retraced his steps, knelt, and opened the lower left-hand drawer of his desk, removing a looseleaf notebook, and a pile of xeroxed pages, stapled together, flagged with multicolored tags. Some of the edges were dog-eared to mark various places in the stack. He cleared space for the papers on his blotter.

"A beautiful book." My hair was beginning to dry. My wet shirt clung uncomfortably to my spine.

"Listen." He thumbed excitedly though the pile. "Listen. "Here. Here it is. There's no picture. None of the reproductions survived. Here: 'The colors are reputed to be as sharp and clear as glass, the Hebrew written with a quill so fine that the calligraphy looks like lace.' "

"Calligraphy?"

He read, " 'According to the fashion of the time, the work was named for the scribe who lettered it—the same famous scribe who did the Pentateuch currently displayed in the British Museum. It is called the hagaddah of hagaddahs, as Eliezar is called the scribe of scribes.' "

"How big would it be?" I asked. "What size?"

"You've seen illuminated manuscripts?"

"Done by monks in the Middle Ages? There were no Jewish monks."

"Yes, true, but there were wealthy Jews and Jewish artists and scribes. Anybody who was anybody in medieval Christian Europe had a Book of Hours. You could pay an incredible sum for a Book of Hours, the cost of a house. They were status symbols. What did rich Jews have that was comparable, what could they buy to impress one another? A Torah is for the temple; you don't own a Torah. You own a haggadah. Do you know what that is?"

*Freedom stories,* Gwen had said. *And the Jews when they came out of Egypt.* A haggadah is the Jewish book of ritual and prayer used at the Passover service.

"Don't let the red hair fool you," I said. "I know."

My grandmother used the haggadahs that came free with Maxwell House Coffee. My mother and her comrades penned their own socialist Passover manifesto with hardly a mention of the word *God.*

Hohen was still paging through his notes, a tight-lipped smile on his face. I took a deep breath. "And let's say we're talking money."

"For the Eliezar Haggadah?" His smile broadened. "Many, many zeroes."

"But it wouldn't belong to you, would it? If it was sent to your grandfather for safekeeping."

"Then whose is it?" He spread his arms wide in an encompassing gesture. "The Rosenblum family was wiped out. Who has a better claim?"

*After all, who owns a thing? The one who's cared for it? Suffered for it? Loved it? Who should own it?* Valentine's words came back to me with such clarity it was almost like hearing her voice. I'd assumed she was speaking about her apartment, that she'd put labor and love into her dwelling, that she hated Peritti, the owner.

"I'm not saying it shouldn't go to a museum eventually," Hohen continued, "but even a finder's fee, an agent's fee, on the money this could bring at auction would astound you."

"At auction," I repeated. "If you had it, this haggadah, is that how you would go about selling it?"

"There are several avenues."

"Am I right in assuming that you'd try one way if you had a clear legal right to sell, another if you didn't?"

"Absolutely. Let's say you were to find the haggadah and with it, a bill of sale, a piece of paper with words to the effect that my grandfather legitimately bought this thing from Rosenblum, or traded for it, well—"

"What?"

"With a proper provenance, a chain of established ownership, I could deal with the giant auction houses—with Christie's and Sotheby's. Suppose it went into Sotheby's fall antiquities auction. Big institutions—the Morgan, the British Museum would bid. Auctions stir the blood. A rare item at auction becomes a prize and bidding is irrational. The chance of getting top dollar would be maximized by a well-publicized auction."

"And without the bill of sale, the provenance?"

"I'm not saying the big auction houses wouldn't touch it, but I'd be looking to make a private sale."

"Why is that?"

"The more publicity the item gets, the more chance there would be of losing the sale entirely. Suppose there's a great-nephew of the Rosenblums alive somewhere? You've read the stories in the newspapers. In New York, two paintings by Egon Schiele were seized as evidence in a grand jury investigation over disputed ownership. There's a group that admits stealing works of art they claim were looted from Jews during the Holocaust."

The Jewish Reclamation League. Front-page news the day Gwen hired me as a "security consultant."

"You know where it is, don't you?" Hohen demanded. "Is there a bill of sale? Do you have it with you? Can you get it?"

"It's been stolen," I said.

"But does the thief know what it is? Does he have any idea?"

"Yes. I believe it was taken, at first, simply to be appraised. By someone Valentine had every reason to trust—"

"And once the value was known, the thief decided to keep it? I see . . . I can even understand, a little."

"Do you understand killing her to avoid giving it back?" There was no coffee left in my cup, but I raised it anyway, touched the smooth porcelain to my lips.

"No. I don't," he said softly. "No, but my God, it must have been a temptation."

*Cops fight temptation all the time,* I wanted to shout. There's money on the streets, drug money and gambling money, small change and big bills, dirty money and dirtier money. But this—this was wealth beyond measure, with only a lonely, elderly woman standing in the way.

"I want to hire you," Hohen said, "to get it back."

"I'm not sure I can do that."

"You're going after the thief, aren't you? I'll pay you to look out for my interests."

"Mr. Hohen, who was the man who approached you about Valentine? Was he related to the Rosenblums?"

He shifted his glance to the window. Wind drove the rain diagonally against the pane.

I said, "If I'm going to help you, I need to know."

He opened the top drawer of the wooden desk. "He left this behind. He asked me to call if I remembered anything, or found anything. I don't know why I kept it. I was busy. I did nothing. Then, later, I got curious."

Reinhardt Levesky Klaus's business card was off-white with engraved lettering. The address was New York City, the Upper West Side.

"That's not his real name," Hohen said when I glanced up.

"How do you know?"

"No one by that name lives at that address, no Reinhardt Levesky Klaus at all, not in New York, not in Boston."

As he spoke he removed a checkbook from the same center drawer. He wrote swiftly, decisively, without asking me to name a sum.

"I assume you tried the phone number," I said.

He handed me the narrow slip of paper. "Yes," he said. "It's registered to the Jewish Defense League."

# THIRTY-NINE

In the less damaged part of the house, the major reminder of the fire was the continuing, but lessening, stink. After wriggling into dry clothes, I set up a temporary office in my bedroom, summoning Roz when I heard her spike-heeled footsteps on the stairs.

Her kohl-rimmed eyes made me think of a football player fighting late-afternoon glare. Her long skirt was transparent; lesser mortals would have worn tights under it.

"Are you available tonight?" I sat cross-legged on the floor, balancing a notebook in my lap. My hair was wrapped in a towel.

She pouted her bottom lip. "I can be."

"I need a witness, with a camera. I'll want the negatives developed and printed by morning."

Roz has guarded my back before. She's not a SWAT team, but she couples good instincts with karate, and she's a photographic whiz. I hesitated before raising the sensitive topic of the boytoy, but this time she didn't seem to mind.

To the best of her knowledge he spoke no Spanish. His gun was licensed.

"Any idea why in hell he was downstairs firefighting in the wee hours?" I inquired.

"Hey, I assume because he heard the alarm. You should be grateful."

"I am. Were you with him when he heard it?"

"I woke up, he was already gone."

"Most people I know, they hear an alarm, they call for assistance, do a nine-one-one."

She shrugged. "Hey, don't worry, I got rid of him. Too serious, too uncool, although he was fun for a few nights, randy, hard as a rock in two seconds—"

"Roz." I raised my hand, palm outward, to forestall further revelations.

"What time do you want me tonight?"

I checked my wristwatch. Five-fifteen. "Take Paolina to Gloria's; I've arranged for her to spend the night. What time can you get back?"

"Rush hour? Give me forty minutes."

"As soon as you're home, we'll go over camera angles. Count on an all-nighter."

She swung an abrupt one-eighty to exit. The hell with tights, I wasn't sure she was wearing underwear.

I studied the phone, ran my fingers experimentally over the push buttons. The instrument in my bedroom had been restored to full working order. I had only to lift the receiver to summon a dial tone.

Dumping my notebook on the floor, I stood and restlessly examined the smudges on the windowsill. The screen Roz had removed the night of the fire leaned lazily against the wall. Did I have time to replace it?

Did I have sufficient evidence to present my case to Mooney? Maybe. If the suspect had been anyone other than Teri.

The sheets on my bed were just as I'd left them Friday night, tangled, the hem of the top sheet trailing on the floor. Where did they sleep together? Not at Moon's place, not with his battle-dragon mother on the prowl. A hotel room? Teri's apartment? If I told him what I feared, could he take over the investigation? Could he turn to her in the night, keep his knowledge secret?

I grasped the receiver, swallowed, and dialed.

I might not reach her, I counseled myself. Might have to wait till tomorrow, reschedule. Five-fifteen is transition time, people go and come, travel the workday roads.

Her supervisor agreed to patch me through. I knew that meant the call would be taped. I didn't mind; I preferred it taped.

"Hey, sorry to bother you on duty." My voice sounded so easy, so relaxed. My hand was almost crushing the phone.

"What's up?" Teri Kiley sounded close enough to be in the next room.

"I interviewed Gregor Daly today."

"The witness, right? Kilmarnock Street."

"Thought I ought to clue you: You're going to need more than Daly. If he's your best witness, you're asking for it."

"We take what we get, you know that." She did sound sweet on the phone, just like Frank Hennessee said.

"Have you got further corroboration?" I asked.

"Mrs. Daniels on one."

"Well, you'd better hope she's not a racist, because that's the way Henry Fine's going to go. Take my advice and consider the departmental P.R. position before you put a bigot on the stand. Remember the picketing preachers."

"Daly came off racist?"

"Regular Ku Klux Klanner." I mentally begged the man's pardon.

She gave a snort of exasperation. "We arrest 'em, lawyers try 'em, juries let 'em go."

"So, you enjoying your new assignment?" With the supposed burden of my message delivered I decided it would sound natural to revert to small talk.

"Yeah, it's fine. Is that all?"

Good, she was in a hurry. I had little desire to prolong the conversation. "Nice talking to—hey, no, it isn't all. Gwen's lawyer, the P.D., Henry Fine, asked me to speak to Mooney about this, but since I've got you on the line, you can pass it on."

"Sure, no problem."

Damn, if it was hard for me to believe she'd deliberately with-held Mrs. Phipps's medication, smashed her telephone when the dying woman tried to call for help, how would Mooney react?

"Tell him I'll be dropping some stuff by his office first thing in the morning. You remember all those boxes and stacks of newspa-pers in Mrs. Phipps's hallway?"

"You bet. I went through 'em, every one."

"No," I said.

"Huh?"

"You didn't search them all. Mrs. Phipps gave one to Gwen, and she's eager to return it, cooperating fully and all that."

"A little late."

"Well, it's not like she was hoarding the old lady's diamonds. Tell Moon it's mostly full of papers, you know how people keep things. There's a receipt—for a painting or something—dates way back to the forties, I swear. I guess Valentine thought Gwen might enjoy browsing through this stuff in her spare time, sort of like a scrapbook. A lot of it has to do with the lady's first marriage."

"Can you drop it by the station?" she asked. "I wouldn't mind taking a look."

"Never mind. Mooney'll sort it out."

"But he's so busy. I can handle it."

"Sorry, but I'm busy, too. Time's tricky for me, what with the fire. Hell, I'm still staying at a motel."

"Which motel? I could come get it." She edged the words in quickly.

I paused, as if considering a crowded timetable. "Damn. Wouldn't work. The box is at my house and I've still got work to do at the courthouse for Henry Fine. I'll have to stop by my place in the morning to pick it up. Tell Moon I'll get it to him by nine."

"Okay." She sounded reluctant, but resigned. "I'll tell Joe it's on the way."

Mooney's mother calls him by his given name, Joseph; I couldn't remember the last time I'd heard a colleague call him Joe.

As soon as I hung up, I loaded fresh double-A batteries into three separate tape recorders. Then I made a tape for Mooney, speaking clearly into the microphone, keeping my voice neutral and flat, like a computer-generated automaton. When I finished, I decided to send it by messenger along with the photos, as soon as Roz developed them. I'm a coward, I suppose; I knew I couldn't stand to be there when he learned, to watch the muscles tighten in his jaw, watch his brown eyes change, harden, and focus far away, as if he were staring out at some remote planet.

As I tucked my gun into my waistclip, settling it against the small of my back, I pictured K-Rob framed by the window, escaping the fire.

# FORTY

I sat on the sixth step in darkness. The green glow of my watch said 2:47. 2:48. 2:49. From my perch I could see the fire-blackened foyer below, plus half the living room, including all four windows.

She might not come.

I'd offered temptation: the dream of doubling, tripling, quadrupling whatever sum she might realize on the medieval manuscript. I'd threatened discovery: If she knew the first thing about Mooney, she'd never risk letting him scrutinize any documents relating to Phipps's first marriage.

I'd tried to cover the bases.

Roz, camera poised, would be watching from my bedroom window, well hidden, responsible for getting an approach shot. Once she snapped it, she was backup. After the target entered the house, she'd move to a better vantage point. The two of us had run various scenarios, marking creaky floorboards with glow-in-the-dark Xs so she could avoid them.

Did Teri have the nerve to wait till morning, intercept me as I approached Moon's office? Might she send an accomplice tonight?

As a cop she'd have met scores of lowlifes who'd think nothing of burgling a house for fifty bucks. But would she trust an accomplice? I felt like a scientist gazing down at a giant lab maze, exploring each wooden tunnel.

I'd made it easy, but not too easy. My back door has an excellent dead bolt and chain. To make that approach even less attractive, I'd left a work-light burning in the back foyer. The damaged front door was heavily boarded. While the living-room windows were boarded as well, I'd removed one plywood panel, propping it carelessly against the wall instead of renailing it. It looked natural, as though a workman had needed the light to see by.

The rat came for the cheese at 3:15.

Shadows shifted as the panel moved. There was no moon, only a handful of stars. A figure was outlined against the glow of the streetlamp. Nothing she wore would have made anyone look twice. She could unzip the dark nylon shell, yank off the black watch cap, go to work, and no one would raise an eyebrow.

Balancing my night-vision binoculars carefully on a step, I picked up my Vivitar, far less complicated, but also less reliable, than Roz's 35-millimeter Nikon with infrared film. Framing the cop as she wriggled through the glassless window, I released the shutter twice, hesitating each time till I could clearly see her face. The motor-drive's noise was negligible, blurred by a white-noise generator I'd plugged into an outlet in the upstairs hall.

The remains of my damaged furniture had been hauled away the day before. I'd moved the dining-room table into the stripped living room, set a canister of pencils dead center, a stack of writing paper to one side. Four file folders and two manila envelopes lay scattered across the surface of the table.

Having snapped the approach shot, Roz would now be inching her way to the dining room via a set of tiny back stairs built long ago for servants.

I placed my camera next to the binoculars.

I'd considered challenging her. I craved Teri's self-incriminating voice on tape. But I had no doubt she could manage a glib excuse: "Hey, I was curious, I was driving past, and remember how you jimmied the door at Mrs. Phipps's? You're not the only hotshot housebreaker around." In the end, I'd opted against confrontation. If she'd been a thief, I'd have chanced it, but murderers play in a different league.

I shifted my limbs carefully and began crawling upward, keeping to the side of each step, where the wood stayed silent. I planned to observe from a hiding place near Roz, close to the sheltered dining room. I'd planted the tape recorders only because I know things go wrong.

Things went wrong.

I can't say whether I heard movement or voice first, but the loud noise startled me so much I almost stumbled, and I wasn't sure if it was Roz who'd yelled "Stop!" or Teri. At the same moment, I sniffed gasoline.

I'd offered attractive bait, dammit, an aged box from my own attic. I'd jammed the file folders full of old news clippings, carefully composed a phony receipt. The rat takes the cheese and exits. It doesn't turn and bite uncornered.

What had Roz done? Why had she abandoned my script?

"Don't even bother to say she isn't here," I heard Teri say coldly. "Don't even fucking bother."

I was in the kitchen in the dark. From Roz's indrawn breath, I guessed she was staring at a sight I'd already faced: Kiley's eyes over the barrel of a gun. I found my .40 in my hand.

"Talk!" Teri prompted harshly. She yelled, "Dammit, Carlyle, you are messing this up." Then, more quietly, to Roz, "She's here, right? Am I on tape? Christ, I'm on tape."

"Take it easy," I called.

"Carlotta!" Roz's voice was shrill. "She's going to burn it down again! She's got—"

"It's okay, Roz. She knows it's over. She can walk away. No one will try to stop her."

"Are you kidding?" The cop tried a laugh, but it came out wrong.

"You can have the tape," I offered soothingly. "No evidence, no crime. You know that."

"Eyewitnesses," she said.

"Eyewitnesses are crap. You were somewhere else at the time."

"Come out. Let me see you."

"No."

"Fine with me. I shoot this bitch."

Dammit. Between us, Roz and I could have smothered the beginning of a blaze. Teri wouldn't have lingered to watch it burn. Why the hell had Roz intervened?

I eased the gun into my waistband. "Relax, I'm coming through the doorway. Not from the hall, from the kitchen. Okay?"

Teri said, "Wait."

I heard a retching grunt followed closely by a thud, but I wasn't sure what the noises signified till Teri gave me the okay to enter the living room and I saw Roz slumped to the ground. Teri must have kept her motionless with the threat of the gun, knocked her cold with the police baton she wore tucked in her belt. Smart. One cop can't deal with two targets.

Three gallon jugs of gasoline crowded the makeshift desk. From the bulk of Teri's backpack beside them, she'd come prepared with two or three more. The fire would be for destruction, not show, this time.

The cop said, "You give me the tape, you give me the file, I'm gone."

I thought, *Sure, I give her what she wants. She shoots me, or knocks me out. With both of us unconscious, she pours gasoline over us, torches the place. Plenty of fuel this time.*

"I should have smelled a fucking trap." Her voice was low and rushed.

"Hey, you couldn't take the chance."

"You're still registered at the motel."

"Yeah," I said, "I'm so smart you've got the drop on me."

A blow from her police baton would have cracked Valentine's telephone like an eggshell. Had it marked the baton? Was there physical evidence, identifiable material, on the baton?

"Where's the tape recorder?" she demanded.

"I'm sure we can work this out." I heard the faint creak of a floorboard upstairs. I thought I might be hallucinating.

"You're not holding any face cards."

"But I might be."

"I don't think so."

"Walk away from it, Teri. Nobody's going to stop you at Logan. What you've got, you can sell anywhere. You have it, don't you? You didn't leave it with the appraiser?"

She seemed to consider my words.

"But if I walk out," she said, almost regretfully, "and you're still alive, you'll spread the word that it was stolen."

"But you'll have the receipt."

"The receipt is real?"

"Take a look."

She held the gun in her right hand. She wore dark gloves.

"Nice try," she said.

"No rush. You'll have plenty of time to study it on the flight to London."

"The auction houses are in New York."

"Don't kid yourself. They have plenty of auctions in London. You don't even have to put in a personal appearance. Keep flying till you get to some country with no extradition treaty, then hire yourself a shady lawyer for a middleman."

You don't need to kill two more people, that's what I was trying to tell her. Roz stirred. I wasn't sure how hard she'd been hit. Maybe she was trying to signal me, but in this light, how could I tell?

"The recorder's duct-taped under the table," I said.

She nodded at the motionless Roz. "Get it for me, and remember, you're not my only target here."

I crawled under the table and retrieved the tape. The gun barrel stayed trained on Roz until I resurfaced. Then Teri shifted it back to me. I placed the cassette on the tabletop.

She slipped it into her backpack. "I'll just bet you have a ton of enemies. Peritti runs with the mob, and the rumor is, so do you. A wise guy was shot in your house, wasn't he? Right in this room?"

"I don't run a tour."

She wouldn't want to shoot me. Bullet holes show up in autopsies, even with badly burned corpses. There'd be a moment, when she shifted her gun from right hand to left, seized the baton, prepared to strike—

I sucked in a breath, yelled, "Mooney!"

I didn't expect a reply, and when the deep voice boomed, shouting in a foreign tongue, I was already diving under the table—not because it was a half-decent shelter, but because it was the only shelter. Teri's gun popped, and I thought, *Silencer,* and the pain in my thigh was a searing flame. I thought, *No, no, that didn't happen,* when all the time I knew it had.

My gun was in my hand, but I couldn't fire because I didn't know who in hell I'd be shooting. With half my vision blocked by the table, I could see legs, sets of running feet, like an army brigade, lit strobelike by errant flashlight beams.

The beams crossed, six, eight, ten beams, flooding the room. Black-clad men spoke a half-familiar language that turned to gibberish the more I tried to follow it. To my left, a man groaned loudly. Teri, prone, yelled and squirmed. A man in fatigues shoved his knee into the small of her back. She no longer had a gun.

"Come out. Put the gun away. It's over." Kneeling at the side of the table, K-Rob, Roz's ex-boyfriend, defender of murals, reached a gloved hand in my direction.

"It's over," he repeated.

Speechless, I obeyed, dragging my leg, clenching my teeth to keep from crying out. My mouth was dry, and the pain sharp. Someone said, "He's okay, just a graze," and I felt like saying, No, I'm a she and it's no graze, but they were talking about the groaning man, one of their own, not about me.

I recognized Yale, Hohen's secretary, as one of the black-clad group, almost indistinguishable from the men. K-Rob called her Ya-el, not Yale. Yael.

Hohen's secretary, who'd been hired *after* the man with the JDL phone number had come to call . . . Christ, no wonder Hohen hadn't returned my phone calls.

Someone said, "She's hit, too."

A hand grasped my leg and I heard myself scream. A bass said, "Missed the femoral by an inch."

K-Rob murmured something and the bass muttered a response I couldn't understand, and that panicked me. Were the words really in another language? Was I losing consciousness, fading into a nightmare?

"I need a doctor." I don't know whether I mumbled it under my breath or shouted it at the top of my lungs.

K-Rob, kneeling beside me, spoke slowly. "Is there a phone upstairs?"

"Yes."

He barked orders I couldn't understand to people I couldn't see.

"We've disabled the phones on this floor. But we won't cut the line. Understand?"

I'd have to make it upstairs to call for help. That would give them time to get away. He waited for me to nod before he continued.

"We're taking her." He indicated Teri, who'd quit struggling and lay still as a corpse. "She'll give us the haggadah; I have no doubt about that."

"You're speaking Hebrew."

"Yes."

"The Jewish Reclamation League."

He said, "The Jewish Reclaimers. They got the name wrong."

"Is Roz okay?"

He disappeared briefly. When he came back into view, he was smiling.

He nodded once. "Give her my best regards."

When they left, the sudden silence in the room buzzed and hummed in my ears. Cautiously I lifted my hand from my leg. Dark blood covered my palm. I wanted to lie there, sleep, because any movement summoned the fire. I felt cold and shivery, nauseous. I thought, *Shit, how can I play volleyball without a goddamn leg?*

It took me twenty minutes to crawl upstairs to the phone. The dial tone was a blessed hymn.

# FORTY-ONE

Lights flashed red and white, and sirens blared, beeping at cross streets. During my second trip of the week via careening ambulance, I was definitely the patient. I doubted these were the same EMTs, but they wore identical orange jumpsuits. They strapped me to a stretcher that grew wheels once we hit the ground floor, and then the ride was bumpier, but level. I demanded to know where Roz was, and Teri, and I ordered them to call Mooney, but I couldn't get his number out, and I wasn't sure if I was entirely conscious, but I was sure as hell that my leg was on fire and no one had a fire extinguisher.

My teeth were chattering. An orange man tucked a blanket around me. He did something to my right hand and when I looked down I'd sprouted an IV line.

"You're doing fine," he said encouragingly.

Harsh lights after darkness made me squint, but I was afraid to close my eyes and shut the light out completely.

I grabbed a doctor by the wrist. "You're not taking it off."

She called, "A liter of normal saline, type and cross for six units of packed cells."

I said, "Did you hear me?"

"What's your name?"

I told her.

"Where were you shot?"

"Leg. Dammit, you're looking at it."

"Where else?"

"Nowhere else, dammit."

Another voice sang, "CBC, drug screen, SMA-seven."

I was moving, rolling, and there was a clip on my finger, a blood-pressure cuff on my arm. Someone wrapped a tourniquet high on my thigh, and my leg exploded with pain that washed over me like a hot drowning wave.

The ceiling fixtures were huge fluorescent rectangles.

"When did you last eat or drink?" had me stumped, but I obediently opened my mouth when given instructions. It didn't occur to me that I was lucky to be alive; I was terrified of waking with one leg. I asked if I could stay awake during surgery, because I hated the idea of being put to sleep, put down like an animal. A woman in a scrub suit instructed me to count backward from one hundred. I wasn't conscious of a damn thing after that till I woke up retching into a kidney-shaped pan, panicked till I saw my right leg down to my bare toes, immobilized and swathed in gauze. Then I fell asleep again, helpless as a baby. I was angry with myself for not staying sharp, and knowing where Roz was, and Paolina's mom, and I needed to explain to Mooney, and where the hell was he? I kept falling asleep the moment I'd gathered my thoughts.

A nurse rammed a thermometer into my mouth. I sucked chipped ice. My leg wasn't burning, but it wasn't like a leg, either—more like a numbness stuck on as an afterthought. I thought I'd just blink my eyes against the yellow light, but I fell asleep again.

Mooney was seated in what could have been the same chair under the same round metallic clock with the same sweep-second hand. It could have been the morning after the fire, when Paolina had been taken away for tests. Then my hand groped for my leg.

His voice seemed to come from far away. "I listened to the

tapes. One was addressed to me; we found it up in your room. Then the team found two recorders fastened underneath the table, one still running, the other unloaded."

I blinked my eyes.

"You were muttering in your sleep. I'm sorry if I woke you."

"Did I say anything I'll regret?" My voice sounded almost as far away as his.

"No."

"Am I at Mount Auburn again?"

"They took you to the General. That's where the gunshots go."

His shirt was sky blue, his jeans faded. I wanted to reach out a hand and touch them at the knee, where the fabric was worn. I said, "Are you okay?"

He shrugged. "You're the one she shot."

"I don't think Teri meant to do it, Moon. There was an argument."

"I thought I taught you not to argue when the perp has a gun."

"I don't mean last night, Moon. Last week. She was the one who had the argument with Valentine Phipps."

"The downstairs neighbor said it sounded like two women."

"Teri must have taken the haggadah to be appraised. Then she lied to Valentine about what it was worth. It fits. Harry, the hardware guy, said Valentine was like that. When I came into his store and told him I was working for Valentine, he assumed she'd been in the day before to memorize his prices. Suppose Valentine double-checked on Teri the same way, suppose she'd already sent photos of the manuscript to an appraiser of her own. Then Teri says, 'Oh yeah, your book's worth five hundred bucks, isn't that great?' when Valentine already knows it's worth five hundred thousand. Or more."

"That sparked the argument." Mooney ran a hand through his hair. His shirttail was untucked and he'd missed a button.

"Valentine started having chest pains. She rushed to the phone— and Teri lost it. That was the real spark, the flashpoint, that moment when she brought her baton down on the phone. Once she lost it, once her temper flared out of control, it was over. If Valentine had lived, she'd have talked. Teri'd have been tossed off the force. . . ."

And lost a chance to claim how many hundreds of thousands of dollars? What was the haggadah worth?

Moon examined his fingernails. I was sure he was thinking it would have been okay, okay to lose your job rather than watch while a woman died, watch with her life-saving medicine clutched in your hand.

"You could have brought me in on it." With hours to adjust, he sounded controlled, careful, as though he were tiptoeing through a minefield.

"Oh, Moon," I said miserably, "I would have brought you in, you know that, but—"

"She was going to quit the force."

"She told you that?"

"Two days ago." Then he added, "Because of me," and his mouth wrinkled in a self-deprecating grimace. "After I told her how working in the same chain of command had killed any chance . . . for us."

With that remark, I felt like he'd put me beside him in the minefield, on tiptoe in unmarked sand.

He looked away. "She'd have been sunning herself on the beach at Bali—"

"You think that's what she'd have done with the money?"

"Who knows?"

"Did she have debts? Sickness in the family?"

"No. Not that I know of. And what the hell would it matter?"

Even if she'd planned to endow an orphanage with the proceeds of the haggadah sale, it wouldn't change the provenance of her wealth. I tried not to think about the funds that would send Paolina to college. Cash from a drug lord. Is money ever clean?

"Yeah," Moon said bitterly. "Sunning herself on the beach in Bali and I'd have been wondering what the hell I did wrong."

"No," I said. "You'd have caught her."

"Maybe."

"How's Roz?" I asked after a while.

"Concussed. Forgive me, but I laughed when the doc said she'd come out of it normal."

"Moon—"

"She wanted me to tell you she's sorry, but I'm not sure about what. Paolina said that, too, and now Roz."

He was quiet for so long I thought I wasn't going to hear the rest of the story. No details.

"Can I have some water?" I asked.

He held the cup while I sucked through a plastic straw. "Nine-one-one got a weird phone-in, about a cop tied up in her apartment. It took a while for the call to get bounced to me, but once all the messages and alarms got sorted—"

"I'm sorry." I'm not sure why I said it just then, or exactly what I was apologizing for. Maybe for the question I felt I had to ask next.

"Is she in custody?"

"No."

"Did they—"

"They didn't hurt her, the JRL, the Reclaimers—how many of them were there?"

"Six that I saw." Including Hohen's secretary and Roz's pickup boytoy. I wondered how soon the Reclaimers had planted Yael in Hohen's employ after the man from the JDL had questioned him about a manuscript. Yael, or a phone tap, or both, would have led them to me. And me to Roz, trolling for men in a bar.

Moon said, "Kiley told the patrol cops she'd been surprised by robbers who'd stolen her gun. They released her; she was a cop roped to a chair. A victim. What else would they do?"

"Yeah." He called her Kiley now, not Theresa.

"So she's gone. We've got an APB out, and a border alert, but she had a decent head start."

Maybe she'd taken my advice, flown out of Logan minus her treasure.

"What about Gwen?" I asked.

"She'll be released. She could already be out."

I asked for more water, sipped till the straw rasped at the bottom of the glass.

Mooney said, "One thing—how did you eliminate Peritti? He looked good for the fire."

"Inside information." I hoped he'd leave it at that.

"Yeah?"

"Simple. He couldn't have set the fire. Teri could have."

"But how did you know he couldn't have set it? With a classic Mob alibi?"

"I believed one of his witnesses," I said.

"Why?"

"It was Sam."

"Gianelli?"

"Yeah."

"Oh."

That was all: "Oh."

I said, "I haven't seen him, Moon."

I closed my eyes, took a deep breath and a quick inventory. My leg felt prickly with returning sensation, still numb near the wound. How did I feel about Sam? Did telling Moon I hadn't seen him mean I didn't want to see him? Would I walk with a limp like Sam? I cursed silently and repetitively. No, his injury had been far worse than my clean, in-and-out wound. He had metal bars screwed to his bones, pins in his ankle. It must have hurt more than I'd ever imagined.

Sam didn't visit me at the hospital. Peter Breeze did.

"Thanks a whole bunch." He pulled a metal chair close to the bedside while tossing a bunch of street-corner flowers on the thin blanket. "The lost fucking treasure of the Fenway, and you couldn't drop a dime to tell me?"

He'd brought me newspapers with columns circled in red. Background articles on other coups by the Jewish Reclaimers, also called the Jewish Reclamation League and often associated with the Jewish Defense League, although a JDL spokesman refused to confirm a connection. There were details of Valentine Phipps's life, photographs of Kilmarnock Street, where the treasure had been kept for seventeen years, and murky snaps of Teri's Jamaica Plain apartment, from which it had disappeared. A curator at the Museum of Fine Arts called the robbery a wake-up call for collectors everywhere. He was quoted as saying, "Owners would do well to know the history behind their art."

"The whole thing's dead now," Breeze said disgustedly.

"What do you mean?

"The Fenway." His voice sounded as wistful and regretful as Mooney's. "It's gonna go the way it was gonna go, the way of the West End, the way of the Back Bay, and nobody gives a shit. Peritti's gonna sell his buildings in a fat multimillion-dollar block. Harry's Hardware'll be gone, and all those small restaurants, and next thing you know Fenway Park will meet the same wrecking ball that leveled the Boston Garden."

He laughed, but the sound was rueful.

"What?" I asked.

"It's just I'm so fucking naive, you know? I thought, for a minute, maybe two, that Valentine's death would unite the tenants, and they'd scream bloody murder, and we'd get some sort of law enacted, some new kind of rent control, maybe. But it's all about money, isn't it? Money talks and tenants walk."

"Yeah."

"So what do you think?" he asked.

"No comment," I told him.

# FORTY-TWO

I waited to make the phone call, waited two days, during the course of which I was introduced to crutches, and to the hospital's concept of solid food. Paolina and Roz, giggling like maniacs, smuggled me a bowl of Suan La Chow Show—hot-and-sour wontons with spicy sauce and blazing bean sprouts—my medicine of choice. The night nurse couldn't understand why I didn't want the TV service, and my roommate hated my blues tapes, forcing me to listen to Paul Rishell and Little Annie Raines through the dinky earphones on my Walkman.

I'd be incarcerated another day, possibly two, and Dr. Culbertson said I could have the bullet if I so desired. It was no longer bullet-shaped. The .38 hollow point had flattened on impact, ripping through a swath of quadriceps, ruining more muscle than a conventional slug. My limp would fade and disappear in a couple of months. Six months' rehabilitation.

I examined the telephone card Roz had picked up at CVS per my instructions, punched area code 603, followed by seven digits.

A man answered, a casual hello. I asked to speak to Marta.

When I identified myself, she said nothing.

I said, "Please don't hang up. Speak Spanish if you don't want him to understand."

"Paolina is with Lilia?" She sounded both puzzled and defiant, keeping to accented English.

"No," I responded, "but she's okay."

"Good, then."

"She's still your child—and I'm sure your boys miss you, too."

"They grow up fast," she said.

"In some ways, yes."

She switched to Spanish then, but I got the gist of it. "When they leave me, they won't care. I'll be by myself, an old witch with no one."

"Don't hang up. Please."

"What do you want from me? If everyone is healthy, what do you want?"

"What do you think?"

"I cannot come back there," she said in English.

"Why?"

She didn't mention the money she owed Diego. "It's not a life."

"Do you love this guy, the one who owns the cabins? Is that it?"

She laughed derisively.

"I guess not."

She switched to Spanish for the rest. "It's a way out of a rat trap. There's grass here, green leaves, and tall trees that smell good. You walk at night and nobody bothers you with catcalls and whistles, and I think maybe he'll ask me to stay, and I'll be his wife, and his wife wouldn't work except the cooking and the laundry and things around the house like a woman does. This is just the camp, but he has a real house, extra bedrooms, too, he says, so when we marry, after we marry, I can maybe tell him there are more of us. I make a story, my brother's kids, and he dies, so tragic, maybe. I think he would be okay about this, if I wait. And the kids are fine, really. Lilia loves my boys."

"Marta, if you love him, and you really want to share his life, tell him the truth about your kids. If you don't love him, tell me. Now."

"Why?"

"Because there's another way."

I'd come into some money, I told her. Lottery winnings, and while I'd purchased the ticket myself, I planned to share the proceeds with Paolina, who'd helped choose the lucky numbers. Of course, she wasn't an adult, so I'd keep the money in the bank for her until she reached eighteen. In the meantime, she could use a mother's guidance in deciding how to spend her wealth to help herself and her family. It wasn't a great deal, but enough to pay debts, possibly relocate, move from public housing to an apartment near Lilia, or maybe a small house with grass and green trees in the yard.

*Sometimes,* I told myself, *it is all about money. And sometimes I can live with that.*

As for Teri Kiley, she disappeared. She didn't exit via Logan unless she slipped out under a fake passport. Her car was abandoned downtown, near South Station with its multiple rail lines and no-questions-asked cash ticket sales. Any cop knows how to establish a new identity. It just takes time and patience. Luck. She could be a long-haired brunette in California. A Midwestern housewife. But she'll never be a cop again. I take some satisfaction in that, hug the knowledge to my chest when it seems that justice failed. She didn't get what she wanted, I tell myself, and she'll never be what she once chose to be. At any moment her newly constructed life could unravel. She'll never know the luxury of relaxation again, never stop glancing back over her shoulder.

A week after I left the hospital, Paolina helped me pack my crutches into a cab, hobble from the cab to the Y. We watched Gwen Taymore play her quietly eloquent brand of volleyball, anticipating shots, effortlessly digging out the low balls. Her beaded braids danced. She served eight straight points.

We went to Dunkin' Donuts afterward, the three of us. Gwen bought me a dozen assorted to go, stuck a bow on the box by way of thanks. She wasn't sure if the thing with Peritti would continue or not. He hadn't exactly stood by her, but she'd had moments when

she'd imagined him a killer, too. She left at eleven, for a job interview. One of the Roxbury churchmen ran a chain of gyms, thought
Gwen might make a fitness instructor.

"We need to talk," I said to Paolina.

She wore jeans and a jeans jacket, paired with a low-cut white
eyelet blouse, managing to look both tough and feminine, a contra-
dictory blend of babyish and sophisticated.

"We're keeping a secret from your mom. How do you feel about
it?"

She shrugged, then took too big a bite of doughnut. Raspberry
filling threatened to drip. "Uncomfortable."

"Are you okay with that?"

"Do we have to? Could I tell her?" She dabbed at her mouth
with a paper napkin.

"Why do you figure your dad sent the money to me?"

This time the shrug involved her whole body, not just her shoulders.

"How would it make your mom feel if she found out?"

"Angry, I guess."

"I don't know what went on between your mom and dad," I
told her. "People act in ways they regret later. Especially when they
think they're in love."

"My dad must be angry at my mom. To want to make her angry
back."

"You're a smart kid," I said, "always have been. You want to
know about your father, but I don't know anything about him."

"I can live with not telling my mom. For now."

I removed a savings account passbook from my backpack.

"Sixty thousand looks enormous until you realize that Harvard
costs twenty-three thousand a year." I named Harvard although U.
Mass., my alma mater, is less than half the price. I have high goals
for Paolina.

"Will he send more?" she asked.

"No way of knowing."

"Nursing school—," she began.

I cut her off. "Medical school costs even more."

Two months after I swung down the hospital walkway on

crutches, the following squib appeared in the *Globe*. I might have missed it, but I didn't, and later, Peter Breeze sent me a copy by mail.

"Dr. Shoshana Helfant, curator of the Tel Aviv Museum of Art and Culture, announced a rare and precious addition to the museum's collection of medieval Judaica today. The Eliezar Haggadah, sister piece to a manuscript currently housed in the British Museum, long feared lost to Nazi looting, will be displayed in an environmentally controlled case designed by Levi Reisenman, chief architect of the museum, which opened to the public last spring. Mr. Reisenman thanked the donor of the manuscript, Mr. Robert Klein, formerly of New York City, at a function attended by Prime Minister Netanyahu and other prominent politicians, as well as former heads of state. Mr. Reisenman also gave thanks to the Jewish Reclaimers, headquartered in New York City, an organization he termed 'instrumental' in the return of the ancient artifact."

I'm no religious scholar, but I know that the haggadah tells the tale of the ancient Hebrews' flight from bondage in Egypt. Moses leads them forth, across the miraculously dry bed of the Red Sea, but then they spend forty years in the Sinai desert, and Moses himself never sets foot in the Promised Land.

Was the Promised Land the proper resting spot for Valentine's treasure? I think so. Its journey, fittingly, had taken as long as the wanderings of Moses' followers—longer.

Robert Klein. I repeated his name aloud as I reread the article once, twice, then slipped it into a file. Maybe Rob K. Maybe K-Rob. Considering the initials, possibly Reinhardt Levesky Klaus, the man who'd approached Hohen, as well. Who knows?

I sent the check back to Bronson Hohen.

I never did find Paolina's photograph.